LOTERÍA

LOTERÍA

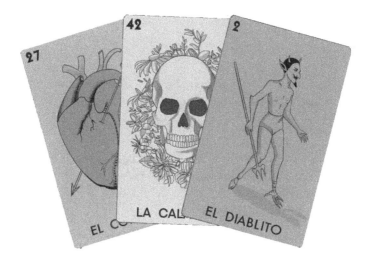

CYNTHIA PELAYO

The following is a work of fiction. Names, characters, places, events and incidents are either the product of the author's imagination or used in an entirely fictitious manner. Any resemblance to actual persons, living or dead, is entirely coincidental.

ISBN: 978-1-957957-10-4
eISBN: 978-1-957957-24-1

Library of Congress Control Number: available upon request
Originally published in 2012 by Burial Day Books
Trade Paperback reissue edition and new material January 2023 by Agora Books
An imprint of Polis Books, LLC
62 Ottowa Road S
Marlboro, NJ 07746
www.PolisBooks.com

AUTHOR'S NOTE:

Lotería was largely written between 2008-2010 and presented as my thesis at The School of the Art Institute of Chicago for my Master of Fine Arts in Writing.

The version of *Lotería* today includes several updates, including a new short story, poems, and a novella. The new works added were intended to maintain the spirit of the original collection.

I hope you find glimmers within these pages of the writer I was and the writer I've become.

Thank you

-Cynthia Pelayo

CONTENTS

EL GALLO

THE ROOSTER

Night blanketed the arid Sonoran Valley. In bed, Señor Julian listened to the rooster outside crow. He massaged his gnarled hands, which throbbed from latching together the heavy barn doors. Closing those doors became more and more difficult with each passing day, but it had to be done alone as there was no one out here to help him. The closest town was thirty miles away, as was the closest neighbor.

A warm wind blew in through the inch open window; the widest he ever allowed at night for fear that *it* would come inside while he slept.

Something outside scurried about the ground feet from his room. It was about this time of night that it would prowl the darkness. It sounded like a dog but faster and lighter on its feet. He held his breath and listened. There was silence. Even if he wanted to peer outside the window he couldn't because there were no lights outside. He had wanted to get a light bulb installed out there to keep it away, but he couldn't spare the money. There was never enough money.

Tonight, things would be fine, he assured himself. There were no more chickens anyway. The cows had been secured in the barn as they had always been. So, there was nothing left outside, except, of course, for the rooster. He sighed heavily and pressed his fingers to his temples. *Did I padlock the barn?* He thought. *Yes, I must have.*

At first, he lost the goat. Then slowly he lost his chickens. Last week it had taken Chanclo, his dog of eleven years. He had always been cautious with the cows, as they were his only source of income. He pressed his palms to his eyes. *I'm getting too old for this*, he thought.

The rooster's cries were abruptly silenced. He sprang up in bed. His hands clutched the bed sheet closely to his chest and he listened to the quickened steps outside across the dry, cracked earth. A door creaked several yards away. The cows shifted and moaned. The barn door was open. It was too late. It had gotten to the cows.

Slowly, he eased himself back down and pulled the sheet over his eyes. In the morning he would deal with it, like he had every morning for the past few years: the puncture marks, blood drained animals, and the sympathetic but disbelieving nods of people who thought him crazy for believing in the small, fabled blood sucking creature—the Chupacabra.

2

EL DIABLITO

THE LITTLE DEVIL

"I can hear them scratching," the chubby-faced, little boy says as he searches through a large box of Crayola Crayons.

The doctor sits directly across from him with his hands on the metal table. "What do you mean, Sebastian, that you can hear them scratching?" The doctor's voice is soothing, hypnotic.

The room is yellow with pictures of the Looney Tunes characters hung around the walls. There is Bugs Bunny on one wall, Daffy Duck on another, Tweety Bird on the third, and the fourth wall has the Tasmanian Devil, which is directly behind Sebastian.

Richard stands in the darkened room, watching his son and the doctor through the double-sided mirror. They could not see him. He wondered if the psychologist sat Sebastian in front of the Tasmanian Devil on purpose.

"I dunno," Sebastian leans his head to his left shoulder. "They just scratch, at night, in the walls." He runs his fingers across the degrees of grays, then blues, and finally stops on the collection of greens. "Scratch. Scratch. Scratch. Inside the walls. Sometimes they do it all night."

The little boy pulls out a dark green crayon and yawns. The harsh, bright lights in the room highlight the dark circles beneath his eyes. His golden-brown hair is messy. He wears a dark blue sweater over his hospital gown.

"Have you ever seen them, Sebastian, the people who scratch? The people who scratched you?" The doctor asked this calmly as he passed a large, plain white sheet of paper across to Sebastian. "You can draw a picture of what they look like here."

Sebastian grabbed the paper. His eyes remained transfixed on the box of crayons. "He said he'd be back for me…and he just kept coming back and back. I told my mom, and she would just cry." Sebastian put the crayon to the paper and began drawing a pointed hat. He looked up and smiled. "This box has all the colors," his smile faded, "but my father didn't want to buy them for me."

Sebastian was Richard's only child with Socorro. They lived a comfortable life in Sarrià, Barcelona. Sebastian attended a prestigious international school by day, and at night he practiced ballet with his mother, a principal ballerina with the Ballet Nacional de España. At first Richard was apprehensive about his son, even at six years old, training for ballet. Yet, when he saw the passion with which the boy moved, he himself could not deny the talent.

Socorro had wanted a bigger home, one with space for Sebastian to train. Richard found her the house of her dreams in Sarrià. It was a historic four-bedroom, three-bathroom house with claw foot tubs and a cherrywood spiral staircase. The house cost more than most people could afford in a lifetime, but it was the home Socorro wanted and he did all he could to please her. After they moved in, it only took one month for their dream to unravel. The house showed Richard monsters he thought only existed in old fairy tales. Even that first night sleeping in their bedroom, Richard could feel something breathing within the walls and watching between the cracks in the floorboards. He was unsure then, but now he was certain that there was something with them in that house.

"Do you have a name for them?" the doctor asked.

Sebastian looked up. He pursed his pink lips and pressed a green crayon into his round right cheek. "Mmmm." He shook his head and then he looked to the mirror with his pained, brown eyes.

Richard didn't care what the detective had said. He felt his son could see him standing in that dark room.

"No, but my father said they are called Duendes."

There was a throaty, smoker's laugh from behind Richard. He knew there was someone standing feet from him the entire time. Regardless, in this observation room with nightmarish possibilities he still felt alone.

The tall figure moved beside him. He was taller than Richard, older, with gray hair and sagging cheeks. The man's laugh was cold, disconnected, but working in such a profession for such a long time Richard imagined one would have to be.

"Sebastian is just a boy! He's six years old. There's no way he could have done anything so…so…torturous," he said glancing over to the detective.

Taking a slow sip from a paper cup, the detective said, "You'd be surprised to find out what any human being of any age would resort to under such…conditions."

"How could he have done such a thing? There's just no way..." Richard's voice trailed off.

"Mr. Torres, I'm seventy years old, and growing up in the northern mountains of San Sebastian long ago, without the comforts of today's technology, there really wasn't much one could do to be entertained. Of course, there was work. I tended the land for my aunt. And, late at night when people from neighboring towns would gather in the plaza, we would tell stories to entertain, and to justify why some thing's happened.

"When I noticed items disappearing in my aunt's home, random plates or old books, she would say it was the Duende; a goblin who was the real owner of the house. One day, I began to hear tapping on my walls. At first it was just one tap that would wake me in the night. The next day it was a flood of fluttering taps all about the room. One night, I saw it, this little bulbous-nosed, flesh-colored creature standing at the foot of my bed. It had the squished face of an old man. It was shorter than me at the time, perhaps four-feet tall. This thing glared at me with two large round black eyes. A dusty and dirtied pointed hat rested on its head. It held a bolt cutter that it must have gotten from out in the barn. Its fingers were long, gnarled, and slimy. This thing, it didn't say anything. It just whipped off my thin sheet and grabbed my left foot and clipped off a toe. Blood squirted, and I screamed. The creature laughed and laughed, rejoicing as I moaned and cried for my aunt who never showed. I wonder now if she was in some sort of trance in her room next door.

"This thing, held up my toe, sniffed it with his large nose, sucked on the bloodied end and then dropped it on its black tongue. I remember those teeth, rotted and yellow, with bits of fur from some animal it must have devoured still lodged between its teeth. As it left my room, it hissed that it would be back for me the next day.

"When I told my aunt the story the next morning, she told me not to worry. Gently, she washed and bandaged my foot. Then she told me that if anyone were to ask me what happened that I was to say I had cut myself accidentally in the barn, as I was shoeless. I was a ragged little child and always barefoot because my aunt didn't have any money for socks, let alone shoes for me. That night, my aunt prepared a large meal and asked me if I had enjoyed living with her. I said I did so, very much. She talked to me on and on about her cousin in Barcelona who would care for me if anything should ever happen to her. She then showed me to her desk in her bedroom, and there she gave me the key to where she kept the deed to the house and the farm. Then, she showed me a trick floorboard underneath her bed where she kept a small savings. She instructed me to set this money aside secretly for my education, again, if anything were to ever happen to her.

"Before bed, she insisted that I sleep in her room, on her larger softer bed, and she slept in my room. The next morning nothing remained of her except for a few bones and blood-soaked bed sheets."

Back in the examination room, Sebastian scribbled away at long, white sheets of paper. There were lines of red and green from what Richard could see.

"Sebastian, did you love your mommy?" the doctor asked.

Choking back tears, Richard said, "Of course he loved his mother. He loved her very much."

"Scratch. Scratch. I don't like it when they scratch. They don't let me sleep. I just want to sleep."

"It's all right, Sebastian. We'll talk more later. You've done good work today, but you're right. Let's get you to bed." The doctor picked up a telephone on the center of the table and dialed an extension.

In seconds there was a light knock on the steel door. The doctor stood up, pulled back the latch, and nodded. A nurse entered, pushing a wheelchair. She positioned it next to the boy.

"Sebastian, just hold steady." The doctor stood at one side of Sebastian and the nurse on the other. Carefully, they lifted the little boy, and as they did Richard saw the bandaged, bloodied stumps where his son's legs once were.

"Your wife could've given herself over to her fate a little sooner Mr. Torres, to protect her son, as my aunt protected me."

"You believe him then?"

"Of course, I believe the boy, but I will never go on record saying that. As far as the law is concerned, he is guilty of the murder of your wife."

The detective tossed the empty paper cup into the wastebasket and walked out of the room.

LA DAMA

THE WOMAN

Jiselle wrapped her hands around the warm mug and looked down at the coffee. "I know what I saw, Detective Aguilar. I saw a woman covered in blood out there and no one seemed to care!"

"Mrs. Bourke," Detective Aguilar took a deep breath and paused. He scribbled on a legal pad and set his pen down on the wooden table. "What were you and your husband doing exactly before you both arrived at the Zócalo?"

Jiselle opened her mouth, but before she could say anything her husband interrupted.

"Honey, really I..."

"Mark, I know what I saw," she shouted above the police precinct noises of blaring telephones, crackling walkie-talkies, and the rapid

Spanish conversations of the dozens of police officers in the large, open space.

Detective Aguilar scratched his black and gray goatee and chuckled to himself.

"I know what I saw!" Jiselle snapped. She turned to her husband who squeezed her shoulders and then turned back to the detective.

"It's all right Mrs. Bourke," Detective Aguilar said softly. "I understand. You are here on vacation. So maybe you've been up late sightseeing, going out to restaurants…"

"Are you saying we were drunk? We weren't drunk."

Detective Aguilar pointed to Mark. "And you, Mr. Bourke, did you see the same thing your wife claims to have seen? This lady…with the blood?" He waved a pencil in the air.

"Tell him what you saw," Jiselle pressed her husband, who had remained mostly silent since their stroll through the Zócalo, Mexico City's public square.

"I…" Mark began but paused. He felt cold, ill, and just wanted to lie down. He was unsure of what exactly to say or even how to explain what it was he saw. The only thing he was certain about was that he did see something, someone.

There was a woman with long, black hair. Her oval face was pale, so pale that he shivered at the look of her. *How can someone alive be so pale?* he thought. She had moved slowly through the nighttime crowd in a floor-length white dress smeared in red. Her arms looked as though they had been dipped in a vat of blood. Crimson droplets fell onto the stone floor as she walked past him, her arms almost brushing against his. The woman's large brown eyes were vacant, fixed on nothing; *no one.* Her blue lips trembled with her words, "¿Los niños. Donde estas los niños?"

"Honey," Mark said as he squeezed his wife's shoulders. "Perhaps we did have a little too much to drink."

"What?" Jiselle said.

Mark gazed into his wife's eyes and shook his head slowly. "We didn't see anything. Come on."

Once the couple exited the police station, all conversation in the room ceased. Telephones continued to ring, but all of the officers in the room turned to Detective Aguilar who was looking down at the two words he had written on his yellow legal pad after listening to Jiselle's panicked report.

He had heard the same story told nearly every week during his twenty-year career. His own father had heard it told weekly during his own time with the force.

"La Llorona," Detective Aguilar said in a booming voice. With that announcement, the officers turned away and resumed their conversations.

It was always the same report; the tortured-looking young woman begging for her children, whom she had presumably murdered herself. It was the same story told each week, by a new person, or group of persons, who had stumbled upon this lost soul, this ghost, roaming the Zocaló since the 1500s.

EL CATRIN

THE MAN

Fernando Silos looked at the directions to the Madre de Dios Cemetery, which his editor had handed to him as he headed to his car. "We'll just need one or two pictures for tomorrow's edition, Silos. Just make sure you get all of the flowers and the other items people have been leaving behind."

Silos clutched the paper and felt a wave of heat wash across his face.

"Silos, it's simple. Just a couple of pictures."

He tucked the directions into his camera bag and smiled. "Sure thing, Mr. Rodriguez. Simple. Just a couple of pictures," he said, holding anything back that could be taken as sarcasm.

This was just his third week as a photographer for *El Diario Daily News* in the city of Juárez, and on this third week, one of the biggest stories of the year had taken place; the Mexican military had killed Antonio "El Hombre" Arbol, the leader of the largest street gang in the city in a twelve-hour shoot out. The funeral was held earlier in the day and reports had surfaced that all day long friends, family, and devotees of El Hombre had been stopping by his grave to pay their respects. Rumors had grown of a mass of flowers, letters, photographs, bullets, and other offerings having been left on El Hombre's grave, and that's the image Mr. Rodriguez wanted shown in tomorrow's edition.

Silos parked next to the cemetery entrance and studied the directions to the gang leader's grave. He slammed the door and rushed down the twisting path. First, he walked past the part of the cemetery sectioned off for simple wooden crosses with names handwritten in heavy black ink across the top. He moved into the part with above ground, gleaming sandstone tombs. The cemetery was empty, except for the occasional statue he would pass of La Virgen de Guadalupe, who kept watch over the dead.

A few yards in the distance Silos saw bright bunches of red, pink, and yellow flowers, many wrapped in cellophane, peeking out from around a turn. He quickened his step. Without looking down, he pulled out his camera and raised it to chest level. *Just a couple of pictures and I'm out of here,* he said to himself, wanting nothing more than to hurry up and flee this place. Retaliations were imminent. No one, not even the Mexican military, could murder the king of the largest street gang and expect peace. More deaths were certain.

Finally, he approached El Hombre's grave, the man feared by many but worshipped by so many more. He raised his camera and started scanning and snapping quickly. There were hundreds, if not thousands of flowers, lit and unlit candles, rosary beads, cards, letters, photographs, cigars, half-full bottles of tequila, and then he dropped his camera and he fell to the ground, overwhelmed by the bloody mess. There, in front of him at the headstone of the gang leader's grave were four decapitated heads of Mexican soldiers neatly arranged.

Revenge was had.

5

EL PARAGUAS

THE UMBRELLA

"I see you preoccupy yourself with the Maya now Umberto."

Umberto Raphael paused mid-dig. His grip tightened around the wooden handle of the trowel. He had held the tool so long it felt like an extension of his very hand. For six hours straight he had been at this very spot, crouching, digging, and sweeping time away from a massive limestone structure. The memory of this place had been abandoned a long time ago. Now, Umberto believed himself to be destined to awaken these objects and reintroduce them to the world.

"Professor Nuñez?" Umberto asked.

The gray-haired professor emerged from the thick of the jungle, mercilessly hacking away at vines. Behind him trailed a young assistant. The assistant looked about nervously, stumbling, and tripping along the jungle floor. These were the signs of an archeologist in training.

Umberto knew these signs well as he was once in that young man's position not even a decade ago.

Umberto massaged his stiff hand. The professor and his assistant set down their machetes and drank water from canteens they pulled from their backpacks. Hopping down from the slippery, stone platform, Umberto extended a hand. "It's wonderful to see you again, professor. What brings you here?" It was a forced nicety, as he knew exactly why the professor was here—to claim Umberto's discovery as his own.

Looking at Umberto's hand with contempt, Professor Nuñez said, "You have always liked to work alone."

Umberto dropped his rejected hand to his side. "I just prefer being able to concentrate without a heavy stream of orders being barked at me." There was an intended iciness to his voice. "With that professor, how did you in fact find out about this dig?"

"Oh, I have my ways." The professor strolled over to a weathered stone statue of a reclined figure. Its feet, back, and elbows were flat on the ground, but its face was turned in the direction of thick trees. "Sacrificial stone, I see."

"Yes, professor. I can only say that some impressive finds have been uncovered that would rival those at Teotihuacan. Not only were there a temple and observatory discovered but an entire E-Group."

Professor Nuñez's eyes widened. "That can't be!"

The discovery of an E-Group, an entire complex specific to astronomical events would catapult the young archeologist's international stature to rival that of his former mentor.

The professor cleared his throat and turned to his assistant. "For an excavation site, of this level of importance, it is clear to see why they brought me in."

"Pardon?" Umberto quickly interrupted.

The professor continued addressing only his assistant, "Notify the government immediately that I will be transferring a portion of my team at Teotihuacan here." He turned back to Umberto and looked at him with contempt. "I see there is much to do."

"Of course, professor," the assistant said cheerfully, pulling a satellite cellular phone from his backpack.

"Wait," Umberto shouted to the assistant as he turned away to begin making phone calls.

"Young man," the professor said, "For this type of work, the clearing of a complete and undiscovered city, you must understand why the government would call me in, a true expert. It would be a national embarrassment for an amateur to, well, mess something up. Of course, if you are interested, the invitation to reclaim your position with my team remains open."

Umberto stood there, his insides burning with anger, and his outsides covered in the dust, sweat, and fragments of a Mayan city. The past had baptized him to uncover the Mayan city, long ago put to sleep by the jungle. "I completely understand…sir."

"Very well. First, you must provide me with all of your notes as I'm sure they will have to be reviewed, edited, and rewritten in most cases…"

"Actually, now that you're here professor, I would like to ask your opinion on something that's terribly perplexed me."

Umberto led Professor Nuñez on to the stone platform where he had been earlier working.

"Yes, very well." The professor looked around at the massive ferns and palms, their large green leaves creating a curtain that shielded the space beyond. "Well," the professor said irritated. "What is it?"

Umberto pointed and the professor's eyes followed. "Ah, yes," he said, pleased. "Now, I see." On the platform were curious but intricate markings engraved on the stone beside his feet.

The professor reached for his glasses in his shirt pocket and lowered himself to inspect the smooth lines. "This will take me more time to decode, but here, this symbol here is for water..."

"No sir, that is not what I wanted to show you, it's this." The archeologist pulled aside the leaves of a nearby fern. "You see, I've seen cenotes before, but none quite this magnificent."

Just feet from them was a sharp several-hundred-foot drop off to a wide circular sinkhole full of brilliant turquoise water. The professor's eyes widened. He steadied himself on the platform and moved farther out. The cenote must have been hundreds of feet wide and easily double that in depth. The massive well below them was lined with sharp, rugged limestone at the edges. Further down its sides, smooth white limestone gleamed.

"This is much larger than the Cenote Sagrado at the great Mayan city, Chichen Itza." Umberto moved closer to the professor. "As you are far more experienced, what is your immediate impression?"

"The cenotes were the fresh water supply to the Maya, as well as where they offered sacrifices to Chaac, the god of rain."

"Interesting, sacrifices you say. Were there any ritualistic behaviors tied to these beliefs?" Umberto took a step back, giving the professor room.

"Certainly." He paused, looking around at the edges. "Offerings to the gods had to be prepared with care. The Maya would dress the selected person from the community with gold plates, masks made of jade, and cover their arms and hands with other brilliant jewels."

"I'm sure that was all very heavy," Umberto said.

"As was the intention. They were made to drink an intoxicating concoction, given great honors as they were paraded through the city and then they were pushed down into the well. They would sink to the bottom in minutes."

"Sounds like a miserable death."

"The individual was very drugged. Therefore, they really weren't in a reasonable enough state of mind to understand the true horror of the situation."

Professor Nuñez turned around. His eyebrow twitched and a look of excitement and plot glazed over his eyes. "You do know that only a handful of cenotes have been uncovered and all of those have been thoroughly excavated."

"You mean that the human remains from the bottom of the cenotes, known to us, have been recovered...as well as the gold and jewels these people donned?" Umberto smiled.

"As you are dedicated to this site, I'm sure we can come up with some kind of *arrangement* to ensure the careful excavation and retrieval of possible treasures," the professor said.

"Exactly what I was thinking, professor."

Umberto took a step forward and slammed his palms onto the professor's chest, sending him tumbling down into the well. A great splash of water was followed by thrashes and screams for his assistant. As the assistant came rushing forward Umberto spun around, grabbed the young man by his collar and sent him hurtling towards the water.

The two men cried and shouted, their pleas reverberating off the limestone walls, and echoed through the jungle. As their calls for help died, and the splashes ceased, a low rumble grew in the darkening clouds overhead. Umberto went back to the far end of the platform, picked up his trowel and returned to his work.

6

LA SIRENA

THE MERMAID

Tomorrow Celia Santos would turn fifteen, quince años, and would now be considered a woman in the eyes of everyone in her community. She didn't feel like a woman, especially since her mother said there was not enough money for a proper presentation; a quinceañera party. The only thing planned for tomorrow was a traditional birthday blessing by the priest during mass. She didn't want to make the forty-five-minute walk to the cathedral, mainly because she didn't have a nice dress to wear during the ceremony.

It's not like she wanted an extravagant dress, like the kind of elegant ball gowns worn by girls from the town for their own Sweet Fifteen balls. Celia just wanted something simple, pretty, and maybe even pink, but again, there wasn't enough money her parents told her. Harvest season was fast approaching in El Norte and all of the family's extra money had to go towards saving to pay for a coyote to help her father make the trek to Florida to pick fruit. Even a simple pink dress for her birthday was something they couldn't afford.

Saturday morning, she awoke to her father's shouts.

"Another baby, Guadalupe!? What are we going to do now?"

Her mother's muffled cries meant less money for her father's payment to the coyote, and more responsibility for Celia who already cared for her five siblings. Another baby, her father felt, would be a major financial strain on a family with very little.

After mass, she and her mother walked quietly back towards their home. As her mother settled in the kitchen, kneading maize for the tortillas for dinner, Celia strolled out back through the cornfields. The clouds were painted in golds, yellows, and pinks as the Chihuahuan sun fell. As she moved further away from her home, she heard voices in the field. She paused, listened, and heard her father and another man speaking.

"Quince mil pesos for such beauty," a man said. "It is the most we will pay. We can relieve you of this problem tonight."

"What will happen?" her father asked.

The other man laughed. "Do not pretend you don't know. You have worked on the farms. You know what happens there when loneliness strikes a man. Don't ask questions you already know the heavy answer to. Brush it from your mind. Take the offer and forget. Many others have made this choice. After tonight, you will have one less burden."

Celia turned and hurried back to the house before she could be seen.

Later that night she awoke to a firm hand pressed over her mouth and a rough voice whispering in her ear to stay quiet or her throat would be slit. One set of hands grabbed her by her arms and pinned them behind her back. Another set of hands grabbed both legs and quickly she was lifted from her bed. Ropes tightened around her skin. The nighttime air kissed her face, but before her eyes could adjust to any shapes in the darkness duct tape was wrapped around her head. She was lifted once again and set down onto a cold metal surface. She tried to scream, kick, and cry, but all she could do was shut down and after hours and hours she fell asleep.

Much later, after the day's heat was extinguished by the night the vehicle stopped. She was lifted off the truck bed. Her legs trembled, her throat was dry, and her stomach twisted with hunger. Her ankles were untied. Rough hands dug into her shoulders and directed her forward.

"Stop right here," she was instructed.

A door unlocked in front of her. Her hands were untied. The blindfold was lifted and the duct tape ripped off. Confusion and terror bounced around her stomach at the sight before her. A pair of hands massaged each of her breasts. A sharp voice said in her ear "Your first man will pay handsomely." He removed his hands and pushed her forward. She fell onto the wooden floor. The door behind her was locked and the man's voice shouted from beyond, "Rest up. You'll be working tonight, Ms. Quince."

Celia looked around the room.

Light streamed in from a single window to illuminate several young women huddled in the corners. They were barefoot. Some were just in thin, sweat-stained cotton dresses. Others wore only a layer of dirt on their naked bodies. Many of the women were young, much younger than she. Some were older, fuller, but they all had that same distant look.

"Where am I?" Celia asked.

A woman, the oldest of them, approached. She had on a pink slip. She grabbed Celia softly by her chin.

"Sometimes the male workers on the farm are lonely and need company. We're their company, and now so are you."

7

LA ESCALERA

THE LADDER

The room was bare except for those items one does not care to take on a long journey. The bed, the refrigerator, the rug, the stool, bookshelves, and a ladder for which to reach those novels at the highest shelf, and a mirror were all that was left.

Lydia stood in the doorway of the bathroom in a white fluffy towel, her hair dripping cold beads of reality, and her naked skin was frozen with worry. The door was locked from the inside, the chain still hung.

How long have I been in the bathroom? she wondered. The sun had barely risen when she stepped into the warm bath. Now a blue-black sky filled her apartment. She stood there alone while a peopled train passed just below her window.

"Delia," her voice cracked, and the walls responded by echoing her own torn despair. The sheets had been removed from the bed. Only an unattached mattress remained. The refrigerator swayed on its hinges, its golden yellow light illuminating the empty white interior.

Lydia stepped in front of the ladder, staring down the imposing frame of rungs and steel like it itself had been an accomplice, the only accomplice to her departure.

"You!" she growled. "You let her leave!" She slammed on a rung with her palm, and then pulled off the diamond stone Delia had placed on her finger just a few nights before. She slipped off the ring and tossed it across the room.

The anger was maddening, sickening, and twisting in her stomach so violently her soul would probably be forever bruised and crippled with deep gashes of anguish. Her cheeks permanently stained where they streamed salted hope for Delia's return. *Where is she? Why did she leave me?*

She crawled to the stool against the window, picked up a gilded hand mirror that sat on top of it, and dropped her towel to the ground.

"Is that where you have gone?" she asked. "Into the mirror?"

She wondered.

She obsessed.

Hours passed by.

Trains charged past, and in those moments she would call to her love, lost in the mirror. She was prepared to sit there forever on that cushion of butterflies, poised and posed, her face staring into that pool of glass hoping to catch a glimpse of her love who had fallen into the mirrored world.

Delia was selfish. Lydia knew that, but still she sat there readily awaiting her lover's arrival, because Delia would come back. She had to come back. Delia had told her she loved her, so wouldn't that constitute enough need, want, and desire to reach out and take her with? She didn't care the conditions of this strange reflective place. There could be lizards that walked upright, lions that dined on plates of hearts and spleens in establishments that only prepared the smoothest virgin flesh, and the devil himself, with miniature demonics that could prance about her feet stinging her toes with their tiny tridents. Lydia waited for her wretched, deceitful, magically cruel and beautiful liar. She missed her and called to her in that pool of glass. Her tears full of panic and of fear.

"Here I am my love. I am here. Come back to me," she cried into the mirror. "Come back for me."

Still, she sits there waiting.

LA BOTELLA

THE BOTTLE

Hair as black as ebony.

No.

Hair as black as a crow's wing.

A crow's wing.

I found her there. Naked and tragic. Tragically exposed in the middle of the interstate. A single crow plume lay beneath her cheek.

"The crow brings the light," I said to myself, remembering the old ones' stories of the rainbow crow bringing the warmth from the southern sun only to fall from the sky with his rainbow feathers burned, the sun having turned them black. But through his suffering, warmth was returned after a harsh winter.

In her left hand she held a small, glass vial.

There was no one outside. In the middle-of-nowhere. It was just me, my idling red jeep, and a dead woman lying on the middle of this nowhere-pacific-Northwest road of dead stories.

She lay as if she had settled down for a night's sleep on a soft bed. Her long, lean legs were wrapped together, and her arms hugged her body. Her face was peaceful. Her body lay on a bed of dark, pooled blood on the asphalt. She had not been hit by a car. There were no visible signs of trauma. It was as if she had fallen there, on the ground, into a red pool from somewhere up above. I kicked the jeep's tire, not knowing what to do. I couldn't call anyone. I didn't have a cell phone anymore. I had given that up. I had given it all up—my job, the credit cards, the internet, everything. I withdrew all I had from the bank, bought this car and drove.

I drove for a long time.

"If I could take you back up from where you fell, I would," I said without knowing exactly why I said it.

I knelt beside her and knew I couldn't put her in my jeep. I was on the run as it was and this was throwing me off track. I just didn't know what to do. I could only look at her. Hell, I could barely look away from her. She was so beautiful. Angelic. Peaceful.

What had happened to her, I wondered. I took off my shirt and laid it across her body as best as I could. Her small breasts were still exposed there in the warm sun. I ran back to the jeep and grabbed a small towel I had in the back seat and with that I covered the rest of her that should not be seen. I felt charged with taking care of her; with sitting over her body and protecting her, even though this meant a police car could easily drive by. I didn't care anymore. I was tired, tired of running. They would find me eventually and seal me in that prison for the rest of my life, a life I wasted away when I took a life. I was done with all of it. I just wanted to sit here, with her.

For hours I waited. Waited, but no one showed. The bottle in her left hand caught the rays of the sun as it departed into the clouds. The bottle was empty, but I had an overwhelming need, no, an overwhelming desire to take that small, glass bottle. There was something in there I felt that I could just not comprehend, and so I reached for it, and I was surprised that the vial slid out from her hands gently.

As I removed the vial, a dot appeared within the center, and with each twist of the cap the object within continued to twist and roll within itself. It was a scroll.

I removed the stopper, the parchment, and read the handwritten instructions that would change my life, change my existence.

Travel between the northlands and the southlands.
That is the travel you must do, child of the crow.
For you will bring the light when cold and darkness folds.
For eternity, this is what you'll do.
If so ever you shall fall from the sky, a replacement will watch over your body and set you free.
And the work will go on, so crow children can continue to light and warm all kind.

As soon as I read the last word the girl on the road disappeared. The blood was gone.

I turned and saw that my car was gone.

The vial now dangled from my neck and as I flapped my crow wings and flew across the great, dark sky I knew it was time to head south, to bring the warmth and light again.

EL BARRIL

THE BARREL

Dark blood ran down the dashboard of the car. Everything looked darker parked here in Humboldt Park, under the shade of this large elm tree. The streetlights nearby were turned off. A huge storm had passed the Chicago area and ComEd was still scrambling to get power on to thousands.

Whatever, she thought to herself. *The darkness works out for me.*

Gurgling sounds were followed by a hacking, wheezing cry. "Why the hell did you do that, Diana? Why?"

"Tommy, your mother is from Argentina. Don't you know anything about the Sayona?" She rested the handgun she had used to crack Tommy across the head with on her lap.

Diana crossed her legs and smoothed out the skirt of her dress. "The Sayona, Tommy," she opened the visor and the vanity light shone on her smooth skin, "is the spirit of a woman, in a white dress, who kills men who have had affairs outside of their marriage."

"But I'm not married, you are!"

"Shut up, Tommy. A sin is a sin."

She applied another coat of red lipstick. "Sometimes the Sayona asks for a ride or a cigarette." Diana scrunched her face. "I always told you that you should quit smoking. It's a nasty habit. Very '90s and it'll just… kill you. But you are nineteen and reckless, so I guess you don't care if you die. Young boys just don't care who they hurt. Even if they hurt themselves. Anyways, my dear, the Sayona is a beautiful woman, clearly." She blew herself a kiss in the mirror. "And after a man offers her a ride in his car, after a few moments, when he looks over, he sees not that sweet face, but a skull with terrible teeth." Diana smiled in the mirror and looked at her perfectly white, straight teeth. She did notice a few new fine lines beneath her eyes. Middle age was catching up to her, but it wasn't anything that the wonders of cosmetic surgery couldn't correct.

She shifted her legs and heard the rattle of an empty Coca-Cola can. "Ugh, Tommy, I really wish you would keep this car clean. You may be incredibly handsome, but oh my, are you just the messiest person I have ever met."

Diana closed the visor and leaned on the doorframe of the passenger car still looking out of the window. She was trying to remember the good times her and Tommy shared, texting each other back and forth for hours late into the night. It made her feel young and vibrant getting to know this young person, and she was excited to learn that he was as unhappy as she, but there was happiness that burned inside of her each time she received a text message from him early in the day saying, "G'morning gorgeous." It was thrilling to be wanted and desired by someone so youthful. They were, of course, complete opposites, but that didn't matter as there was an intense bond, a connection. At least that is what she felt. And so, they planned to meet, and finally did at a coffee shop, and they sat in this very car finishing their coffee joking with one another. Then, on their next date they had laughed after that terribly bad horror movie and then laughed some more when they got lost in that maze of an underground garage. Their next date, and many after, ended here at Humboldt Park listening to music in Tommy's car and just talking and relishing in each other's company. She knew then, on that first night in his car, that she would fall in love with him, and it would be that much harder to kill him.

"I never wanted this, you know," she whispered under her breath.

He cried again and reached for the door handle. She grabbed him by his collar and slammed his head against the dashboard. Blood sprayed from his nose. His glasses shattered and bits of glass were embedded in his cheeks. Blood mixed tears ran from his large blue eyes.

She looked down at her silk, white dress. "You know, I bought this dress especially for you, especially for tonight," she said over his whimpers. His hands shook violently as they shielded his head. "I really wanted this to work. I'm lonely and you were obviously lonely posting an ad practically each night on Craigslist. You were pretty easy to follow. Your ads were always similar. The last one was particularly cute: 'Tattooed Bad Boy Looking for Fun.'"

"You know that's what I do. That's how we met…you're married. You said you didn't care about any other girls that I may be seeing," he cried.

"True, but I'm bored Tommy. You just don't give me as much attention as you used to, and, well, that makes me angry, and to guarantee that my husband never finds out about his lovely wife cavorting with this tattooed, pierced 'bad boy' who whores himself around, I thought it would be better this way. You understand, of course you do my dear." She took hold of his chin, kissed his bloodied lips and then laid both hands against the side of his head, twisting quickly until there was a crack and a pop. Tommy fell flat, lifeless, his movie star face was free from pain.

Diana opened the car door, stepped out and walked over to the driver side. Her small frame managed to shove Tommy's body into the passenger seat. She turned on the car, adjusted her rearview mirror, and, before setting off, checked the vanity mirror, making sure her face was clear of any blood. She applied one more coat of red lipstick and smiled as she saw the blue barrel she had asked Tommy to pick up on his way to get her in the backseat.

EL ARBOL

THE TREE

The tree died, but then it lived,
existing and breathing as we do,
but in other parts

twisted sticks for bones,
tangled strands of mint green
colored Spanish moss plucked

from Southern Live Oaks
and Bald Cyprus trees on nights
when the wind whispered

use this for flesh and use that for blood
string the needle and thread

to seal in its soul

cloth wrapped, covered
to maintain the warmth of your intent
while staring into

unblinking glass bead eyes
you wish you could see what is
truly being done, assemble

stand at your altar and make your cross
wrap the pieces round with string
start at the center

working towards all ends
leading you down into your petition
wish, goal, magick

strings exposed
a button for a mouth
command your poppet

to serve you, service you
feel great pleasure
or ache with pain

drive the needles in
drip hot wax down
success

or a blessing, cursed to feel
great shame, or an instant shock
followed by death

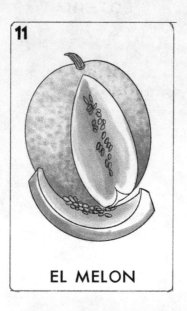

EL MELON

THE MELON

A slice of cantaloupe with every meal, that was Esther's only request right before she stopped speaking completely. I know this because my mother was the intake nurse when Esther first came here to Our Lady of Resurrection Hospital. My mother is retired now, and sometimes I wonder if the story were true, but I don't know why my mother would lie. She had no reason to lie, not about something like this.

This story goes that Esther was moved to a private room on the eleventh floor after she stopped communicating. One day, nearing the end of her first year, something unfortunate happened which invariable extended her stay.

At the time she was sixteen years old, and as she couldn't really do anything for herself, not because there was something medically that prevented her from moving, but because her mind had locked away her willingness to want to move her limbs. In the mornings, a nurse would wake her, get her out of bed, bathed, and into a fresh, white hospital gown. Then, slowly the nurse would walk Esther over to her preferred spot—on the very corner of the bed in her sparse, white room. There, Esther would sit all day until it was time for a new nurse to come in, take her to the bathroom to get her teeth brushed, and then get her tucked into bed.

At night, the first rounds of checks went well. As did the second, third, fourth, and fifth. Every fifteen minutes someone walked down the corridor, peeking into the darkened rooms and making sure all the patients were asleep. However, shortly before midnight, every night, a nurse would always find Esther, awake, sitting on the corner of that bed. Again, quickly and carefully, she would be tucked into bed only to repeat the same routine the next day.

This was her posttraumatic stress nightmare that she just could not wake from.

THAT DAY, THE ONE that extended her stay, the squeak of the wheels announced the approach of that afternoon's lunch. David, the young orderly with sleepy eyes and messy red hair, would stop in each of the patient's rooms delivering their trays. Esther was always last as her room was furthest down the hall.

David knew where she would be, seated on the very edge of the bed. She would swing her legs back and forth, back and forth, so gently that only he could see her movements. The doctors thought he was seeing things himself, but he was sure of this. He was also sure that each time he entered her room that she would smile so gently that, again, only he would catch this. Regardless, he knew that she was paying attention, sensing the world around her, but still a locked prisoner in her own mind, suffering a day that consumed her happiness.

He felt her sadness each time he walked into her bare room. He wondered what she had been like before the murders. Did she like school? Did she sing? Or play any sports? Or did she draw and paint? What he really wondered most was what her voice sounded like. He imagined it was something soft and musical, like a violin.

Wheeling his cart up to her open door there she was like always, sitting. He sighed. He was saddened by the tragedy of a beautiful girl locked away, sad and sitting, always on the corner of that bed. She looked so frail and frightened. Her skin, soft and pale, almost glowed against her chestnut brown hair. Looking down, her head leaned into her right shoulder so that her hair fell down in waves. Her hair was like another person, so full and long, but protective. He imagined it was her shield somehow.

He wondered if she was there, lost in that day, continuously reliving her trauma. He knew she was trapped there as the nurses had reported her cries in her sleep, begging the men to get off of her, to let her brother and parents go, but they did neither. The headlines reported the crime; a family of four stopped and dragged out of their car along a lonely road in Chihuahua. A multimillion-dollar exchange was going to take place in minutes by an international crime ring and the family's passing had disturbed the exchange. A mother, father, and adolescent boy were tied to cantaloupe trees. The teenage girl was taken a few feet away. As two men pinned her down, her brother began to cry, and his throat was slit. The parents were then each shot. A knife was held fiercely against her neck. The sharp blade dug into her skin with each of her movements as she kicked and screamed at the two men pinning her down and ripping off her shirt. The knife slipped. A man was cut. She took the moment of distraction and ran. She ran and ran until she found help.

"Where are my slices of cantaloupe?" she asked as David set her tray down beside her on the bed.

Startled, he nearly tripped backward. Her voice was a violin.

"I don't know..." he said nervously, flipping through pages on the clipboard on his cart hoping to find something, anything from the doctor. "Here," he said. "The doc just said he wanted you to try some other things...that maybe taking cantaloupe away would help..." He stopped, knowing he probably should not be reading this to her.

She did not look pleased. He set the tray down on the counter and pointed to a bowl of grapes, two slices of toast, and a bowl of chicken noodle soup.

"I have a cantaloupe with every meal." She whined. "It's for them. It's the last thing they saw and smelled, and I need that for them. I can't forget."

Her sad, hazel eyes stayed on him as she straightened her head and sat up. Her long hair fell away from her neck exposing a knotted necklaced scar from where they knife sliced her skin during her fight. The shiny, pale pink skin slowly turned red, bright red until droplets of blood emerged on the surface and rolled down her neck, staining her white gown.

"It's OK, Esther!" David held both hands in front of him. "I'll get it for you. I'll get you whatever it is you need."

He ran out of the room, and shouted to the nurse, my mother, to watch Esther, that she was ill. My mother covered her cut with bandages and gauze, but the blood kept flowing. She shouted for a doctor, but no one came.

When David returned to the room with the slices of cantaloupe the blood was gone. From that day on he made sure she had her cantaloupe with every meal until he grew very old, and she grew old. He cared for her until she died today, as best he could, even if all she wanted was to live in her tortured mind.

12

EL VALIENTE

THE BRAVE ONE

J immy dipped the brush in red paint one final time.

Seated at his wooden bench, in his one-bedroom, wooden casita set atop a hill, he looked out at the great sleeping giant mountain of Adjuntas, Puerto Rico. The sun was setting, fast. Magnificent golds, reds, pinks, and purples blended into one another in the sky. Outside, the coquis, the tiny tree frogs of the island, sung their co-kee song much earlier than he could ever recall. It was as if the world was bidding him farewell. His thoughts took him back to that day the King of Spain presented him that golden idea, "When your enemies are charging towards you, ready to plunge you into death, show them the devil. Maybe then you'll have enough time to save your own life, and the lives of millions."

Adjuntas was the land of the sleeping giant. It was a tiny mountain town, on a tiny island, where the Swedish had once settled because it was an escape from the seething hot temperatures of San Juan.

Jimmy looked at his work once more. This mask was his best piece— ever. Many Carnivale masks were crafted by his hands, thousands he would guess. Carnaval Ponceño, part circus, part festival, but always partly masked.

His fingers were stiff, but he gently brushed the tip against the curved right horn of his final creation. He pulled the brush away, tilted his head and then held what he knew would be his final Vejigante mask in both hands. Sitting at his workbench in his kitchen he looked out the window at the sky. Pink and violet clouds were moving in, washing away the sunset he had been enjoying.

Against the wall, on his workbench was a small hand carved statue of a saint. He set the brush down on a sheet of newspaper, lifted the wooden santo, closed his eyes and breathed deeply before setting it back down. On the base of the weathered statue were the crudely carved words *St. James.*

This mask he had just completed was modeled using his own face, pressing tin foil against the curves of his chin, mouth, nose, and cheek bones. After he removed the foil the impressions of an ancient man looked back at him. It was time. It had been time ages ago, but now he was ready. He had carefully cut out two large eyes, punctured two holes for the nose, and cut out a large piece where the mouth would be. This mask was going to have a large, open, menacing mouth, with over a dozen sharp white teeth. Later, he rolled out the horns with cardboard that would curve out from the top of the head; two large devil horns and then smaller ones growing out from those horns. There were horns growing out from where the nostrils should be as well as the ears and from the chin. After the mouth was shaped and set, the teeth glued, and the papier-mâché construction was dried, painted, and set, the mask looked like an enraged demon ready to pounce.

Holding the mask up to the light Jimmy nodded in approval. Granted it wasn't constructed in the traditional style, fashioned out of a coconut, as they crafted to this day in the town of Loíza, but Jimmy enjoyed the smooth feel of papier-mâché against his wrinkled, sun-spotted hand.

"Jimmy!" A young man's voice called from outside. "It's almost time! We must go." The shouts were repeated, and with each time they grew closer and closer, and even more urgent.

Now, there was pounding at the door. "Jimmy, please Jimmy. You're going to miss it."

The door finally gave, and in broke in a young man with shiny black hair. He was in gray slacks, a white shirt, and around his neck was the collar of a priest.

"We used coconuts," Jimmy said, as he thought of a faraway time of another life. "We made ghastly masks out of the coconuts and that is how we won the battle."

The young priest dropped to his knees. "Saint James, please. It was because of you the battle was won."

"That was the twelfth century, my son. I have seen much across these decades, centuries, and I am tired."

Saint James patted the young priest on the shoulder. He then eased himself from the wooden stool and shuffled over to a large chest in the corner of the room. He unlatched it and out he pulled a Vejigante mask, fashioned out of a coconut.

"It's your turn." Saint James held up the mask.

The young priest took it, with no reluctance in his heart, but only fear of the great burden he would now bear.

"Wear this mask every year on my feast and you too shall live, well, as long as you want to live. As long as you live, my son, light will continue to shine. When you grow tired, create another like this.

"And what will happen to you?" shouted the young priest after Saint James, who was now walking out towards the door.

"Now, I rest."

13

EL GORRITO

THE BONNET

"To dream of a Sunday in Alameda Park," Juan-Carlos said to the young woman who lay across the bed. A melon-scented breeze wafted in from the windows. Outside, the fruit sellers had stationed themselves all along Humboldt Boulevard, in front of their brownstone mansion. From here, he could see old pickup trucks stocked with ripe watermelons, oranges, tomatoes, corn, and bouquets of fresh flowers.

"We will go out for a stroll soon, my love, I promise, to get you some air, perhaps even to get you some lovely fruit or a bunch of roses. For now, though, there is still work to be done. Much, much work."

The young woman did not stir. She continued to lay there, motionless, faced down in her short pink, A-line satin dress.

The room was spacious and airy. The two large windows flooded the room in warm light. At one end of the room was the cherrywood king-sized bed made with cream-colored silk sheets. A few feet from the bed were his cabinets and trays that held his pencils and pens, markers and acrylics, oils and charcoal, and canvas.

Still looking outside of the window, over the north side of the park, he began to whistle a cheerful tune, and suddenly he stopped. "This light is absolutely magnificent. My love, I implore you to wake up. I just cannot stand the idea of missing this light, especially when we are so, so close to such perfection."

The lady remained silent.

"You know, my love, I could die in Diego Rivera's painting. And I could die there with you, in that *Dream of a Sunday Afternoon in Alameda Park*. Oh, the park, the sweet smells of the park; fresh grass, the trees, but it is nothing like the smell of paint." He spun around, pointed to her, and walked back to his easel, inspecting the canvas.

"To me, there is no work more perfect than that painting. Funny," he leaned away from the easel, looking back to his wife. "Berenice, my dear, really do wake up. I just need a few more moments of your lovely face looking towards me. I just need to catch the light, how it falls onto your face, and penetrates your chestnut hair. I just need to be sure, Berenice. I need to be sure!" he shouted and flung a pencil against the wall.

There were sirens in the distance, they grew louder and louder until they passed the house.

"Dammit!" He gathered a bunch of brushes set on a metal stool beside him and threw them all out the opened window. "I need to work!" he screamed, holding both handles of the window as he slammed it down.

As he leaned his back to the window, he looked at the reproduction of Diego Rivera's painting that hung above their bed.

"That painting," he gasped. "I tell you! The beauty! The magnificence. The golds and greens and browns of the trees in the background, and the people! The society, the high society of the day—women in lovely dresses and hats, men in suits and bowlers, and of course there were peasants in the painting, but Rivera just wanted to show the then against the now and, my love, we are the now!"

Still, the woman did not stir.

"I had hoped you would like your gift, love it in fact. It was a difficult find to locate such a beautiful representation of *La Calavera Catrina* that matched José Guadalupe Posada's vision. This one was one of his own, an antique from 1913. Beautiful what one can create with their own hands."

He took up another brush and held it to the surface of the canvas. "Dear! Please sit up! Your face will gain creases from the sheets."

Dropping the brush on the floor he stomped over to the doll on the nightstand and sat her up. "Catrina." He caressed the white porcelain doll in both hands, gently adjusting the bonnet on her head. The skeletal doll of high society looked back in him. There were those empty eyes, gaping black holes, and that wide bone-colored grin. Her gown was white as cold death.

Still holding the doll, he sat on the edge of the bed. "The Catrina doll is an icon in Mexico. Did you know this, my love? Her face is one of the most seen during the Day of the Dead, the elegant, fashionable woman with her ornate hat and with the golden air of richness and fashion. She shows us that no matter how wealthy one is we are all susceptible to death."

He threw the doll against the wall and it shattered into pieces.

Standing up, he rolled over his wife. Vacant eyes looked back at him. Sliding her up on the bed, he propped the fair, slim, lifeless body in a sitting position against the headboard. He adjusted her dress, smoothing out the wrinkles. Delicately, he positioned her hands on her lap. He gently brushed her hair away from her face, letting it cascade onto her shoulders.

"We begin again. To perfection!" he said and walked back over to the easel to finish her portrait.

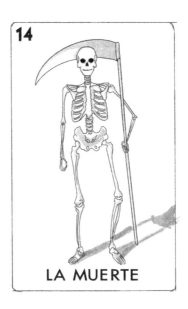

LA MUERTE

DEATH

The last burial at El Panteón de Belén was in 1896. It was held at the base of the monstrous columnar juniper tree on the south side of the cemetery grounds. There is no record of who, or what, was interred at that site, but dark rumors had made it so that locals didn't really want to know.

Even though funerals here had ceased over two hundred years ago, the living and the legends, continued to visit. Instead of mourners shedding tears on the grounds' manicured lawns, joyful couples and families walked the lush grass and strolled down cobble-stoned paths lined with white cedars on sun-filled afternoons.

At the gate, Hector Ramon pulled out his wallet and paid the five-peso entrance fee, like he had for the past ten days. The ticket attendant,

Gabriel Suarez (from the silver nameplate on his red vest), tore off a ticket and handed it to Hector.

It was on Hector's fifth consecutive visit that Gabriel made a comment: "I see you can't seem to get enough of the gardens."

"Research," Hector quickly explained. "I am a professor of history at the University of Guadalajara researching the ancestry of those buried here, and so I'm conducting a somewhat of an informal survey."

Gabriel slipped off his eyeglasses, wiped them on the bottom of his vest and then looked out over to the feared juniper tree and sighed deeply. At first Hector felt guilty about lying. He already knew all of the names that were possible to verify from the faded, crumbling headstones. There were the names of the wealthy men who were laid in the Rotonda de los Jaliscienses Ilustres. Then there were the names of the famous-poor, lucky enough to have a marked resting place. He had committed these names practically to memory in his quest to unravel the riddle of who was buried at the base of the juniper, but no matter how many times he read and re-read the names, and listed out their known histories and family trees, he could not determine who was buried at that tree.

On his daily visits, Hector strolled through the vast, barren lawn where the poor from the cholera epidemic were buried in unmarked graves. Beginning at sunset, he would move over to the weathered memorials and the sinking concrete tombs where the wealthy rested. When the moon hung in the black sky, pale and bright, and when all of the visitors had left and the gates were locked, Hector would go and sit at the base of the juniper, exhausted, his chest aching, but still he would wait. Each night, right before he would sit, his rotting insides would twist with excited panic.

On this night, as Hector's eyelids began to droop, he caught a shadow floating across one of the three doors at the circular mausoleum of Capilla de Vejacion. He sprang up from the tree and sprinted towards the stone structure after the quick moving black mass. He ran up the steps, two at a time, and stopped, panting and in pain—the cancer gnashing away at his lungs. Leaning on a ceremonial granite table, where the bodies of prominent citizens were put on display for their funerals, Hector wheezed and gasped for air.

A soft whistle startled him. He straightened up and turned. There, around the corner stood a black figure. He made out the silhouette of a man, dressed in dark slacks and a jacket.

"What is it that you want?" the man asked coolly, his back turned to Hector.

"To live forever," he blurted as he dug into his pants pocket, wrapping his fingers around a set of rosary beads his mother had given him on her own death bed.

The man laughed once. "You're a fool. There is no peace in forever."

"There is when you are already damned!" Hector pleaded, the beads now digging into his skin.

The figure moved away from the wall and walked slowly toward a thick group of trees on the edge of the grounds until he was enveloped by darkness.

"Come back!" Hector screamed. "Come back!"

Hector had failed.

LA PERA

THE PEAR

There's a secret a pear holds
in the ways in which you keep
and care for it

sprouted seeds, scattered
with complex destinies of
movements here, nor there

everywhere there's feeling, and
sometimes we lose meaning
along the way

walk North, keep going
entrenched, entranced by
something better, different

hopeful purpose, across a constellation
of warnings
that ring true of what is

known that the sun will radiate
and the heat will blister
and we will beg

to be quenched of a thirst
that is infinite, because
we walk East now, no

West, perhaps there's some salvation
South?
Or, there's no relief for these

hands will blister and bleed
packages weighed,
and gates closed, there's no

break when we're meant to splinter,
so there's more shifting, and watering
standing,

there's always standing,
movement that bends and aches,
repeat it

once more, and there's this seed
that will be planted and it will sprout
and it will grow

across this land where we walked
North, South, East, then West, and
its roots will tangle in and out,

and we must care for the great
fruit tree, because if it is not loved
if it does not feel light

it will sprout sharp thorns as daggers
so that when we can no longer walk
or bend, we will toss

ourselves into our work
and allow ourselves to shatter
under the weight of dreams

16

LA BANDERA

THE FLAG

t all began with an earthquake. If you live in California, then you are likely accustomed to preparing for earthquakes, but when a large one hits, well, it's something that just rattles your bones. Since that night, my nights were stolen from me. I felt the soft crunch of sand beneath the balls of my feet, the grains between my toes, and then I began to sink. I heard the crash of the waves, the tumbling of wooden planks, stairs, and doorways. Windows all rocked and tumbled to the ground. Horses squealed. Men shouted. The women screamed. The sky turned black and blacker still was the flag that flapped off the shore, on that vessel, with the glowing white skull and crossbones. "Dear God," a woman cried, but I knew that God didn't have anything to do with that ship.

The next moment, I was seated, screaming so loud it sliced into my throat. A woman was standing at my bedroom door. She wore blue jogging pants and an oversized gray T-shirt.

"Henrik?"

The woman flipped on the light and approached me slowly. The palms of her hands towards me.

"Henrik!" Her voice cracked and repeated the name louder, but I didn't know who she was talking to and what she meant when she said this, this Henrik. All I could do was scream, and scream, and scream, and then she grabbed hold of my shoulders and shook.

I awakened. That ship, that flag, imprinted on my mind forever.

FOR YEARS DOCTORS TRIED telling me that my nightmares were nothing more than recurring dreams. Occasionally one of my advising doctors will ask me how my nights have been. As always, I lie. I don't think they'll fail me for admitting that my problem persists. Who would fail a medical resident because they are not getting enough sleep?

I suppose, it would just be odd to come out and admit that my problem has lingered all this time. The reality of my nights has never left me. Each night, since I was a fifteen, they have always been the same. A recurring dream seemed far off from what I was experiencing. This was no weekly or monthly dream of flying or arriving nude to school. This was an existence that repeated itself each and every night. There are no nights without dreams, and it's always that same dream. It's always that very same. When I sleep, I always find myself there, at that beach, with the sand beneath my feet, the ocean before me, the warm sun on my skin, but then it all shifts. The crumbling, the cries, the brand of pirates—skull and crossbones, the Jolly Roger.

When I was a boy, the dreams terrified my mother as much as they terrified me it seemed. The first time she took me to the doctor to talk about my nightmares she was still in her own pink medical assistant uniform. She stood beside the bed, rubbing my hair, and answering the doctor's questions for me.

"Henrik, do you watch television late at night?" he asked.

"Yes, Doctor Rumilla. Yes, he does," my mother answered quickly, but I didn't watch television late at night. I countered my mother's response, and the doctor tapped his foot on the laminated floor and crossed his arms.

"Then, Henrik, are you playing video games late into the night?"

"Yes. Yes, he is doctor," my mother said through tears.

"Mom," I whined and pushed her hand out of my hair. "No, I don't! You know that."

"Then what can it be?" she pleaded with me. "Something is making you wake up so late screaming like that."

Her face was in front of mine now. My mother was so beautiful. She had me very young, I learned from my grandma. No one knew who my father was, and she would never say. All I knew is that it was someone from her home of Jamaica. After I was born, my grandmother and mother moved to California and neither of them ever returned to their home. Each time Jamaica would come up, they would seem unsettled and push the mention of it away, like the ghost of something long dead.

My mom's boss tried all he could. Dr. Rumilla asked me more questions and finally he rolled his stool over to his desk. He then took out a silver pen from the breast pocket of his white coat and scribbled something on a pad of paper. "Kalissa, have him take one of these every night before he goes to bed. Let's see how it goes from there." The doctor handed my mother the slip of paper, rubbed my head, and left.

The pills didn't work. That same night I was being wakened by my mother at my bedside, screaming at me to wake up. She was still in her medical assistant uniform I remember. I was seated. The blanket had dropped down to my waist. Sweat dripped from my forehead and my mouth was opened wide. I woke as the last shriek tore from my throat. The look on my mother's face was beyond that of panic. She was frightened. When she saw that it was me now, coming out of my night terror she gave me a tight hug and cried, "My Henrik! Why? Why are you doing this to my Henrik?"

I wondered who my mother was talking to.

My mother tried to live like this for a few more weeks, but the dark circles under her eyes were indicators that it was all taking too much of a toll on her. When she finally told her boss that the pills didn't work, Dr. Rumilla wrote her a referral to take me to see someone at The Stanford Center for Sleep Sciences and Medicine. This made it all the more jarring for her. She tried to prolong the visit as long as she could, until the need for a decent night sleep had become desperate.

At the hospital, we passed through a busy lobby. People were on cell phones directing family members to their whereabouts. Others were standing in line, checking in to visit a patient, while orderlies rolled newly healed patients to the exit doors so they could board a car home. The elevator left us on a surprisingly quiet floor. Everything was white, the floors, the walls, the doors, but no jarring, bright fluorescent light. It was a dim floor. No pictures lined the walls, and no one was in sight. Mom took my hand, and she followed the signs to room 919 and then knocked. The door opened to a small room, with a bed and a nightstand. Inside were Dr. Rumilla and a doctor half his age that introduced himself as Dr. Milam, the sleep specialist who would be monitoring my sleep, he said.

A young woman in navy blue scrubs entered and said she would be the technician. She told me not to worry, to relax as she placed stickies on my temples and connected them to a small dock on the nightstand. All the while, the doctors and my mother were telling me to relax, that all I needed to do was to fall asleep. The doctors eventually made their way into the hallway with my mother, and the technician told me it was all very simple.

"My name's Viviane," she smiled. "This does not hurt at all. All we want to do is learn why it is you're having trouble sleeping."

"What if you don't figure it out?" I asked and all the while I could see it there in my mind, the skull and crossbones.

"What do you mean?" she smiled. "I'm sure the doctor's will be able to make sure you get some good rest soon."

I wondered then if I should be holding it all back, but what was I going to tell them? That each and every night my sleep would take me to the same place, where a town would crumble, the black waves would crash ashore, my feet would begin to sink in the sand, and out in the ocean I would see the tall, black, ghostly, ghastly pirate ship. It was blacker than anything I had ever seen before, and it eluded such vile evil that its very approach shook the land. I stared at it, the flag flapping in the wind, fearing what was on that ship. Who was on that ship?

"You're right," I lied. "I'll get better soon after all this."

As everyone left the room, I wondered how I was supposed to fall asleep in a foreign place, but as soon as I sat back against the headboard a weight pushed itself down on my shoulders. At this point, I hadn't slept much in weeks. A few more minutes passed, and Viviane's voice came on softly overhead. "Now Henrik, I just need to test the sensors here on my end to make sure we can read the signals. I'm going to give you a few simple instructions." With that, I followed as her voice instructed me to look up, look down, raise one arm, raise the other, and the same with my legs.

"Everything looks good, Henrik. Just relax now and take your time, but overall, feel safe here. We're all here watching."

Time passed there in the darkened room, but eventually I did fall asleep.

This time, instead of just my mother standing over me trying to calm me down there were three other people, both doctors and Viviane holding down my arms and legs. I tried to kick and fight but then I awakened. In my dream this time something had changed. Now, I was not sinking in the sand. Instead, I was at the shore when the ship docked while behind me destruction tore through town. The crew of the vessel had gathered; rotted teeth and toothless grins silently greeted me. Yet, those weren't real faces. What looked back at me was rotted and wicked, and only small patches of skin covered bones here and there. All of them were dead, but that didn't matter. The skeleton crew waved me aboard.

"The Flying Dutchman!" I cried as I came to, the name of the ship written across the hull. My mother screamed as I called out that name.

AFTER SOME TIME, WE went into Dr. Milam's office. It was painted sea green, and his desk was lined with seashells, similar to the ones I had seen in my dreams.

"This is all very simple," he began. "Henrik here suffers from pavor nocturnus…"

"What?" My mother asked, confused.

"Night terrors," Dr. Rumilla responded as he looked over a chart. "They are usually more prone in children ages two to six, but they can happen in children of Henrik's age, fifteen. We even have adults come in with this condition. It's rare, but it can occur. They are characterized by a sudden arousal from a slow sleep wave with a piercing scream accompanied by manifestations of intense fear. People are also known to thrash around violently, unaware of their surroundings. You may also be unable to talk, comfort, or fully wake the child while they are having one of these spells. Thus, what we are seeing with your boy."

My mother looked at me and for a moment she looked afraid. "Are you sure that's it? I mean, can this be cured?"

"There's therapy and treatments. We can try to see how well you will respond, Henrik." The doctor rose from his seat, and he sat on his desk in front of me. "Henrik, that's a fine name. It's Dutch you know. My great-grandfather was a Henrik. Well, I'm sure you'll be able to move out of this stage of your life soon."

Before leaving the sleep center we were made to schedule several other polysomnogram tests. I had no intention of ever coming back for further testing. Out in the parking lot, while my mind was racing with possible ways to get out of testing, my mother saved me. As she opened the car door she said, "Don't worry. You'll never have to do that again."

As I slipped on my seat belt, I asked my mom "Is it true then, my name is Dutch?"

She nodded as she looked in the rearview mirror.

"Why a Dutch name, Mom?"

"Because that was your father's." And that's the only thing my mother ever told me about my dad.

Eventually, my mother took me off the medication Dr. Milam had prescribed because they were useless. My dream was there, and it was never going away. I just learned to control my body and my physical space so I wouldn't scream or thrash about—too bad—as I slept.

MY MOTHER WOULD LIVE to see me through medical school at least. She died young and she will forever be a secretive, young, beautiful woman to me. Her heart attack came suddenly on the beach one day with friends. Funny thing is, my mother always feared the ocean, strange for someone from an island, but after years in California a group of her friends finally convinced her to meet up at a beach and that's where she died, with the sand beneath her toes.

Today, I'm a resident at the very facility my mother brought me to years ago as a child. My job is to understand why it is people's nighttime sanctuaries are polluted with fear. I've studied them all, teeth-grinders, sleepwalkers, children suffering from night terrors, and adults reporting severe cases of sleep paralysis. Just last week, we had an extreme case where a teenage girl's night terrors were so brutal, during the sleep test, while still asleep, she stood up, jumped a few times and then ran across the bed and charged into the wall in front of her. Like most people suffering from true night terrors the young woman could not explain what had happened to her.

I'm months away from being a doctor, but how can I be expected to help people like that young woman when I can't explain my own condition? The last few months I've taken to forcing myself to write detailed notes about my dreams, and that place, that ship, that flag, and that crew. The Flying Dutchman I learned is a ghost ship destined to never make port as it has been cursed to sail the ocean forever, with its crew of the dead. There have been plenty of reports over the centuries of the damned vessel being seen, especially in the Caribbean. I don't know what that means. I don't know what any of it means. I just feel that somehow my dreams are shouts from a supernatural realm demanding me to go to this physical place, but why? What will happen if I go? I don't know, but I expect I'll soon find out. My ticket has been purchased, my bags have been packed and I am flying out in the morning to Jamaica to find the remnants of that sunken town and to look out into the blue ocean to see if there is indeed something out there calling for me.

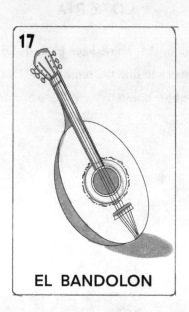

EL BANDOLON

THE MANDOLIN

C ampus security would like to alert all female students to remain indoors tonight. There was yet another reported incident yesterday evening. Like the last three attacks this month, the assault occurred shortly after dusk. The patterns are strikingly similar across all cases, and therefore we are asking you to remain vigilant. Women, if you must venture outdoors, walk in pairs or in groups. We also recommend that you tie your hair up into a bun or wear a baseball cap. Do remember to walk along well-lit paths and please do not cut through any heavily forested areas.

The description of the assailant remains the same as in previous attacks:

Gender: Male

Height: Four Feet

Weight: 65–75 Pounds

Eye Color: Brown

Hair Color: Brown

Last seen wearing: A black shroud with a shiny, thick belt around his waist, black boots, and a large, wide-brim hat that flops down and covers most of his face.

In this case, as in previous cases, the woman was cutting through the forest to get to the main street when suddenly she heard loud footsteps approaching from behind. When she turned around, she saw a small man standing before her. The man had two small, long-haired dogs with him. Each dog had a braided tail. The man smiled, reached behind his back, and produced a small guitar that he then used to serenade the young woman. When the woman ignored the bizarre behavior and attempted to continue on her way, the man chased her and tackled her to the ground. The man then laid the woman on his lap and proceeded to braid her hair, while still serenading her.

When night approached the woman complained of hunger. The man then pulled out a small silver plate from his pocket, filled it with dirt and presented it to the woman as her meal, which she declined.

In all cases the women escaped after the man fell asleep.

Some residents believe this is a repeat prankster who is dressing up as El Sombrerón, the legendary bogeyman who is also referred to as Tzipitio or plainly a goblin. Legend says that if El Sombrerón finds a woman who corresponds to his love that he will rope his mules in front of the woman's house and serenade her—forever.

Additional reports of similar incidents dating back to the 1940s said there was a wave of panic in this area that led to parents cutting their daughters hair to deter the advances of El Sombrerón. All of the women victimized had long hair. We are not asking that you cut your hair. However, we are going to suggest it. Local hair salons in recent weeks have reported an increase in business.

18

EL VIOLONCELLO

THE CELLO

I decided to do this. You didn't decide it for me because you would not have decided this for me. I don't think anyone really would tell their friend to go along with this idea, and so, I guess that's why I have no friends. Another year and I age. Another year and I rot. Another year and well…you know, you all know, because you are here as well… many of you. Yet, many of you will not meet this end because well, it is a sin, now isn't it? If you believe in that sort of thing. This is a grave and serious thing. It's believed that you are the property of God and destroying his property is asserting your dominion over what is God's. So, if you break something that's not yours the owner typically will get pissed, but I didn't care.

Hey, at least you can't say I didn't try. I tried. I went to high school. I got expelled. I got my GED. I worked as a receptionist in a doctor's office. I went to community college. I met this mysterious guy at a club, dated him a few times, and we even moved in together. Don't blame any of this on him. He's not the reason I'm here. He wasn't the whole religious type anyway. So he wouldn't think my plan would have some sort of spiritual repercussions. Actually, the guy was the opposite. No, not an atheist or agnostic, but a proud ol' Satanist. My mom was none too pleased. Lukasz and I didn't last too long. I threw Satanic Statement number five right back in his face when I caught a nasty case of gonorrhea from him, "Satan represents vengeance instead of turning the other cheek." So, I packed up his clothes in some garbage bags, poured in some bleach and changed the locks.

The next day I got fired. Maybe it was karma for ruining Lukasz's stock of black Armani shirts. A few months later my mom died of kidney failure. It was like this endless line of tragedy. And then a few weeks after burying my mom, I found the lump. Stage IV metastatic breast cancer, at age twenty-six. With no job, no insurance, no mom, no boyfriend, and that old high school drug problem slowly creeping back, I said screw it. I'm done with life.

I always wanted to get out of Milwaukee because who doesn't. A trip someplace far, far away; a place that would be my perfect ending. My mom was really into churches, weird ones. We had visited every weird church in the Midwest—cathedrals and crumbling old buildings that were once visited by Pope John Paul II. Hey, some people's moms are into knitting or drinking, my mom was into churches. I don't know why. Maybe because she grew up Catholic and eventually just became nonreligious all together, but I think something about churches reminded her of her parents or her childhood. So, it was a way to tap into old, good memories, not the ones from the last twenty-some-odd years. I was probably the beginning of her end.

She got pregnant at sixteen and the only thing her adult boyfriend had left behind was an empty cello case. Who the hell leaves behind an empty cello case? A violin case, maybe? But, a cello case? He obviously played the cello, but for whatever reason, he just lugged that huge instrument out of the house, without its case, and never returned. My mother would go on to get kicked out of her house after a huge fight with her parents. She worked as a waitress and lived in a small one-bedroom apartment until her death, but she always displayed that case. We used it as a wobbly sort of coffee table. Maybe she thought he'd come back for it one day. Who knows?

The voices began a few nights ago. At first it was a soft hum. I thought the microwave was on in the kitchen, but when I went to check on it the thing was surely off. Little by little the humming grew clearer, sharper. The words took shape and form, and it then became like the vibration had moved out of my head altogether. It settled, in my apartment and everything in it vibrated with that rhythm.

I sat on the floor of my apartment, in the corner furthest away from any window and I listened, carefully. I proceeded to write on a pad of paper with a pencil the words being spoken to me. Hours went by. It took days for me to clearly and confidently be sure what was being said, but eventually I got it; that loop of syllables and sounds, I finally got it.

Nós ossos que aqui estamos pelos vossos esperamos Nós ossos que aqui estamos pelos vossos esperamos Nós ossos que aqui estamos pelos vossos esperamos Nós ossos que aqui estamos pelos vossos esperamos Nós ossos que aqui estamos pelos vossos esperamos Nós ossos que aqui estamos pelos vossos esperamos Nós ossos que aqui estamos pelos vossos esperamos Nós ossos que aqui estamos

pelos vossos esperamos Nós ossos que aqui estamos pelos vossos
esperamos Nós ossos que aqui estamos pelos vossos esperamos
Nós ossos que aqui estamos pelos vossos esperamos Nós ossos
que aqui estamos pelos vossos esperamos

Nós ossos que aqui estamos pelos vossos esperamos

After logging those words, I fell asleep and woke up that morning
with the lump more painful and tender to the touch. It was time. I
wasn't going to wait around any longer to wither away in some county
hospital or in that depressing apartment. After a few online searches,
I found a really messed up church abroad, maxed out my credit cards,
and a few my old boyfriend forgot to take with him, and packed a
suitcase. In it I included a bottle full of sleeping pills. Before I stepped
out of the apartment, I grabbed that stupid cello case. I wanted it with
me on those final days.

THIS IS HOW I came to be here in Portugal, standing beneath this
stone arch, at the Capela dos Ossos standing under the words that
called me here, "Nós ossos que aqui estamos pelos vossos esperamos."
At the airport, I had snagged a travel guide and found that these very
words mean, "We, the bones that are here, await yours." Fitting for
someone who came here to take their own life.

Inside, I knew what awaited me. It is what awaits us all. We all
must remember memento mori. Here it is, reality. The only light that
streamed into the room came from one of the four small windows
ahead. The muted light fell gently on the hundreds of packed, stacked
and carefully positioned grayish-white shapes. From the doorway,

it looked like a simple, Gothic cathedral. The arched ceiling was painted with soft, delicate floral patterns, but the walls were made up of something more than dirt and stone and concrete. Stepping over the threshold, a chilled air kissed my cheek. I walked slowly taking in the walls crafted by skulls once covered by blood and flesh and hair. Hundreds of skulls were stacked upon each other, bulging craniums emerging from the walls. Sternums and lumbars, femurs and ribs were all used to create this very room and decorative patterns. I felt thousands of empty eye sockets watching me as I silently approached the center. A desiccated adult corpse dangled from a chain at the front of the room and beside it the remains of a small child. A sixteenth century Franciscan monk had started the construction of this chapel with the remains of those from nearby cemeteries, because space at those cemeteries was limited. He wanted this place to be a beautiful tribute to the dead, and he thought that this space would bring one into contemplation that life is transitory.

I had nothing. No mother. No boyfriend. No job. I was a pretty girl, not vain, but with cancer ravaging my body, what was the point in fighting anything any longer. I was tired, frustrated, and mad. I had lived a life consumed by loss and misdirection. It was as though everything I had ever sought was to be laid right here with these exquisite corpses and gleaming bones.

My decision had been made and what else could possibly hold me back? I was angry and empty. No one would be with me in my final moments, and I didn't need anyone here. All I hoped was for everyone and everything to feel as hopeless as I felt.

Suddenly, I heard a snap behind me. There was a click and then a series of bright lights pulsed. An older man, in a checkered cap had snapped a photo. A woman, in an ankle length blue dress and black walking shoes, milled nearby. They exchanged a few words between the two of them, Italian maybe, and then left with their arms around each other. I hated them. Hated them for their happiness in their old age.

I looked back to the front of the chapel and wondered if I should write a note asking for my remains to be left here. I wanted to be here for eternity. Anonymous in death as in life. I dug my hand in my purse and pulled out the prescription bottle of sleeping pills that I coerced a doctor friend of mine to give me. I pushed down on the safety top with the palm of my hand, twisted it opened and then I paused. The rusted, iron cross beside the hanging corpse led my eye to the skull to the very left of its base. I stepped closer and noticed that this skull seemed smoother, more defined, and just different than the rest. I approached the cross. The wall from which it hung was made up of dozens of horizontally positioned fibulas. I reached out and, with the tip of my finger, lightly brushed the dusty cranium.

That simple move, so light and thoughtless changed my life.

The skull fell from its place leaving a gaping hole in the bone design.

There was a cough from behind me.

"I must say, I didn't think it'd be a woman so young, but I do suppose it all makes sense."

"I'm sorry. I barely touched it," I said, embarrassed and shocked all the same. "I didn't think it'd fall..."

Remembering the bottle in my hand, I quickly closed it and shoved it in my sweater pocket.

The man laughed. I thought he was a security guard at first but after the panic subsided, it was clear he was no security guard or even a museum or church attendant. He had wavy black hair that fell right above his shoulders. He wore gray slacks and a gray jacket with a white undershirt. His face was narrow, and he had a sharp, prominent nose. I tried to look away but couldn't. I felt like he was reading every part of me, my misery and failures.

"Well? Are you or aren't you?"

"Aren't I what?" I was frozen there.

"There, in your pocket." He waved a hand holding a pair of sunglasses in my direction. "The pills…" He smiled.

"What pills?" My face, voice, and yes, the orange bottle of pills in my hand betrayed me.

"Very well. Then, take a look there and see what you've done."

I didn't need to look again. I had destroyed the wall. "I'm sorry. It was an accident."

"Take a look inside," he pressed. "There's something there…"

His words hung in the air for a moment until I turned around and inspected the hole in the wall. Indeed, there was something there. When I turned back, he motioned for me to remove the object, which I did. It was covered in a light brown cloth sack and weighed as much as a small bowling ball. Carefully, I undid the tie and slid the bag back over the object. The man gasped with pleasure and then laughed.

"Bring it here," he said gleefully.

A smooth, brilliant skull made of a single piece of crystal looked back at me. I didn't know what to do, so I did as told.

He looked at it as if it were a newborn child, with bright eyes, and a mouth opened in awe. His eyes took it in completely and then he spoke to me, without removing his gaze from the hidden treasure.

"You don't really have much time now do you?" He glared at me before returning his focus to the skull in his hands. "I'm going to ask you this just once. Would you like the opportunity to be gainfully employed, to travel to locations where I have specified for you all within three months' time? You'll be paid handsomely, travel in luxury private arrangements, and get to do whatever else it is you want to do before you must get back to your task at hand. I just need you to do what you did here five more times. I am missing five more of these skulls and need them all for my collection." He covered the skull carefully and tied the sack.

"What are you talking about?"

"You were able to see what no one has been able to see for a very long time. Not many people have that ability. So, do you accept?" he pressed.

"If you're not lying then yeah, sure, why the hell not? I don't have anything going on right now anyway." I figured he would laugh at me, say he was kidding and then I'd rush out, alert security, the guy would get arrested for being stoned or drunk or just plain crazy, and maybe I'd go off myself in my hotel room, but none of that happened. No, instead, he carefully slipped on his black sunglasses. He flashed a sharp canine smile, then he turned and proceeded toward the exit. My heart sank. I knew he was crazy. As I turned my back on him to face the altar he called from the archway.

"The helicopter's outside. Let's be off."

The job sounded simple. Do what I had done and find five more crystal skulls. The man in the gray suit was sure they could be located in other bone churches. I struck out with this one, so it should be easy enough.

I was supplied with an unlimited credit card but limited time. Three months was all the doctors had given me and coincidentally that's the time the man in the gray suit gave me to find the missing skulls. I didn't know what the punishment was for failing. I guess I didn't really think about it much. Maybe he figured I wanted meaning, something to hold on to before I let go. Something I could say I accomplished before abandoning life. Maybe that's why I went along with it.

"I DON'T UNDERSTAND HOW the cello comes into play." Gabriel said.

"The cello comes into play at the end," I remember telling Gabriel as he helped me set the cello case in the SUV for my final trip.

In a sense, I regretted bringing him here, but from the moment I met him there in the dark, I didn't want him to be away from me.

By the time I had gotten to Paris, I was so ravaged by depression I didn't think I could continue. Little by little I learned the terms of my new employment. My employer was more than just a collector of the macabre. In our ongoing correspondence that included prepaid cell phones, email accounts that would have to be deleted after a single use, and the use of couriers, one of which shot himself through the mouth after communicating my employer's message—led me to wonder if they all killed themselves after passing our messages. I learned that the man in the gray suit believed himself to be a Nephilim. Time spent traveling alone in private train cars, buses, and private jets was time I used to study and research. I learned that no one really knows who, or what, the Nephilim were, or are. They are mentioned in the Bible as the "sons of God," and the "daughters of men." They were described in the Bible as giants who inhabited Canaan, but of course, no one really knows what that means.

Some theorists believed them to be the offspring of relations between angels and women, while others believed them to be the offspring of demons with women, or just fallen angels altogether. A website I had to crack the code to get into stated that there is an underground belief that Nephilim are plotting the end of the world, attempting to acquire the Sword of Destiny, the sword that pierced Jesus's side on the cross, for the belief that whoever holds this sword will rule the world. Another speculation is that the Nephilim want to obtain all thirteen of the mythical Mayan crystal skulls to destroy them because the destruction of all of the crystal skulls would set in motion the end times.

I didn't know what to believe.

Staying up all night, breaking into crypts, and locating skulls started to make me feel like a crazy person, and soon, I just wanted this job done and over with because the pain in my chest became unbearable without drugs. After weeks on the road, I had made my way through ossuaries in the Czech Republic, Ireland, Poland, and Italy where in the tiny chapel of San Bernardino alla Ossa, bones were carefully set in the dark walls and in the center, skulls formed a large cross. It had been easy to find the crystal skull there. It was almost as if I had x-ray vision because tourists that stood directly beside me seemed oblivious to the sparkling lump of crystal in the wall. There it was, plain in sight, stacked at the base of the cross.

In Paris, I was staying in a bed and breakfast off of Rue de Cuer. I found myself sitting outside the Cathedral of Notre Dame, preparing for a long night through miles and miles of underground passages. It was going to be a long, dark night, so I strolled over to the Latin Quarter for some wine, lots of it. After midnight, when most Parisians were in bed, I broke into l'Ossuaire Municipal. The remains of six million were down here and so I figured I would be in Paris for quite some time, spending my days above ground sleeping and my nights below ground searching for one of the few remaining skulls on my list. In fact, after this one, I would just need one other.

I had bumped into Gabriel in the dark as he searched for his friends who had also broken in. They had crept down here for a night of drinking among the dead, he had said, finding it an exciting outing. Gabriel never found his friends that night. Instead, he and I spent hours talking over a couple of bottles of wine, no one to listen to our conversation except the remnants of the once living. His fingers through my hair, down my neck, and my back pressed against the cold floor made me forget about bones and death, for just a few minutes. His hot breath on my cheek felt like it brushed away the stain of the job I was soon to accomplish. When I turned on the flashlight to get dressed, I spotted it there, in the wall, the fourth crystal skull. Just one more and my job would be completed.

"THAT STILL DOESN'T MAKE any sense." Gabriel said. "The cello comes into play at the end?"

He had followed me to Valladolid, Spain, and I wanted him to. Up until now I had been consumed with so much anger and hatred but something about Gabriel set me at peace and gave me immense joy. I needed him near me. He made me feel safe and clean and whole and loved. I didn't know how to explain to him the private jet and the black SUVs driven by bodyguards, and so I lied that I was the daughter of an ambassador. He didn't seem to really believe me, especially as we drove up to the Church of Santa Maria outside the village of Wamba, Spain. I told him I wanted to play tourist and visit another ossuary. The ossuary here held the bones of people that spanned centuries, from the twelfth to eighteenth centuries in fact.

"No, really, what is in the cello case," Gabriel pressed as our car left us in front of the church.

"Just, something I picked up in Paris," I said. Really, it was where I held the last skull found in Paris. Up until now, the man in the gray suit had met me to collect each skull, but he had not made it to Paris to collect this one. I didn't know where to store it, and so I placed it in cello case of the father I never knew.

Inside the church Gabriel stopped and pulled me by the arm over to an inscription. He read, "*Como te ves, yo me ví. Como me ves, te verás. Todo acaba en esto aquí. Piénsalo y no pecarás.*" It means, "As you see yourself, I saw myself too. As you see me, you will see yourself. Everything ends in this. Think about it and you won't fall into sin."

The piles of bones were everywhere. In other ossuaries the walls were made up of bones, but not here; here bones were scattered about us in organized piles. Gabriel pulled on my arm as I stepped to make my way toward one of the piles. I had seen it, there, almost instantly. Glowing and white. Distinct from all others. This was it. The fifth and last skull owed to the man in the gray suit. "Everything does end in this," Gabriel repeated. "Think about it and you won't fall into sin."

I knew then Gabriel wasn't who he said he was, and now searching through that foggy night we first spent together I realized he never did say where he came from. I had just assumed France, but he wasn't from France or anywhere near here.

Kill myself or contribute to the collapse of the world, or both. This was the path I had chosen, and now Gabriel was asking me what would be my next move. I could feel the cell phone in my pocket vibrating. The man in the gray suit was calling to check in on me. I turned to face Gabriel and he was gone. I ran outside and the car was gone, the case, the fourth skull, Gabriel all gone.

Back inside, I stared at the inscription in the bone church and as the inscription said, I thought about it, thought about what I had been lured to do while I was weak. The phone continued to ring, and I finally answered it.

"Just one more. Do we have it?" he asked.

"It's not at the Church of Santa Maria. I'm going to go back and search another location. I think maybe it was back in Czech Republic, at the Sedlec Ossuary, in Kutná Hora."

"Very well," he said before hanging up.

I unzipped my backpack and pulled out the bottle of pills I had been carrying with me for weeks. The pain in my chest burned so powerfully that I needed to lie down, anywhere. I found a small spot in the corner where I curled up on the floor, surrounded by bones, and slowly I took each pill, thinking that no matter what, I would fall into sin, but at least I would only be responsible for my own death.

19

LA GARZA

THE HERON

They'll always come to discover—a new fruit, a new root, medicinal miracle or simply to cut
blades, saws and steel machines will pull and rip the jungles
twisting, sky touching breath
branched arms reaching upwards, always upward while inhaling sickness and death
exhaling life for those who destroy—but she's here to kiss the scars of her forested home

and lead away murderers to where they will worship her, as she consumes their souls
a new sacrifice is what she needs now—heartless logger knowingly casting destruction

she sits cloaked in stars, the moon hangs against the sky, the Amazonian River glows

the lady listens to the shrieks of the forest, her children are chopped, gutted, her life cut

tears roll down her glistening cheeks as she mourns her rainforests soul

she kneels on the ground, bathed in the moonbeam, and prays for the return of her river's breath

lonely is she. Seeking love, but the only ones near are those charged with the death of her home

she'll rest this day. Many come, but she sits waiting for her chosen, love in death

when the buzz and yells and the corpses of her trees tumbling awaken her from death

and the great blue heron submerges its harpoon beak, breaking through the river this night

her dreams of land are over. She herself will die if she does not soon return to her watery home

searching the sounds of their hearts she listens and finds one. A saw is out, sharpened to cut

pressed against the tree's bark they pull, back and forth. The ancient god cries and ceases breath

their spiritless carcass is rolled across the floor, prepped, wrapped—an empty soul

she herself falls, her flesh itself beaten and whipped by the forest's reduction of souls her frail form finds comfort in the cool mud, but she needs her river, and a death

a motor charges. More people enter. Empty vehicles, to transport the lifeless, the deceased breath
she cries. Wrapping herself in muddied earth, covering her body, wishing she herself were night
so that she could no longer feel the wrenching within that stabs and stings her shape. It cuts, it
pierces. It mutilates her thoughts. She is hungry, starving, raving, and it's time to go home

the jungle beats her name, freshwater name telling her it's time to go home
Lara, ancient Guaraní, our lady of the lake—the freshwater maiden, we're losing souls
beautiful woman, the river calls for your green hair, your fair glowing skin, your eyes that cut
any person's desire, any heart—your lure is any honor for anyone's death

pretty lover, beautiful spell the forest calls you back to your home, to sleep away your long night
return to land after you bring us a sacrifice, but first heal and swim and halt your breath
it is day again. Buzzing returns. It vibrates the jungle floor. She listens through the breath
she finds him. Her lover. Her lover of loves. He thinks of her now, feels her home

seated on a log, she stares at the great blue heron, patiently seeking its prey to envelope night

"Come love me," she whispers musically as she feels his feet step away, he runs through souls

no human sees as he rushes past, removes his gear, work belt and helmet embracing death

at the riverbed, he meets her, an angel, a nymph, his siren, his mermaid—she reaches and cuts

She breathes in his soul
Her home, her waters become his death
Night takes over and she'll return again when the trees tumble

20

EL PAJARO

THE BIRD

Ancestor's songs pulsing with the scent of salt-sea air
Lull of a coqui call tucked between El Yunque roots
Stargazers whisper wishes to an infinite black sky
Dotted by stars, puncturing the present, pained by past

It's silent in the morning, we weep with mouths closed
Wondering, shuffling, laminate floors, pouring coffee cultivated
Here? Or, there? El campo? I miss, but no, we can't reminisce
We who are abandoned by the Bermuda Triangle impossibility

And so, we'll sink, and they'll call us wretched
And so, we'll drown, and we'll be prosecuted for our own deaths
Across a plane, down highways, crowded in neighborhoods

That aren't really neighbor-ly, what did Pedro Pietri say:

"They worked and they died," and so we die, with a Lottery Ticket
Unfulfilled promises staining our lips, staring at that cloudy gray sky
Not our sky, begging and dreaming, for her, 100X35, last hopeless breaths
Clinging on to the desperation that we'll spot the great beating green wings

Of our endangered island parrot ushering us back home

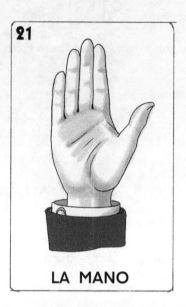

LA MANO

THE HAND

"*Chupacabra!*" The old man snorted. He patted his chest pockets until he found a half-smoked cigar and a withered matchbook. Holding the cigar between his teeth as he struck a match he said, "I don't believe in some stupid goat killing, blood sucking little monster." Taking a long puff and then blowing it out from his nose, it was like his anger came out through his nostrils. He seemed angry at me for having asked him if he believed in the stories. Then again, here in Tlaxcala, weren't all people made to believe in the Tlahuelpuchi?

It was getting late. The sun had begun to set over the plaza and the old man, my sleeping daughter, and I sat there on the wooden bench waiting for the bus. Sitting here, in silence, watching small children kick a soccer ball around the plaza as the sun set felt unsettling. We had lived outside of town for a few months. People didn't bother us there. I had found a good Catholic school for Rebecca where prayers and religiosity were enforced beyond the classroom, with mandatory volunteer work to be carried out at the church during the weekends. Knowing that she had a constant duty to God made me feel like she could be saved, somehow.

Rebecca had come to me that morning with a disturbing announcement: She had become a woman. Her blood had started to flow. My daughter, at only eleven years old, had potentially become something that I could not control. This morning she went to school in her uniform: a navy blue jumper, white polo, Mary Janes, and frilly white socks. It was her day to help sweep, mop, and dust at the Convent of Our Lady of Assumption. I called the sisters and told them Rebecca was ill. As soon as I hung up, I told Rebecca that we were going to take a little field trip.

The ruins of Xochitecatl were located eighteen kilometers from the city. My mother had brought me here at about the same point in my life. She was relieved to find no glow in those darkened rooms, so we left. Back in New Mexico, I had studied and eventually married—with the intent to never have children. Although, after a few years of marriage my husband became persistent that he wanted to become a father. He loved me and did all of the things a good husband would do—changing the light bulbs and sweeping the garage. I thought maybe we would be lucky, have a boy, and then there would be nothing to worry about. The day of the ultrasound, when we found out it was a girl, I knew that she would carry the gene. It was something I had felt in my blood.

As soon as she turned eleven years old, we left our lives. I torched my car out on some back country road. I paid cash for a small jeep and we drove all night. I had saved enough money over the years, just in case, to live a simple life—away. In a few days, I had purchased us a small white stucco house, some furniture, and all of the other little items that make a life: clothes, dishes, and linens.

"Your daughter?" The old man turned to me. "Did she like the ruins?"

I stared him down with curiosity. I had not mentioned that we had visited the archeological site.

"You asked me if I believed in the Chupacabra and I say no. You ask me if I believe in Tlahuelpuchi, the female vampire, and I say yes. People who go to the ruins ask such questions."

I could feel Rebecca's heartbeat as she slept against my shoulder. "Yes, she did like the ruins." I squeezed her a little tighter, perhaps too tight.

Rubbing her eyes, she groaned and stretched out her arms.

"The bus here yet, Mom?"

"Keep your hands in your jumper pocket." I pulled the hood of her sweater over her head. "No, you can go back to sleep."

"But I'm hungry," Her hazel eyes burned into me. She was just so pale.

"We'll get you something at home."

"I'm just so hungry now." Her voice was a strained whisper.

"Baby, there isn't anything around here now. You'll just have to wait," I pressed my cheek against hers. "Get some sleep. The bus should be along."

The old man removed the cigar from his mouth, holding it out with two fingers and looked from Rebecca to me, and then over to La Malinche, the volcano in the distance.

"It's getting dark. The bus should be along soon," he said. Still looking out to the mountain. "Your girl should be able to get something to eat tonight."

Rebecca had fallen asleep again.

"Why didn't she come with her class to the ruins? I know they take school children there frequently on class trips."

The answer to that was none of his business, as the answer to that was to prove to myself that I had done the right thing, ripping myself and my daughter from the life we knew to prove that she indeed was a threat to those who loved her most.

"Just because I wanted to see them too," I lied.

"Did you see The Pyramid of Flowers?" the old man asked, leaning forward now, and shuffling through a shopping bag that sat between both of his legs.

"Yes. It was on her list of places to see for school."

"Right, for *school*," the old man chuckled.

From the bag he pulled out a small salmon-colored clay statue. It was of a little girl, an indigenous child with an elaborate headdress of a serpent, its fanged teeth decorating her head like a crown.

"You know they found the bodies of thirty children in there when they first excavated that pyramid. Another odd discovery was made leading up the stairway. They found thousands and thousands of little clay figurines, like this one." He turned the statue in his hand. "They were all of women from different stages in their life, from little babies to old women. All of the statues had individual clothes carved. They were all unique. What was most strange was a second stairway where they found mythological figures of the goddess Xochitl, a beautiful woman who can turn into a snake. But that is folklore, and I assume you, of all people, know about folklore."

I felt my hold around Rebecca tightening.

"Do you know why we don't believe in the Chupacabra here, miss? Because we know that the Tlahuelpuchi exists."

I squeezed Rebecca's arm. "Wake up, baby. We're going to walk."

"What?" She stretched her arms in front of her and yawned. I took her hands and shoved them in her pockets.

"Keep your hands in your pockets, baby."

Her large eyes glittered and looked up at me pleadingly. "Mom, I'm too tired to walk."

"We have to go!" I raised my voice and stood up, yanking Rebecca's arm and forcing her to stand. The old man remained calm throughout.

"Does your daughter know the legend of the Tlahuelpuchi vampire?"

"No!" I snapped. "Come on, Rebecca." I put my arm around her waist.

The man shouted over my voice.

"The Tlahuelpuchi are born with this curse and they cannot avoid it. They learn about their true nature during puberty and most are female. They feed on the blood of infants at night and the only way to identify one is by their glowing aura, or if they are detected by a shaman." The man removed his hat and lowered it over his heart. "And shamans, young lady, have a pact that we do not turn in your kind." His lips quivered and his eyes watered.

The sun had set. The children in the plaza had left and we were the only ones there. The bus came towards us from down the road, stirring up dirt. Right before its headlights reached us, Rebecca removed her hands from her jumper pocket and reached for the old man's hand. An emerald glow emanated from her fingertips.

The old man stood up, took her hands in his, and shook them. "It's very nice to meet you, Rebecca. Can you help an old man with his groceries onto the bus?"

My daughter smiled at me. It was a fresh, happy smile.

"Mom, he knows too. I can tell." Her smooth round cheeks were like small apples. "Sure, I'll help you."

"Such a fine daughter you have raised. She will be fine, like those before her, she will be protected by all of us."

"All of 'us'?"

"There are many people like me. There are many people like your daughter for you to meet. I will introduce you to them all, after the girl eats of course."

As we boarded the bus, we passed a woman seated alone with a newborn infant by her side. The old man leaned forward and whispered into Rebecca's ear. I was so close I heard him say, "Your first lesson is never to eat in public."

22

LA BOTA

THE BOOT

"And why is your hair sticking out so much?" She pointed towards my face; the broom clutched tightly in her other hand. I felt around my ears, looked at my reflection in the microwave and tucked a few loose strands of wavy dark hair back into my hijab.

"I ran home from school and my hair must've got loose," I said as I tossed my school bag on the kitchen table and pulled up a wooden chair.

I moved over to the refrigerator and poured myself a glass of coconut water. I was seventeen. We had moved to the island when I was five, after my father was promoted as the head of mechanical operations at Bristol Myers Squibb, a global pharmaceutical company. Puerto Rico is strangely a hub for pharmaceutical manufacturing, and even stranger, it has a sizeable Palestinian population, and so there are quite a lot of Muslim families.

My grandmother resumed her sweeping, the bristles made a scraping sound against the white tiled floor. At the kitchen table, I tried to reconstruct my thoughts.

"In class today while we were talking about mythology, what is good and what is evil, some idiot brought up genies and said they are, well, evil. I think he said it more to mess with me," I fumed.

"Genie? What is a genie? There are no genies. There are jinn. You call them jinn and you better not let them hear you insult them in this house or elsewhere, ever." She closed her eyes and placed her hands on either side of her head. One of her headaches was coming on.

"I'm sorry," I said quietly, but she waved me off. Grandmother wore a silk flowered headscarf. She had been balding for some time because of the chemotherapy, and so a thin scarf was all she needed to cover her head.

"There are three beings Allah created…" she paused, waiting for an answer from me, I guess, but I just shrugged.

"You need to read Quran more," she said. "Allah created the jinn, the angels, and humans. The jinn are like you and me. They have their own house, their own world, but our world, they can enter anytime…. and…" She stopped abruptly. Turning her head slowly. She peered into all of the corners of the kitchen, almost as if she were searching to see if anyone was listening in on our conversation. She lowered her voice slightly and said, "Like humans, there are good jinn and there are bad jinn."

I laughed. She frowned, clearly not amused.

"They don't grant wishes, then, right?" I tore off a piece of flaky baklava sitting on the table grandmother had prepared and popped it into my mouth.

There was the clank of metal against glass as she added heaping spoonfuls of sugar to the tea. "Really, Noor?"

A car pulled into the driveway next door, with pulsating Spanish reggaeton beats blaring. Victor, my neighbor and secret boyfriend, had just come home.

Grandmother looked out of the kitchen window over the sink and pulled back the blinds. "That poor boy. I don't know how his mom allows him to go off to war."

"I want to join the army after high school," I said.

"For what? To march around in boots? To kill your own people?"

"No, to help people. They need women in the army, Muslim women that can speak Arabic, that can help, and I know I can help."

"All those boots will do is guide you to nothing because you don't even know what needs helping."

"Yes, I do," I said, admittedly unsure.

"What is happening right now in Palestine?"

I shook my head slowly. I really didn't know.

"Go outside and check on the shawarma. Your dad should be home soon."

"But what about the jinn?"

"When you learn the history of Palestine, you will learn more about the jinn. Now go and get your father's dinner before it burns."

I pushed the screen door open, and back there, in our yard full of mango and coconut trees, my life changed forever.

They're made of fire and smoke. As a little girl, my father told me, "When you put out the coals from the grill never, ever toss them out because someone can get hurt." I never understood why until that day. Instead of throwing water over the coals I tossed them into the fire pit quite haphazardly. What followed was the panicked scream of a little girl. I'll never forget that scream of pain and terror.

I turned around to find her there. Her eyes flamed red and gold. Her long, black ringlets fell down her angelic face and past her shoulders. Her dress was a pale blue, and it was singed and dirtied with ashes. A life-sized doll, that's what she looked like. A pretty little girl, no more than ten. She raised her still hissing arms and inspected her injuries. Large, red sores oozed on her skin. The smell of burning flesh stung my nostrils. She approached me with a wicked sneer, presenting her still smoking arms to me. I fell back onto the ground.

"Stupid girl! What is your name?"

"Noor," I choked back terror.

"The stupid girl who hurts her sister is named Light?" She tilted her head, looked down at me curiously, and stepped forward. "You'll burn for this!"

She opened her tiny hands and in each were two large, fiery coals.

I kicked backwards on the ground, but she was on top of me. She was strong. She had me pressed down onto the grass and I couldn't move. I tried to hit her, to push her off, but each time my hands reached upward to touch her, they shot back, repelled by an invisible shield. I covered my eyes and screamed.

"Stop. It was a mistake." There was a glittering laugh all around me.

My arms were beginning to burn, stinging cold at first and then blazing under the shock. The heat moved toward my face, getting hotter and hotter, and seconds before it touched my skin, I screamed. "Stop! I'll do anything!"

"Anything?" The girl said sweetly.

I opened my eyes, and there we both were sitting outside on the grass on a sunny, cloudless day. The air smelled crisp, of fresh salted ocean air and citrus fruit. My arms were fine, just covered in blades of grass and dirt. The little girl sat properly in front of me, legs crossed, and hands folded on her lap. The burns were gone, and her large, doll-like eyes looked up at me lovingly.

"You'll come back home with me." She smiled wickedly.

"No."

"Oh." She bowed her head sadly, her curls falling over her face. Those red and gold eyes looked up and she said, "Then I guess you'll just have to die now."

A circle of flames erupted around me. The child laughed, and through the fire, I could see her skipping outside of the circle. The wall of fire began to close in on me, closer and closer until I could smell my hair burning.

"I'll do anything," I cried. "Just stop please!"

The flames disappeared.

The little girl threw herself at my leg and hugged it tightly. "You'll be my new slave."

"What?"

The enraged ruby and amber eyes looked at me and a deep, rough voice erupted from the child's throat.

"You'll be my new slave...unless of course," her girl-like voice returned, "You can tell me my name." She pressed her lips to my cheek, an iron hot kiss.

She stood up, dusted herself and said, "I'll be back for you, Noor, in seven years. For now, I'll grant you three wishes, whatever three you think of right...now." There was a quick pause, an all-consuming silence. I could feel her invading my thoughts and then she said, "Very well then, those three things you just thought shall be granted."

"But wait I didn't say…"

"These are my rules. In seven years, I will return for you, and you will be my slave.

Unless, of course, you can tell me my name."

And then she was gone.

GRANDMOTHER DIED A FEW years later. It was a peaceful, painless death. The kind of good death I had wished for her. I tried bringing up the jinn again to her, but she had been spooked, I guess. She didn't even want me mentioning their general name in our house after that day. I always wondered if the little girl had gotten to her. The day I went to the hospital to gather my grandmother's items, I had found an envelope with my name tucked into her Qur'an. Inside of the envelope was one verse from our holy book—that was my second wish.

The seven years have gone by and sometimes I think I was silly to have made the pact with the jinn. Yet, I look at my life now, one of the youngest medics and most decorated officers in the US Army, and I know that my third wish came true. My life hasn't come without great pain though. It has come with terrible loss and suffering. Victor is serving life in a military prison for the brutal murder of a family in Afghanistan, and my father suffered a horrific incident at his company, losing both arms in a freak accident inside an industrial sized machine.

As I slip on my boots, I remember my grandmother's note. I take off my left boot and tuck the note inside. I already know what it says. I've memorized it. It was that verse that brought me here, to this point in my life about to embark on a humanitarian aid mission on a flotilla into Gaza. I think about the land that I walk now, the land I walked before. It's all of me, all my identity, and all my history. I also worry about what I've learned in the past few years about the jinn, the wicked ones, and wonder if I'm ready to take more of them on, more fires, and more legends—but it's what I promised I would do—help.

I tighten my laces and take a deep breath. The seven years pact will be up in a few hours, about the same time that I would find myself on the aid boat. I gather my bag and throw it over my shoulders. As I pass the bathroom door, I turn and look in the mirror, at the black hijab that covers my hair securely, and I smile.

I turn off the lights of my hotel room, and as I reach for the door, I hear a little girl's giggle.

My fingers tremble on the door handle. "You're early," I say.

"It's exactly seven years to the very time in Puerto Rico," she says matter-of-factly. "So, Light, what is the name of Smoke and Fire?"

I drop my bag, whip around, and she's standing there in the middle of the room, the same little girl in a pristine blue dress with dark, wavy hair falling past her shoulders. Her eyes blaze and sparkle—crimson and gold. She is the eternal child.

"The Quran says, "We have adorned the nearest heaven with an adornment, the stars. And there is a safeguard against every rebellious Shaitan.""

The little jinn laughs. "You don't know my name." She shakes her head mockingly.

It was grandmother's hint that helped me, that put me on the seven year's path to find her name. It brought me here, to the Middle East, to my history, and so I found it with time, but still I found it.

"You are Marid, the Jinn of the sea."

"No," her voice cracked. "I'm not."

I recite the words given to me by my grandmother. "And lo! We had supposed that humankind and jinn would not speak a lie concerning Allah."

The little Jinn shrank back and began to cry, screaming and wailing. The room erupted into flames. I was thrown against the door and blanketed by black smoke. The smell of sulfur stung my nostrils.

NAMES HAVE POWER.

You give something a name, something you didn't know what it was before, and you call it by this name so it seems that much more real. You do the same for a person, and they too, become that much more real; holding shape and form in your memory now because you have uttered their name.

I don't really understand yet what Marid is exactly. I've done more research during my time here in the Palestine. I've spent a lot of time with the people here, those who claim that they too have been attacked by jinn, and I help where I can. I've become somewhat of a ghost hunter around these parts—specializing in the jinn. My research continually stirs up interesting things about these beings. I found that there's a belief that the jinn will sometimes whisper evil desires into your ear late at night. I don't know if that's true, and it's not technically a universal belief among all Muslims, but sometimes, late at night, when I'm alone and tired, I do hear wicked little things being whispered in my ear.

I've even heard that little jinn's voice tell me she's the one who tempted Victor to go and massacre that family. The same voice also came to me in my dreams and said that she's the one who made my father delirious with mania, forcing him to crawl into that machine where he lost his arms. When I wake up at night, after hearing that voice, all that's left is a faint smell of smoke and what almost sounds like a glittery laugh outside my window.

23

LA LUNA

THE MOON

I hated the campo; the rural, dusty, blazing hot land that modern time refused to acknowledge. Driving slowly onto the gravel road, I could feel the dozens of curious eyes on the shiny, black government issued car. I don't know why they gave me this car for this trip. It didn't seem appropriate, a vehicle that goes from zero to sixty in 5.4 seconds in a land where midday traffic was generally cattle being herded by a couple of cowboys. It's as though they wanted me to stand out, like I really needed a car to do that. *It's just one day,* the orders had promised. Just one day. That sounded simple to them, but torturous to me.

There was no need for me to drive here to see these twisted and pained faces. I could tell you easily what happened here—God abandoned this land and these people, a long time ago—hundreds of years ago. The account of what happened throughout the Americas was not documented objectively in most history books. What I learned all came from him. What he learned all came from others like him, charged to keep the truth and damned to protect. Their accounts were never written, just recited.

They arrived from the other world in colossal vessels. The old ones thought these newcomers to be centurion gods. Their pale faces were covered in thick hair and their bodies were wrapped in silver. The gods looked at the old ones curiously, but there was something behind their eyes—greed, lust, and hunger. There was awe, silence and then the presentation of the two gilded, perpendicular bars accompanied by foreign words. Confusion and madness followed with the roars, the blows, and the savagely shed blood. The newcomers were not gods the old ones quickly learned—they were men, and these men brought with them devices of death and their own version of the curse.

I drove onto a sunburned patch of grass and past that familiar small, blue wooden house. Two young police officers, a man and a woman, watched me as I parked next to their squad car. They stood there with their hands on their hips, set strategically above their black leather gun holsters. Superstitious judgment was evident in their eyes. They were uncomfortable with my presence. That was clear from the way they shifted their feet and clenched their jaws. Whispered theories floated between them. I couldn't hear what they said out there, but I could sense them talking about me.

What is that man doing here?

Him? Really? This is the help that they provide?

Several yards away, beside the house, a half dozen woman and children were gathered. They looked on in silence. Further out, beneath a tree, a few elderly men and women stared on. The men in the community were still tending their lands, I assumed, while the rest of the community had come out to bear witness. Their fear was thick and heavy, and I breathed it in as their eyes stayed latched onto me. If they wanted to continue staring at the back of my head, then let them. They would keep staring. They would always stare. When one believes evil is near, there is a curious excitement, an attraction almost, that attacks, making it terribly difficult to look away. I glanced sideways to the police car I had parked beside and laughed to myself. That old, dented thing was more valuable as scrap metal than a vehicle to pursue criminals.

Then again, the small farm town of San Ignacio didn't even really need a fancy police car. There were only four cops in this small town, the young man and woman on the porch, and two angry old men. I admit, I am surprised those two old officers have not yet allowed their rage, possibly due to boredom, to consume their existence. The mean ones never die I suppose.

Crime rarely, if ever, occurred here. What was there to steal in this town anyway? Someone's starving goat? Everyone who lived in town was either a poor farmer or the family member of a poor farmer. With so much seeding, watering, plowing, and harvesting to be done people weren't afforded the time to even think about committing a crime.

It had been many years since I had left this town, and nothing had changed. Even the dent across the driver's side door that read *Policía San Ignacio* remained. That dent was put there by me, on accident of course, during my first week as a police officer. So much time had passed since then. Even now as I look into the rearview mirror, I am surprised to see the stubble, the dark circled signs of sleep deprivation, and the bitterness that looks back at me—wearing sunglasses, of course.

The sky was growing brighter with the blast of the unforgiving Argentine sun. With each increasing notch of light in the sky, my eyes would ache further, and I could imagine the pain could be much worse if I hadn't located these sunglasses. A few hours' notice was not enough time to prepare for this forced trip. I rushed back to the precinct after the call yesterday evening and tore apart my already disorganized desk searching for the right pair of sunglasses.

I had amassed a significant collection of sunglasses over these months. They were everywhere—in my desk drawers amongst files that read: *Criminal review per orders from Interpol*, tucked between manila folders of recent crime scene photographs, and in the glove compartment beside my spare Bersa Thunder 9 and Bersa Combat Pistol. It was a specific pair of sunglasses I needed, the pair I had set aside for such emergencies. They were optimal for use in open landscapes where the sun beat down without mercy. I had never used these sunglasses before, but I knew in my blood that someday they would be needed, and that day was today.

Pushing the car door open, I felt the warmth of the brutal sun immediately as the heat penetrated the dark fabric of my suit. A group of men wearing faded jeans, sweat-stained white cotton shirts, and tan work boots walked up from the road towards the house. Dust from the dry, cracked earth swirled about their feet. One of the men rushed ahead. He stopped at the wooden gate, pulled off his faded baseball cap, and pointed at the open door of the house, which barely still hung on by its hinges.

"You see. It is true."

The other men had now gathered around him.

One of the officers, the woman, hopped off the porch and ran past me toward the group. Her run turned into a sprint as the large man opened the gate and stepped onto the property. The officer shouted a host of verbal warnings to them to stay where they were. The crowd to the side of the house had grown. More people had come out from their homes and walked up the hill to see if it was true—if death had come to their town in the night.

The large man remained at the gate. He slowly slipped on his hat. "I can see from here," he waved a large hand to the open door. "The windows have been broken. The furniture has been overturned. That beast, that boy, was the one who did this to Father Marco Antonio!"

"What boy?" I said as I removed a handkerchief from my breast pocket and wiped the sweat across my forehead.

"El Séptimo," a raspy voice said from the crowd of men. It was a strained, bitter smoker's voice. With that voice, the sweet and heavy smell of hand rolled cigars wafted to me from my childhood. Forward, a gaunt-faced, elderly man stumbled from behind the mob. His leathery, wrinkled face was twisted into a look of revulsion as he pointed one shaky, knobby finger.

"I thought Don Pedro died two years ago," I said under my breath.

"The old mean ones don't die that easily," a male voice responded.

I turned to see the baby-faced male officer standing behind me, bobbing on his feet.

We watched as the female officer directed the group of men across from the property, where the larger group stood in wait. As Don Pedro shuffled slowly away, he looked over his shoulder a few times at us.

"Hell, I was told he was run over by a horse."

"He was." The young officer laughed as he pulled out a satellite phone from his front pocket and handed it to me. "Your phone, sir. The commander insists you keep it on you at all times. They're just *worried* I expect."

"Thanks," I said through my teeth as I took the phone, turned it off in one move, and slid it in my back pocket. I had just thrown one of these out of the window a couple of miles back, and I didn't want another one. I didn't want my commander tracking down my each and every move, especially if one of those moves was me leaving here sooner than expected.

"You don't seem too excited to see your uncle, Detective Melendez."

There was no surprise to know that this young officer knew my name, and some family history as well. People in this town liked to talk—seeing as how there wasn't much else to do. Lucky for them my family history lent itself to the kind of small-town gossip that spanned decades.

"The only family members who I care to see are the ones who died a long time ago. The ones who are still living, well those, I couldn't care less if I ever saw them again."

"I'm sure all of your brothers will be pleased to see you, sir."

They would be pleased to see me with a bullet in my head, I thought. "I don't plan on seeing anyone, officer. I'm here to get this site inspected."

"The land here, it's in our blood. So hopefully your visit home will not be too much of an inconvenience."

The young officer seemed painfully optimistic for this early hour. He held out his hand. "Officer Martins," he said with a smile. "I'm looking forward to working this case with you."

"There's not much work that needs to be done here. I'll be out before dark."

His hand hung there in the air, waiting for a promise, I supposed, that I would stay; that I would care. What young Officer Martins did not know, that all of the other officers and officials in the central knew, was that handshakes bothered me. I don't see the need for them, or for pleasantries, or small talk for that matter. Niceties are for people who lie to themselves and don't mind being lied to. All I wanted to do was go inside, inspect, write up my report, and go home.

I walked towards the house. The officer was probably baffled, but that young man had to learn one way or another that the world doesn't care. Officer Martins reached me at the bottom of the steps and quickly gave me an unrequested detailed account of the past few hours.

He explained how the priest had never arrived to give his daily tour of the ruins of the San Ignacio Mission yesterday evening. Tourists still continued to come here daily with promises of legends and ghosts said to stalk the crumbling missions. There are no legends here, just dust covered stories, told and retold, to give some kind of meaning to the destitute life on these lands. And as far as ghosts? The ghosts are these empty people here, standing around this crime scene.

And so, Fathers José Cataldino and Simón Masceta were called. They demanded the old ones to be protected. The Guaraní were to not be enslaved and were never to be removed from their land. In 1610, a magnificent church was built that surrounded a main square. A monastery was erected. Homes were built and security was given. The slave hunters, los bandeirantes, tried to destroy the Guaraní some years later, but they failed. The Guaraní lived peacefully—always keeping their secrets, and their legends near.

"Everything has been left just like we found it," Officer Martins said.

In this town, there were only two families with the surname Martins. Depending on which of the two families this officer came from I would know whether to keep my gun's safety on, or off.

"Obregón?"

Officer Martins stopped mid-sentence, startled. "Yes, that's right, but how'd you...?"

Good, safety on, I mentally noted. "Doesn't matter," I said.

The young officer opened his mouth to press on, but I shook my head slowly. *Don't question me, ever.*

"Detective Melendez, as I was saying, we wanted to wait for you, especially since we were told you would be here so quickly. Thank you again for committing to assist during the preliminary investigation."

"Don't thank me. If it were up to me, someone else would have been here, but some people's orders you just can't ignore."

"Of course." Martins laughed. "I get it. We are always at our commander's mercy."

"It wasn't my commander."

"Really? Who then?"

"My godfather."

Martins-Obregón stood at that bottom step, probably in shock, as I made my way to the door. My godfather was the ultimate authority, the President of Argentina. I followed his orders, not because he was the president, but because, ultimately, it was he who took me away from here and moved me to Buenos Aires when I was a young man, saving me from my soulless existence. Let Martins-Obregón and the rest of the town believe whatever else they wanted to believe. Let them whisper on about my family's shadowy secrets. Let them obsess about myths and legend. I cared for none of that. I didn't choose my family, but my godfather had chosen me. He had given me a job. I did my job very well, and that is what I came here to do—a job.

A Guaraní Legend:

The supreme being, Tupã, created the good spirit Angatupyry and the evil spirit Tau. One day the evil spirit fell in love with a human woman, Kerana, The good spirit and the evil spirit battled for seven days and nights until the evil spirit was defeated and banished to the underworld. Tau would not be defeated and so came back to the land and kidnapped Kerana. Kerana birthed seven children, each cursed by the goddess Arasy. Tau and Kerana's children were feared and revered for they each possessed an ability.

Teju Jagua, the man of lizard and dog who protects the fruits.
Mbói Tu'ĩ, with the head of a parrot protects the life in the waters.
Moñái, a giant snake who guards the fields.
Jasy Jatere, the fairest of all fair children protects peace.
Kurupi, an ugly little man who is the god of sex.
Ao Ao, a monstrous sheep who watches over the hill tops.
And the final male child Luison, the man who is dog, and the lord and protector of death.

Right now, I just wanted to get these preliminary results done so a new detective could be transferred to this case. It was a strange request, even from my godfather: Drive out several hours to my boyhood town, where I hadn't been in years, to investigate a disappearance. He refused to tell me whose disappearance until I reached town. When I did, the

GPS on my car triggered the call. I pulled over to the side of the road, answered the phone and he told me the priest had been killed.

I knew then what this meant for me.

It was time.

I tossed the phone out of the window and rubbed my eyes. If they had needed me to drive out here at night, I would have surely killed myself. My eyes were failing, quicker than what the doctors estimated, and soon, nighttime driving would no longer be possible. So, I needed to get this done, quickly.

Walking up the creaky wooden steps onto the porch I saw them—deep claw marks had been dug into the side of the house and across the door frame as though a bear had tried to enter. From the scrapes and scratches on the porch leading into the house, it looked like whatever animal it was had managed to get in.

The door was hanging from its hinges, and a light breeze made it creak and sway. Splintered, bloodied bits of wood jutted out from the edges. The smell of rotting flesh was present in the air. As I stepped into the house, something squished beneath my foot. I knelt at the entrance mat where a clump of cottony white hair, with a chunk of pink flesh still attached, lay.

"Martins-Obregón, get over here."

Martins-Obregón was next to me in seconds. Eager kid. "He left through the front door," I said, pointing down at my discovery as I crossed the threshold.

They clearly had missed this piece of evidence in their initial search, which made me feel as though I was not entirely useless—yet. My eyesight may be deteriorating by the day, but at least my other senses were compensating for their loss. I could smell the soil that had been dragged into the house on the offender's feet. I could feel the electrical charge that pulsed within these walls. This was a home in violent disarray.

"Sir, you can call me Martins you know."

"Why the hell would I do that?" I said as I ran my fingers along the edge of the door, trying to determine the height where the door was struck with the most force.

"No, because Martins is that other Martins, and I don't like that other Martins. Understand Martins-Obregón?"

"Yes, sir." Martins-Obregón looked at the mat and then out towards the expanse of gravel, dirt, and rock. "Sir, I know that your eyesight may not be that good but…"

"And you know that how?"

My time in the field was limited, but I didn't need some new officer reminding me of that. That's why my godfather had gotten me the best eye specialists he could find, so that they could torment me with their expert opinions. As of now, their opinion was that retinitis pigmentosa would make it impossible to get around unaided at night. In just a few years, I would be completely blind. It was maddening as is to know that this would take my night vision, but it was worse knowing that there were already other people ready to take my job.

"Your commander, sir. He called last night and just told us to make sure you got here safely," Martins-Obregón mumbled quickly. "Sir, I'm just thinking that if Father Marco Antonio was dragged out of the front, we would have seen something…markings on the ground..."

"There aren't any markings because Father Marco Antonio was not dragged out of here. He was carried out."

The single room house looked as if a fight to the death had taken place. Only an optimist would find it believable that the weakest person involved in this fight would be out there somewhere, alive. During my career thus far, I had seen it all; gang brawls in maximum-security prisons, the calculated work of serial killers, and brazen political assassinations. My job was to both protect and detect. I protected my godfather at all hours, patrolling the presidential mansion at night waiting for hopeful assassins, and there were many. He had made significant enemies during his political career, those unhappy with his repeated wins, and those unhappy not to reap the benefits of these repeated victories. I stayed out of politics. I stayed out of corruption. I stayed out of his business. As long as I performed, I lived, and I did so comfortably which meant being left alone, away from people.

In so many years at this I have not seen, or felt, the intensity with which someone fought to stay alive. It wasn't that Father Marco Antonio was afraid of death, the man was old, exhausted and would probably welcome a peaceful end, but it was not his time, and people like Father Marco Antonio choose when to die. This room bore the visible signs of a man's struggle to stay alive just long enough to make his required arrangements.

Hand-carved chairs had been overturned, a table was flipped on its side, and a large wooden bookshelf beside a broken window had been cleared of all of the books, which were now scattered across the floor. Heavy, hard covered tomes, brittle paperbacks, and loose sheets of paper exposed Father Marco Antonio's reading interests. Passages of gospel, reproductions of antique maps of the New World, and historical texts lay where they were last tossed and thrown. A copy of La Santa Biblia looked as though its black leather cover had been mauled by a dog. Torn, yellowed pages from the Bible floated in a pool of blood in the center of the worn, wooden floor. Next to the gruesome stain lay Father Marco Antonio's most sacred and prized of his church's antiques split in half; a thick golden cross that had originally hung in the San Ignacio Mission the day it was founded in 1632. Against the wall was a blood splatter that ran from the floor to the ceiling. This is where he stood, I expect, trying to protect this cross.

"Not the kind of case you'd want to come back home for, I guess," Martins-Obregón said.

Ignoring the young officer, I walked around the room reading the titles of the books strewn about the floor. Three books in the corner, which were stacked atop of each other neatly caught my eye. On top of the stack was Ovid's *Metamorphoses*, Dante Alighieri's *La Divina Comedia*, and at the very bottom the copy of Miguel de Cervantes's *El Ingenioso Hidalgo Don Quijote de la Mancha* I had given to Father Marco Antonio.

"Detective, did you find something?" Martins-Obregón shouted and in seconds was by my side, bending down trying to read the titles.

Sticking out from the inside cover of *Don Quixote* was a torn sheet of notebook paper with the priest's handwriting. At the very top of the sheet of paper read:

For Brother Gubbio.

I didn't need to read further. I knew what it was, and whom it was for. Handing the paper to Martins-Obregón, I walked back to the door, removed my sunglasses, rubbed my eyes, and looked out to the crowd of Father Marco Antonio's parishioners who came to pray, question, and cry.

"I don't understand. Is this a poem?" Martins-Obregón asked. "Interesting writing for a priest, don't you think?"

I began to recite the song from heart; it had been burned there many years ago: "Be praised, my Lord, through Brother Fire, through whom you brighten the night. He is beautiful and cheerful, and powerful and strong."

Martins-Obregón followed along, amazed. The words came to me with ease, even though it had been years since they were recited by me.

"...Be praised, my Lord, through our Sister Bodily Death,
from whose embrace no living person can escape.
Woe to those who die in mortal sin!
Happy those she finds doing your most holy will.
The second death can do no harm to them.
Praise and bless my Lord, and give thanks,
and serve him with great humility."

"Father Marco Antonio didn't write that song," I said. "He just copied it down there by hand." I knew in my bones these were the last words he wrote, but not the last words he had uttered. The last words for the followers of St. Francis of Assisi were always Psalm 141.

"It's the "Canticle of the Sun," or some call it the "Praise of the Creatures." It was a song written by Saint Francis of Assisi a long time ago. It honors the connection between the animal world and man."

"Saint Francis of Assisi..." Martins-Obregón looked at the paper again, as if the document would tell him something that wasn't already there. "You know, Father Marco Antonio told us a story, well, a legend I guess," he shrugged nervously. "A long time ago about how Saint Francis of Assisi in the town of Gubbio went into the woods to tame a..."

His eyes widened, and in that moment, I could finally see, and feel, his fear. A floorboard beneath his feet creaked. His weight shifted. He was getting ready to step away from me when someone came running.

"Martins!" The female officer shouted, and in moments she was standing in the doorway panting. "The men say they're going to Familia Medalla's house now!"

"So, let them," I said. "Has anyone checked the hospitals in the next few towns over? How can we not be sure he's not at a hospital nearby being treated?" I knew the father wouldn't be at a hospital, but I wanted these two out of my face.

The female officer didn't seem too convinced. "Yes, we'll check, but what about the mob..."

"Let them go. They're not going to find what they're looking for because it doesn't exist. It's a legend of the old world and the new. It's just a damn fairy tale, officer..."

"Leyenda," she said with equal intensity. Her hand closed around the keys to the squad car tightly and for the first time her eyes met mine. The eyes were piercing, yet there was a childlike curiosity as she looked at me with those round brown bulbs. "Detective, these men are ready to go out there and kill that little boy!"

I laughed, not because of the officer's comment but because the only remaining book on the fallen bookshelf was a massive reference listing of Argentinean civil codes from 1900–1990. How fitting for the occasion. I bent down and dusted off the cover.

"Here." I flipped to the law I had hanging over my head since the day I was born, pointed to the passage, and handed it to Officer Leyenda. "Read them Decree 848 that should relax them for a bit."

"Sir, this isn't funny."

"I'm quite serious. Right here." I pointed to the first line beneath the decree's title and began to read:

"El Siglo XIX, que el Presidente de la Nación sea nombrado 'padrino' del séptimo hijo varón."

Officer Leyenda nodded and pulled the book away, closing it with a snap. "If anyone were to know the law of the seventh son it would be these people. It was written because of them, so that people would stop being so darn frightened and stop killing their seventh consecutive born son. It's a rare occurrence as is, having seven boys and people here are still superstitious about such things."

"That boy is the president's godson, officer, and he is not to be touched by you or by anyone. He is under federal protection."

The loud, roaring sound of old mufflers approached. I peered out of the window. The glare of the sun bounced off of two rusted, black pickup trucks. In the cab of the first truck were twin men, in their forties, with dark brown hair. In the truck bed was a larger man, bald-headed with a scruffy red goatee. In the truck behind them was a single man with a silver beard and a gaunt face.

"Oh hell," I said beneath my breath. Officer Leyenda pushed through and looked out the window and then back to me. "They're here just like everyone else because they're worried."

"I don't need those men coming in here stirring up any trouble," I said. "I want them removed from the property now…"

"They're your brothers, sir," Officer Leyenda pleaded.

I could hear the sound of gravel crunching beneath the truck tires until each of the pickups came to a stop. The heavy doors opened, and the voices outside intensified with renewed energy with the arrival of my siblings.

"That boy is a murderer!" A deep voice called from outside. Surely, it was one of my brothers shouting.

"He's a beast. We want him dead," a female responded.

Shouts were growing within the crowd. "The devil lives within the body of that child."

"I don't care, Leyenda," I said. "Get out of my crime scene now or you're suspended." She didn't move.

I headed towards the door, but she darted and blocked my exit.

"What about everyone else?"

"Remove them all. I don't want anyone within two hundred yards of this property."

I stomped out of the house, fuming, blood rushing to my cheeks, but simultaneously nervous as I had not seen my family since I left to the city. I was tired, I was hungry, and hell, I needed a damn shave. So, I did what I did better than anything else—I took my anger out on people.

"No one is to go near the Medalla Farm," I ordered. "If I learn of anything happening to that boy, this entire town will be dragged down to the pits of hell!"

My oldest brother ran his fingers across his silver beard. Joaquin was the only one of them who acknowledged me, his baby brother. He straightened himself up, gave me a nod, and gently brushed the rim of his hat with his pointer and middle finger. None of my other brothers would ever look at me then, nor did they now.

I turned on my heel and stomped right back inside, flashing a sly smile to Officer Leyenda.

She didn't look too pleased.

"Great, nice, just real nice, detective. You've probably scared the hell out of them."

"They were already scared."

The voices outside fluttered around us. The murmurs increased to yelling, and soon to loud, angry shouts.

"If you don't do something to stop this boy, we will!" One voice shouted above the rest to immediate agreement.

"Go out there and move those people, officer." I turned away from the door, patted my jacket pocket, searching for my cigarettes and then cursed silently to myself. I had left them on my desk. A sign I should quit.

"Sir, really, I understand you may be tired, and you may be retiring soon, but you were the one they sent to help us because..."

"Go ahead, say it," I said, leaning on the windowsill, looking out at the weathered, panicked faces. An elderly woman, with small sad eyes sunken in her head and stringy white hair pulled back in a bun stared at me. She signed herself and mouthed, "En el nombre del Padre, del Hijo, y del Espíritu Santo."

"Sir?" Leyenda called and, sure enough, there she was standing closely behind me. It was as if she had awakened me from a dream, and here she was waiting for an answer. I caught her as she and Martins-Obregón exchanged looks.

"No, there's no easy out here, officer. Martins-Obregón can't even save himself. Look at him." He pointed in his direction, looked out the window again, and the old woman was gone. Turning back to Martins-Obregón, there he was, a clumsy, fumbling mess, balancing a stack of books tucked under one arm while he turned a book upside down, shook out its pages and waited for another possible hidden document to magically fall out. "I highly doubt you're going to find anything tucked away in any of those books that would be of any use. The note the father left us was obviously planted by him."

"Sir, but really," Officer Leyenda took a deep breath and then relaxed her slim shoulders, releasing the accumulated tension.

I smiled.

She scowled.

"They sent you because this is your town. He was your priest, and if anyone would know the signs and be able to piece this together for us, it would be you."

"Nice save, officer," I tapped the side of my sunglasses. "But there's nothing to piece together." I walked to the dusty corner where the neatly stacked collection of books lay on the floor. I brushed away a small spider creeping across the cover and picked up the copy of *Don Quixote*, tucked it beneath my left arm, and headed for the door. "Careful searching through those books, Martin-Obregón. You may give yourself a paper cut."

There was the sound of books tumbling on the floor as I moved to the door.

"Sir, where are you going?" he called.

"To find some damn breakfast," I said.

"We have food at the station."

"No thanks, officer. I'll go to where my kind is welcomed." *Since there's nothing worse than eating with people who think you're a monster,* I thought silently.

Outside now, a group of women were kneeling on the ground, praying a rosary, the beads dangling between their fingers while a group of children sat in a circle nearby watching.

"Sir!" Martins-Obregón shouted. He came running after me.

I was already in my car, seat belt fastened, air conditioner blasting, and Miguel de Cervantes seated comfortably in the passenger seat next to me.

Martins-Obregón rushed to the window and banged on the glass with this palms. His round cheeks puffing air in and out as they flamed red. I lowered the window, and he brought his voice down to a harsh whisper. "Sir, what do we do now? Fingerprints? Analysis? What's next? We've got to tell these people something. They need some kind of idea of who did this. For comfort."

I placed a hand on the cover of the book, hoping that whatever it was that Father Marco Antonio was trying to communicate to me would make sense later. In that moment I couldn't even think of a lie. And so, I went with the truth. "Tell them it was just some wild animal, and not one of their own."

THERE WAS NOWHERE IN this town to sit and have a cup of coffee in privacy. No matter where I would go, mothers would whisper in their children's ears to stay away from me, and men would mentally check if they had a bala bendecida in their revolver. There was one place in this town of five thousand that I could eat without having to sit with my back to a wall—a small roadside sandwich shop a couple miles down from the Medalla farm, the one owned by that other Martins family.

I pulled the screen door open, and there she was behind the counter. I wasn't surprised she was there. Where else would Carmela be?

"David."

She was wiping the wooden countertop with a white rag. She straightened up from cleaning and blinked back tears.

"I heard you were here, and I wasn't sure if you would stop in…"

I pulled up a stool at the counter, leaned my elbows on the cracked wooden surface, and interlaced my fingers to prevent myself from reaching out and taking her into my arms, and begging her to leave with me. "Hello, Mela."

I felt complete inside looking into those welcoming eyes. The world had built up a barrier between us, but it didn't matter because we both knew we were the others' only real love.

"Have you seen Raphael and Esteban?"

"Yes," she whispered and rolled her eyes, like a teenage girl hating to admit she had to be home early otherwise her parents would kill her. "Your brothers are out back with Gabriel. You want me to get them?" She joked.

"No, just Gabriel," I joked back.

Gabriel Martins wanted me dead because the whole town wanted me dead. I wanted him dead because he had the luxury of marrying the only woman I ever loved.

"Just tell them their brother stopped in to say 'Hello' and don't tell Gabriel anything. Just let him be jealous knowing you and I were alone for some minutes."

"Oh, I'm sure they'll all be thrilled to hear you stopped in."

"They'll know sooner or later; the others were up at Father Marco Antonio's home."

She looked away from me, pretending to focus all of her energy on an unseen spot on the counter, wiping vigorously. "So, is it true? The father's been murdered," she raised an eyebrow "By one of *our* kind?"

"Where were you last night, Mela?"

Stopping abruptly, she raised her face towards me, pained that I would even ask. "In the barn."

I slammed my fists on the counter and stood up.

"Where else, David?" she groaned. "Where else am I supposed to be at that time?"

"The damn moon. Come back with me, Mela. To Buenos Aires."

"Don't blame the moon, David." Her voice was gentle.

"I curse the moon."

"It's fine," she said, turning over her shoulder to check the door. Her jaw tightened. She wanted to say something, paused for a few moments and then finally said, "It's fine, David, I swear."

Her eyes pleaded with me to sit. "Oh my David. My dear David. There's nothing either of us can do now to change my life…" Her voice trailed off. She brushed a strand of hair that had fallen over her left eye.

I moved the chair. The metal legs of the stool scraping against the wood was the only sound in that small diner. I sat back down.

"This is what was meant for me. It was too late for me to go. I already had Lola."

"How is she?" I lowered my head.

"Beautiful, David. She's just beautiful. She loves school and all she talks about is how she will be able to go to university soon and live close to her Uncle David."

Mela rubbed her fingers through my hair, and all I could do was press my palms to my eyes, to keep the tears away. "Is she alright, I mean…is she…"

"She's just perfect, David," she kissed the top of my head.

"There was no way I could leave her and go and do what you do. That boy, please tell me you have come to take the boy back with you."

I removed my hands from my eyes and nodded.

"Then there is a chance for him, just like there was a chance for you."

"But none of them know about you. You can come and stay with me."

"And the children?"

"Bring them all."

"And what if any of them ever has a fit?" she laughed. "I wouldn't risk it. I can control the fits here."

"A fit that requires that your husband sit feet from you with a rifle, chamber fully loaded? Mela, just come with me. We can have a better life."

"Someone has to remain here, David. How can I leave with Father Marco Antonio gone? There always has to be someone, just in case."

I curled my fingers through my hair and fought back a scream. "This is madness, Mela!"

I reached for her hand, but at that moment she turned away.

Our timing was always off.

"Cheese empanada with coffee?" she asked, turning on the water, running the white cloth under it, then squeezing it out. I just watched her, watched her movements, even sensing a sad smile sweep across her face. I wish I could just tell it all to stop, tell the years of damnation to disappear and give me the life I wanted, to give me Mela. A life with her far away from this town, maybe even in another town like it, with our own land to farm, with Lola and the others and nothing but fresh and simple minutes passing us each day. That is the life I wanted for her, for us. Sometimes I wish I had never met her so that we didn't have to suffer this daily ache of existing without having the other by our side.

"Well, David?" She dried her hands on a towel and returned to the counter.

"Just the coffee, Mela."

"You're just so thin, David. You really should take better care of yourself."

"I can't be happy after what I did to you."

"You, existing out there makes me happy." She took my face in her hands. "It was an accident."

As she tilted her head, her hair shifted from her shoulder, and I spotted them, just for a second. The three long, pink scars where she had been clawed.

"Be happy, David. That's all I've ever wanted for you."

"I am happy, right now, sitting here, looking at you."

Mela bent down again and whispered in my ear, "Me too, my love."

I had my coffee. Kissed Mela on the cheek and left all without my brother's or Gabriel knowing I had been there. I was family. I had my right to be there if ever a quick sanctuary was needed, but other than that I was banned from ever stepping foot into any of their homes, and if I ever did, well, there'd be a bullet in my face in minutes.

Back in the car parked along the dirt road that led up to the Medalla farm, I could tell quickly that no other cars had driven down this way in some time, as only hoofmarks were present. Sitting with the motor running and air conditioning as high as it could go, I read the second note from Father Marco Antonio, the one Martins-Obregón didn't see because it was written on the back blank page of *Don Quixote*.

The Olmecs, one of the oldest of the pre-Columbian cultures had a name for them, but I cannot recall what it was exactly. The Maya called them Jakaltek. In Central America, they were called the Nagual. The Aztecs even had a tool, the Tonalpohualli, a sacred calendar that they used to calculate a person's Tonal, animal spirit. In Guaraní mythology, they are called the Luison. The Europeans called them werworlf, or werewolf. The Españoles called them Hombre Lobo. In modern day Argentina we call them El Lobizon.

A Lycanthrope. A Shapeshifter. An anthropomorphic, transformative birthright. A curse. The Europeans believe in many ways one can become a werewolf—by ways of black magic, through a pact with the devil, an infection, drinking the rainwater from a footprint of the beast, a full moon shining on a man's face as he sleeps outdoors, tasting human flesh, the bite or scratch from a werewolf, the call of the wolf spirit, or, in Argentina, being born the seventh consecutive son.

"Jesus Christ, what am I supposed to do with this?" I shouted. I shut the book, looked in the rearview mirror, and saw a black, rusted truck was sitting idling a few miles away. There were no houses nearby other than the home of the Medalla family down the road. So either the car behind me was waiting for me to leave to get to the Medalla's house or was waiting for me—period. I swung the door open and stepped into the thick heat. The truck spun in a wild U-turn and drove away even before I could close the door.

"Well, I guess that's my sign to get moving."

THE MEDALLA FAMILY FARM sat off the main road. It was a shabby little house, with peeling gray paint, slightly elevated from the rest of the property. In the yard, there were empty wired crates. Two large fighting roosters, each tied to opposite ends of a wooden tool shed, and small brown horses tied to nearby trees.

A teenage boy in a blue and white school uniform was seated on a concrete step as I drove up. I parked the car in front of the wooden gate. The boy had not stirred from reading a book that sat upon his lap. Watching him for a moment, I wondered if he was just ignoring me. I approached and as soon as I touched the wooden gate, the child's head snapped up, and realizing I was a stranger, he dropped the book and took off running around the house.

Swinging the gate open, I spotted an emaciated brown and gray pit bull. The animal lowered his head and let out a soft whimper as I passed. As I walked up to the house, the roosters hissed and lunged toward me, only to be yanked back by their ropes. The horses kicked, cried, and retreated as far back as their ropes allowed. Clapping my hands together twice, I whistled sharply, and the animals quieted. I had grown up on a farm and knew how to handle excited creatures.

Easing on to the cracked concrete step, I figured this was the place where I should sit and wait for the boy to return with his father, or possibly with a shotgun to put me out of my misery. The door behind me leading into the sparsely decorated house was wide open. I had grown up in a similar house, a small kitchen in the back, which only really held a clay oven and a refrigerator. One larger room to the side was where everyone slept, and out back was a latrine.

There was the patter of small feet from behind, the hesitant moves of a small child.

"Are you the man who's come to take me away?"

I turned to spot a small boy dressed in a green T-shirt with white stripes. He had large, sad brown eyes and smooth black hair.

"You're the meager little thing that's got this town mad, huh?"

The little boy didn't say anything. He recoiled back into the house. His eyes fixed on a point behind my shoulder. It wasn't just fear in the little boy's eyes—it was pure and simple terror. The boy walked slowly backwards until he ducked into the bedroom and was gone.

"He's not going with you!" A man shouted.

I raised both hands slowly above my head. I could smell the gunpowder in the air.

"The boy's godfather is concerned for his safety," I said, turning to face a scrawny man. The teenage boy from earlier stood directly behind his father.

"He's my boy! Not the government's property."

"Hector!" A woman shouted from inside the house.

"Stay in the house, Gloria!" Hector, the boy's father, cocked a rifle. He wasn't going to shoot me. He needed me.

"Hector, please stop. The boys."

The sun had begun to set, in yellows, golds, and pinks.

"I have the letter here, from your wife, giving us permission to take the boy." Slowly, with one hand, I reached in my jacket pocket and produced the letter.

Hector came closer and snatched the paper from my hand. Opening it with one hand, and keeping the other hand on the rifle, pointed at me, his lips began to tremble as he fought back tears, reading his wife's words. I don't know what the letter said exactly. All I knew were my orders—to bring the boy back to Buenos Aires. Nothing at this point could keep the child here. The priest, his protector, has been murdered, and so it was time for him to be taken into the care of his godfather.

Gently, Hector eased the rifle onto the ground. He wiped the corners of his eyes and called his son to him. "Reynaldo, come here to Papa." The child hesitated, but after his father called him again, he came running. Hector squatted down and hugged his son tightly, clutching the letter with force in his hand. "You're a good boy, Reynaldo, know this please, that you are a good boy."

"The sun is about to set any minute." I pointed out. "It's time to get him away."

I knew it was time. I felt it beneath my feet as the land began to rumble and vibrate.

People were on their way. They appeared in the distance, two sets of headlights, and far behind was a third set with a flash of red and blue on top. "That Martins-Obregón is a good kid," I said to myself.

"Hector, Gloria, get all of the other boys in the house!" I shouted. Hector reached for Reynaldo's hand, but I told him to go ahead.

"Trust me," I growled.

Hector and Gloria called out to the fields. Their remaining sons, older teenaged boys, came running out. Hector shuffled his family inside.

The pickup trucks were now just a few miles down the road, probably full of men who wanted this seventh-born son dead. Trailing them closely was the defender of the law, Martins-Obregón charging along. To do what exactly? I really wasn't sure. I only hoped this kid knew what he was getting himself into.

I squatted down and looked at that little boy's chubby face. I remembered being seven years old and a man coming to my house, in a black suit, having the same talk with me that I was going to have with Reynaldo.

"When the sun goes down and the full moon rises, you will become a werewolf. You are the seventh son and as the seventh son you are set to protect the President. You will be his bodyguard. You will kill anyone who attempts to kill him. You are at his command. Whatever it is that he asks of you, you are to do it. Do you understand?" It felt silly telling this to a child, but it was law. The rules had to be communicated.

Reynaldo tilted his head and looked at me curiously. "Are you a werewolf too?"

"I am a seventh son."

The trucks arrived, and the men jumped out.

Hector opened the door to the house, and my brother, Raphael, raised his pistol and fired once through the man's chest. Gloria released a scream that tore through the dark sky.

"Get inside!" I shouted.

Martins-Obregón raised his gun. "Drop your weapons!" he shouted as the rifle shook in his hands.

"What are you going to do? Protect that monster?" Esteban said, approaching Martins-Obregón with a knife.

My back cracked and popped, but I remained standing. My hands burned, as if metal iron rods were being shoved beneath my fingernails. The moon was in control.

"Stop, Esteban. They've given you no trouble!"

"No trouble! He's a monster! Carmela is a monster because of him and now this one, this child! Father Marco Antonio protected him for too long and so…"

"And so, you took Carmela to his house the night of a full moon to kill our protector."

"Of course! She wouldn't know what she had done. She wouldn't have remembered because she can't remember anything after the change, unlike your kind."

Raphael snuck around from the truck, running towards Reynaldo, and Martins-Obregón fired once. My brother fell face forward, a bullet in his back.

My eyes began to burn. My bones rattled, and my limbs twisted and tore, broke and bled. There were shouts, cries, screams, and then fire raged in my blood.

Paws on the ground running, charging, colliding with bodies into the crowd. Holding panicked, flailing hands and legs down. The taste of flesh, blood, and bone, and then night fell.

"THIS IS FROM YOUR godfather." I handed the envelope to Reynaldo, as custom.

Reynaldo looked to his mother with wonderment and moved quietly alongside the house. Some of the boys sat on the concrete step. Some with blood on their hands, the blood of their father. Others leaned against the peeling paint of the house with swollen, pink eyes. Their tears still fresh on their cheeks.

Reynaldo's large brown eyes took in the envelope as he reached for it with his small, dirty hands. Carefully, he tore the yellow paper from end to end. He pulled out a folder and quickly handed the documents to his mother.

"Oh," she said as she looked at the white sheet of paper clipped to the front of the folder, with the presidential seal. She was unable to make out any of the foreign lines and symbols other than the famous signature she had seen before on her son's baptism certificate.

"Sebastian, come read this for you brother," she said.

The tallest boy took a step forward and said, "Father Marco Antonio was murdered. Father is dead, and you support this all?"

"It is what we are meant to do." Gloria whipped around and held out the packet to her son. "God forbid you speak to your mother like that again. Come read this for me, now."

Sebastian walked over to his mother and took the folder. "I do this only for you, not for him." And by him, I assumed he meant his little brother, Reynaldo.

Gloria stood in front of me, and her little boy in front of her.

Dearest Godson,

Bless you and your family on this glorious of days.

Reynaldo, please send my dear wishes to your mother who has loved you unconditionally all of these years. I still remember when we met at your baptism years ago. She held my hand and told me that her son was going to be a good man. And so, we baptized you, and I, as your godfather, will ensure that these next few years of your life will be lived without sickness or menace because no illness exists within you.

Enclosed you will find the proper documents to begin your next few years of boarding school here in Buenos Aires. By law, all expenses will be handled by me.

Please, pack your belongings immediately. I am sure that under these circumstances we both would like to ensure the safety of your community, especially that of your family.

Your loving godfather,

El Presidente de Argentina

"Sir!"

"Yes, Martins-Obregón."

"Sir, what do we do about…the mess." He motioned over to the cornfields where the bodies of my brothers lay.

"I'll discuss that with my godfather, and we'll see how he wants to handle this."

Reynaldo settled in the front seat, moving the copy of *Don Quixote* to his lap.

I adjusted the rearview mirror, seeing Martins-Obregón standing there, shocked and bewildered. I knew what I had to tell him, but I didn't really want to tell him because I still was not sure if I liked him or not.

"He did save your life," Reynaldo said.

I looked over to the little boy, my fellow lycan. "Did you just read my thoughts?"

The little boy smiled.

"Well, don't do that again."

I grumbled beneath my breath and shouted, "Martins-Obregón." I beeped the horn, and he ran over.

"Hey kid, can you hand me that..." As soon as I turned to look, Reynaldo was already passing me the copy of *Don Quixote*.

"Thanks," I said. I wasn't going to like having to train this one, but it was time for my retirement, especially because of the failing eyesight and all. If it wasn't for the kid there by my side last night, I, too, would have been shot with one of those silver bullets that had gotten his father in the chest.

Handing the book over to Martins-Obregón I told him what Father Marco Antonio would want me to say.

"You're the new protector. Since the Jesuits built their missions hundreds of years ago near here, this job has been taken up by a priest, but I like you, and I think the kid likes you." I looked over and found Reynaldo bobbing his head. "It's your duty now to protect us. When the next seventh son is born, it's your job to make sure he has all he needs."

"Wait!? What?! I didn't sign up for this."

"I didn't either."

"I don't understand, sir. Who is going to be the next seventh son?"

"Your son."

I rolled up the window and we hit the road to Buenos Aires.

EL COTORRO

THE PARROT

"Why are you doing this!? Why are you doing this!?" The parrot cried as Machi filled the water dish.

"Down the stairs! Down the stairs!" The bird cawed.

Machi laughed to himself. His nearly three-foot tall, emerald green macaw was like a tape recorder, playing back words and phrases exactly as she heard them. Repetition—that was the trick. The more she heard something, the more likely she was to attempt to say it, practicing those repeated words over and over again until she sounded almost human. Many neighbors had moved out over the years, with most citing that bird's eerily sounding cries as a major motivator.

"Sawing a woman in half," Machi said, as he rubbed his gray-haired goatee. "Can you say sawing a woman in half?"

Of course, the parrot couldn't. His pet had learned to say almost all of the names of his acts except for that one, the once highlight of Machi's world famous magic act.

She was a quick learner and that is why he brought Kalku with him to New York from Chile over fifty years ago. The allure of show business back then was enticing, magical—not like what show business was like presently. Today, the masses mostly looked to multiplex movie theaters, video game consoles, and the internet for their entertainment.

As a boy in Chile, tourists would surround him at his card table where he would guess repeatedly which card they had drawn from a deck. One day, a local businessman, who was a skeptic, brought with him his own newly purchased deck, unwrapped it, and pulled a card to which Machi guessed correctly. He was not a fake. He was just a boy who had grown up in the Chiloé Archipelago, a town where witchcraft had been practiced for ages and ages, and where magical abilities were honed and celebrated. Machi soon learned to make things appear and disappear, and soon after, he left his card table and stepped onto the stage.

He came alive under the lights, in front of audiences who would remain silently transfixed as he glided across the stage commanding objects and people. He mesmerized and hypnotized with tricks and illusion. Soon he became a great illusionist traveling the Americas until the real America called, New York. His assistant, Marlena followed. With them, they brought exotic animals he had accumulated over time—the rabbits and doves, snakes and tigers. They also brought with them an impressive collection of custom-made props; human-sized boxes and water tanks. There were also the hats and scarves, suits and gowns. Of course, there were also chains, handcuffs, and well-sharpened blades and knives.

The day he was to make his great appearance on the New York stage, a storm began to move into the area. Charcoal-colored clouds looked down. The air grew bitingly cold and the world began to rumble. There was something he had once seen his elders do—appease the great sky. Quickly, he scrambled to perform that same trick and suddenly the sky cleared. Marlena was lost, but still the show went on. New, lovelier assistants came along to join his act, and each time weather threatened audience attendance, another assistant went missing.

His talents flourished and soon he could make a grown man disappear. He could conjure a tiger from an empty box. Most impressively, he had learned to break free from a straitjacket in three minutes while suspended over a bed of knives as a flame burned the rope that held him in air. He was the master until television, movies, special effects, video games, and the internet turned everyone away from true magic.

"Let me go! Let me go!" the bird screeched.

A snowstorm was reported to be moving in tonight. High winds knocked on his window begging to enter. As Machi dressed himself in his finest, a sleek black tuxedo, and before he slipped on his white gloves, the bird screeched again. Tonight, the stage came calling again. A televised special to showcase new magical talents, men and women who performed and looked more like pop stars than magicians, but still who were inspired by him, Machi El Sorcerer.

Flurries of snow kissed his window, and he knew it was time to revive his old trick. He walked over to the corner of his tiny, garden apartment surrounded by the ghosts of his magical past; dust covered top hats and picture frames holding the essence of his fantastical years—posing alongside movie stars and celebrities.

"It hurts! It hurts!" "Kalku, please stop."

Machi went back to his parrot, kneeled, and pushed aside the large rug in front of her massive black metal cage. He pulled up on the ring and opened the door that led below. He descended a flight of steps, feeling against the stone walls as he walked slowly down. At the bottom of the stairs, he flipped on the light and smiled when he saw the colorful life-sized poster of him and Marlena.

In the center of the concrete room, a gagged beauty hung, suspended from the ceiling. She wore a green taffeta gown, the Swarovski crystals on the neckline glittered as she swayed into the light from the single bulb in the room.

Machi moved over to the wall and released the rope that held her up. The woman fell onto the stone surface. Her cheeks blazed red as Machi moved to an opposite wall where knives, blades, and swords hung, delicately displayed. His fingers floated over each one meditatively until he settled on a scythe. Yanking it from the wall and holding the base in both hands, he turned.

"My name is Machi the Magnificent Sorcerer. I am a magician and I learned magic from the great witches of my land at Chiloé. I can make a man disappear and reappear, saw a woman in half and put her back together, and simply enough pull a rabbit from a hat. These are simple things that all magicians can do, but I can control the weather. I can make the rains cease, the clouds part and the snow stop…all for a price of course. All great magic, all powerful magic, requires a human sacrifice."

He raised the scythe and above Kalku screamed, "Saw a woman in half! Saw a woman in half!"

25

EL VICIO

THE DRUNKARD

The shop window was blocked by a glass-sheltered bus stop.

Yet, each morning when the bus would arrive at that particular bus stop, Ariana would crane her neck and try to peer into the little store. She never was able to see anything more than the life-sized wooden statue of a pirate, the partitioned wall behind him, and in front, a rectangular wooden, rustic sign with red all-capped letters that read BOTANICA.

Having a botanica just a short bus ride from her new home here in the Bronx added a level of comfort. There were more connections to her home of El Salvador here in the states then she had originally anticipated. For days now, she had the urge to rush off the bus and run into that botanica, but she didn't really know why. She had visited her pueblo's only botanica with her mother and grandmother, each who visited themselves for two very different reasons. While her grandmother would stop in occasionally to purchase religious items, such as a prayer card, her mother would visit often for a different purpose. On any given visit, her mother would purchase incense, oils, perfumes, a new and strange crystal thought imbued with magical property, and always a candle for whatever spell it was she was preparing to cast.

"Sometimes, Ari, there can be two very similar looking things, but one is good and the other is evil," her grandmother told her one day. "A woman who has encountered evil, and I mean true evil, never walks alone at night, let alone crosses the path of an alley."

"Why?"

"Because that is where the black cadejo lurks, waiting for your weakness to show."

"Why would a cadejo want me?"

Her grandmother squeezed her hand. "If a black cadejo finds you, have faith that a white one should be near to protect you."

That's the last time she ever mentioned those legendary beasts, an evil black hellhound type creature that seeks to kill travelers and a white protector who lingers nearby to ensure safe passage.

THE TRIAL MOVED SWIFTLY, and while it could never be proven how exactly Ariana's mother killed her father, there was no contest as his blood was smeared all over her altar. Ariana was asked to testify, and at the time she didn't know that she was testifying against her own mother. The prosecutor asked her questions about her mother's habits; her altar, the objects she would purchase from the botanica, and any specifics she could provide about the rituals she did see. When her mother was sentenced to life for murder, the last words her mother told her were:

"I curse you."

ARIANA PULLED THE CORD, the bus stopped, and she pushed the door open.

The sign read Cerrado. Closed. She looked at her phone. It was 9:33 p.m. Of course, they would be closed this time of night. She shook her head, tightened her hands around her backpack straps on her shoulders and heard it. A growling and a hiss. Then a tap against glass. Right next to the sign was a large white cat. The largest she had ever seen. The animal clawed and hissed, desperately spraying small droplets of saliva onto the glass.

Ariana backed away, a few steps, stepping into the yellowed streetlight. Still stepping, she tripped onto the uneven alley floor. She could still hear the white cat hissing. It began to meow loudly and then Ariana heard the growl.

It came from down the alley. She didn't need to look because she could already imagine what was there, feet from her, a savage, hoofed, black dog. The smell of urine and sulfur intensified as the growls and snaps of the animal's jaw drew closer. She felt frozen, but how, she hadn't even looked into the animal's eyes. It was fear that kept her there. Ariana closed her eyes, waiting for the animal's teeth to sink into her calf and drag her down.

Suddenly, there was silence.

Blood rushed back into her face, her hands, her legs, and she moved.

Looking down, on the ground, was the large white cat from the shop's window.

She scooped up the animal, its paws bloodied, its snout covered in black grime. She pressed it to her chest.

"Of course," she said. "The white cadejo was near."

26

EL HOMBRE

THE BLACK MAN

Those who read this still walk the world of the living. While I who write shall have long passed, fallen into the world ruled by shadows. Surely bizarre things occur and sometimes truths shall be spoken.

Years and years have passed us and still, with each new epoch, it seems that with equal fervor the undertakers and morticians must prepare the multitude of men and women who will be put to rest in coffins and tombstones, sepulchers and mausoleums. Granted at one time they were buried where the earth was soft enough to dig with one's own hand for a final resting place. This is how those who suffered so were put to rest much time ago. Some fail to believe, to trust that essence of something grave stalking us in the night; us from Ayiti.

We have suffered, a people who were taken, tortured, forced to sail across the Atlantic. It still travels across the ocean to us, seeking to rip apart our bodies to luxuriate in our pained last few moments.

That particular year had been more miserable than the despairing ones that surrounded it. Hurricanes flooded the streets, washing drowned, bloated bodies through neighborhoods. Then the earth shook, tumbling concrete structures, collapsing on to the still breathing, crushing bones, snapping necks, and cracking open the earth to expose the pits of hell below. Fear had been seen, felt, and heard.

Many outsiders, those primarily of the land up north, justified our misery as they wrapped their own reason around their gods. Men of the cloth murmured that this was our price, to starve and to die for a pact our ancestors made in the northern mountains at Bois Caïman. I tell you here and now, that our houngan, Vodou father, Dutty Boukman, sealed no deal with evil. The only deal and desire was our freedom.

This history of suffering goes far back, much farther back then the days of Vodou. The island was paradise once, ruled by chiefdoms, Taíno kings. The stars never unfolded their secrets that vessels of change were on their way. Despair sailed toward them, with the curse of iron chains. The heavens above fell silent and became the passive witness to the monstrous minds of man.

The Cross of Burgundy arrived on the shores. The kings and queens of the island nation and their people were then forced to work their own land for these newcomers. When denials were made, their lovely leader, Anacaona, was hanged before her people. For hundreds of years, the indigenous toiled, farmed, worked, and bled until they could move no more. Death became their salvation from pain. No memorials. No tributes. Their tears are morning dew over the mountaintops.

The land was renamed, Hispaniola. The land then reclaimed after the powers struggled and Spain gave the West to France. Saint-Domingue then became her title in 1697. Did the skies rage and fall then as they rage and fall now? An accursed destiny of pain. The newcomers stole from the island to build their wealth. Ships traveled to Africa bringing back stolen people. The Grand Blancs, the pale-faced aristocrats, planned tortuous schemes, dark imaginations, and black meditations for the hands that would work to grant them immense wealth, unspeakable wealth.

THE PLAN CAME SWIFTLY.

From greed of sugar much blood was shed. Hundreds of thousands of black bodies worked and died on that land. Some broke free, finding freedom in the mountains. They asked their loas, their gods, for help. Petitions were made and then came the day.

A meeting took place there at the mountains. The escaped planned for freedom, planned for a revolt, and a woman began to dance.

She had been willingly possessed by her god. She danced and twirled, sang and rejoiced, and relayed the message.

OVER A GLASS OF rum and within the walls of the National Palace, we sat at night; a group of seven. No lights remained on the island. Electricity had died. We wondered within those minutes if we were the last to remain, but each time we speculated, a cry echoed through the forest. We fell to silence, listening to each cry. I wondered if it was a ghost or the land demanding our lives be sacrificed as well.

To our room there is no entrance. The lofty door has been blocked by a collapsed column. If Georges H. Baussan, our grand graduate of the **École d'Architecture**, could see his masterpiece fallen on to itself, he would slash his own throat. The design of the building was classical and twice the size of the White House. Its simple decoration was often mocked but now we were glad, as there were very few items that could fall onto us. Three wings, which we were unsure of their present condition, ran from back to front. The columns from the main hall, which towered toward the ceiling, we had assumed, collapsed as well. When we attempted to free ourselves from this chamber, all we could see were the chunks of white-painted, reinforced concrete and dust through the forced inch.

The presidential residence was in ruins.

The few feeble candles we located gave sufficient light. Another cry rang out. Blasted shrieks set against that radiant moon that beamed over this accursed land. Evil had not returned because evil had never departed.

My throat tightened as I took another sip of rum. I felt as if I was being suffocated and maybe I was. Maybe my soul was squirming somewhere beneath the rubble, and this was all a dream. Confusion. An earthquake.

A dead weight hung upon us. It hung within these walls, lingered on the dust-covered furniture, and rolled beneath our skin. This weight of knowing, of hiding, depressed us all. Yet we continued to drink quietly in the candlelight at the round, ebony table where we sat. There was a new attempt to laugh as a group, and be merry, because what else could one do now that no one remained out there?

We toasted the silent tenant in our company, at the front of the room in his black coffin—our great president, the young Léogâne. He lay, dressed in what we could best provide, not a suit, but still shrouded in decent slacks and a dress shirt. His countenance was distorted, from the rubble, which had fallen upon his head when the earth opened, and demonic trembles violently shook our homes. His eyes had seen Death as it tumbled from the skies, and when the fires in the great palace were extinguished, we found him there, splayed about the great rotunda, lain on top of a crushed porcelain cup—how fitting that he had been drinking coffee with sugar, the two fruits which damned this land.

It was I, François, who felt that the eyes of the tortured were upon me. Still, I forced myself to gaze into my drink and listen to the song from the mountains outside. Then, it came. It appeared—a dark and undefined shadow, darker than the unseen side of the moon, darker than the hearts of murderers, darker than all of the horrors committed on our soil. It was a shadow; not of a man, nor of an animal, nor of any familiar thing.

At length it rested, in full view in front of the coffin. The shadow was formless and indefinite. At length, I demanded the shadow to address us, the seven who had here gathered.

The shadow answered, "I am SHADOW and my dwelling is near the Catacombs of Bois Caïman."

And then we, the seven, shuddered in our seats, trembling in horror and aghast, for the tones in the voice were not of any one being, but of a multitude of beings, varying in their cadences from syllable to syllable, their voices of the thousands, millions murdered from our island.

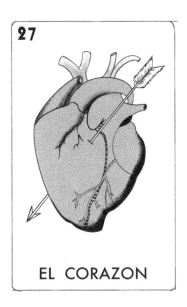

27

EL CORAZON

THE HEART

My name is Ernesto Baez, and this is my final report regarding the nomination of the Humberstone and Santa Laura Saltpeter Works for inclusion into the United Nations World Heritage. Please forgive the state of this report as my laptop's battery died shortly after my arrival here. Therefore, my hand against this battered notebook is all that I can provide.

It was always my dream to work for the United Nations. I remember as a boy my father constantly trying to instill within me his own entrepreneurial spirit. I declined a life revolved around managing businesses, employees, and products. I wanted to be able to preserve the land, not strip it. I felt by doing this, by protecting the world in which we live, I could somehow ease the pain my father had inflicted. I was lucky to have a life where I had the opportunity to use my hands to turn through the pages of books, type out scientific reports, and hold a college diploma. Not many people in Chile are afforded with the luxury of an education.

My father remained busy over the years, tending to his elite corporate duties. I feel, even now as I sit here, my hand shaking as I write this, that my father was disappointed with my decisions in life. That all does not matter now I suppose. Before I forget, I would like to take this opportunity to say how grateful I am to have had an opportunity to serve as a committee member in the United Nations Educational, Scientific and Cultural Organization, UNESCO. As one of twenty-one committee members approving and managing World Heritage Sites, I can only say that I am honored to have been in this role, one that places global recognition, and protection, on locations that should be valued and not destroyed.

Many people fail to realize what a UNESCO World Heritage Site is. They are everywhere and in every country. From the Pyramids of Egypt, to the Grand Canyon of the United States, UNESCO sites are places that hold special cultural significance that tell us something about our heritage and history. I only wish now I could have seen more of them. Of the nearly one thousand World Heritage Sites, I have only caught a glimpse of our world's treasures, all because of my fear of flying, which I can only laugh about now. If my fear had overpowered me in France, then maybe I would not be here right now. I am sickened knowing what I have done.

I wish I never had made this nomination. This place, this vile, wretched place is a living graveyard of the damned, and I only fear that, by the time you read this, my flesh would have fallen from my bones and I, too, would be like these residents.

The formula NaNO3 represents the chemical compound of Sodium Nitrate. Known as Chile Saltpeter, this salt is used as an ingredient in fertilizer, pyrotechnics, food preservatives, solid rocket propellants, smoke bombs, and ammunitions. The largest accumulations of naturally occurring sodium nitrate can be found in Chile. The saltpeter mines of Chile and their associated company towns developed into a distinct urban community with their own language, organization, and customs.

I didn't think I would ever fly on an airplane again after relocating to the World Heritage Centre at 7, Place de Fontenoy in Paris, France. When I boarded the plane for France it was the first time I had ever been on an airplane, and that was more than fifty years ago. I remember that morning still because fear leaves a distinct stain on your memory. As I walked down the narrow aisle to my seat, this ancient woman reached for my wrist. Her hold was so tight and forceful that I fought the urge to scream.

"You are not allowed to leave!"

"I'm sorry miss, but I think you have me confused with…"

"You're Raul. Santiago's boy. You have the same face. They wait for you. All of them. Your father waits for you as well!"

I didn't know what to say. I just looked into her worn eyes sunken so deep into her head, it was as if they were about to fall back into her skull. She wore a black dress with a black shawl around her shoulders. The clothes of a widow, I remember thinking. Her spell was only broken when someone pushed me from behind. A young woman apologizing.

"I'm sorry about my mother." She said as she slid past me and into the seat next to the old woman. "Mom." The woman smiled nervously as she fastened the old woman's seat belt. "Just close your eyes. You look tired."

The old woman looked back to me, her cloudy eyes reading my face. "You are Santiago's boy. I know this. You are the son of a man who lived off the abused backs of thousands. They are waiting…" she said as she raised a bony finger. "You belong there, right with all of them."

There was another push from behind, so I continued walking toward my seat in the rear. I could hear the old woman's excited cries and her daughter's pleas for her to calm down and sleep. I located my seat but could not sit down. Instead, I went to the lavatory, locked the door, and stood in front of the mirror staring at my face. The old lady was right. I did look like my father.

On takeoff, we veered violently to the left. The seatbelt dug into my hip. A metallic grinding rung throughout the cabin. The loud clatter and banging took me back there, to Humberstone. I could see the massive town chimney rising high above everything in the town, even the processing plants. Groups of men, dressed in similar gear—pants, dark long-sleeved shirts, and helmets upon their heads—were walking toward a series of structures and short towers where other men were descending.

The plane dipped.

The grinding grew louder and then the captain came on the speaker. The engine had failed, and we were preparing for an emergency landing. The cries throughout were primal. I couldn't look, so I kept my eyes closed, just feeling my body thrash and sway. I did not want to have my eyes open as I died. I did not want to see the impact that would kill me. I just kept my eyes closed, finding some comfort in the darkness. A jumbled crash came from overhead and then the sound of people shouting. An object bashed into my arm as carry-on luggage spilled out from the overhead bins.

A whining, vibrating mechanical noise pulsated throughout the plane and then we hit the ground hard. I opened my eyes after the aircraft slowed. The plane was evacuated, and on my way out, I saw the young woman trying to awaken her mother. The old woman was the only one who died that day. I learned later on that it was a heart attack.

NOW, SITTING HERE IN the dark, I understand what she had meant. She was right; they were waiting for me. I like taking comfort knowing I had a good life. My years in Paris were good. I met my wife. We had a daughter, and it was the life any man would want—full of joy, comfort, and success. I admit there was always a pang of guilt that rested on my shoulders because I had left Chile. I missed the land. I missed the people. I missed the food. As I grew older, my longing for Chile faded some. Yet, at night, the country would visit me. The sounds of Spanish, folklore melodies, and the smells of empanadas would greet me in the nighttime.

My dreams took me to my boyhood, darting between buildings in my father's mining town of Humberstone. I would sneak out during the afternoon, rush past the living quarters through to the main square shaded by carob and tamarugo trees. The school day had ended, but still, I would peek inside its windows, curious of the world within. I would never go to school there as I went to a private school in the city, and when there with my father, private tutors were arranged for me. In my dream, as in my childhood, I would run around the square and through the basketball court feeling as if the town were all mine.

The town was empty every day during this time. Most people were in the mine. Partners and children were in their homes. Others could be found in the energy house that housed electricity generators, diesel engines, and massive electrical panels. Others more were in the foundry workshop, and even more were in the foundry itself manufacturing nitrate.

Even in my dreams my father would send for me. His personal aides would escort me back to the administrative building. There, my father would be as pale as the salt in the mine. Mechanically, he would tell me not to mill about the area, that it was dangerous for the son of the owner to be out unsupervised.

My dreams always ended the same way. A storm of miners covered in dirt and mud would charge into his office, pull him by every limb, and cart him away. With that they left me there alone, ducking under his desk to cry.

Even after my father's disappearance, my dreams continued the same way. I had never told anyone about them. It is silly now writing about this at this moment. Pointless perhaps? I struggled with wanting to tell someone about these dreams but there was no one to tell who would truly understand. My mother died when I was a teenager, and my sister was too busy being a mother of three and a wife to the owner of the San Jose copper mine. No one needed an old man calling them bumbling on about some nightmares.

Guilt, that is what I attributed my dreams to then; guilt for turning away from my family's intent of me being a businessman like my father. I was doing something instead for our world, for the greater good. As I drew closer to retirement the dreams became more vivid. They were more than nightmares I see now.

It then occurred to me, that perhaps what I could do was to honor my father's memory. Here I was working at all of these historic sites and locations, petitioning for their recognition, but none of them were in my homeland, and so I made a phone call to my sister. Karla had been gravely ill for some time. A woman who had never smoked was being destroyed by lung cancer. Her husband told me that I should plan on a trip to visit her as they were estimating she only had a few weeks. I could not see her, not like that. When I called to tell her my plan, she sounded bright, and her charm emanated through the phone.

"You are calling me? What miracle is this? Aren't you too busy placing value on things? I think I'll call you Jeweler now as that is what you do...look at rough stones and give them a value?"

"Fine, you can call me the Jeweler, but I need you to first give me your permission to claim value to a very rough stone, one that we both own."

Karla went silent on the other line. Her voice was heavy. "What do you mean?"

"I'm nominating the mine and I would like your permission. It belongs to both of us."

"The only reason I continue to hold on to ownership of it is to ensure that place is never reopened, ever. It's not a place anyone with a heart should be allowed to go to."

"It was not bad there."

Karla laughed. "Ernesto, people died..."

"It was just part of the work. It was just...dangerous work."

"They were murdered, Ernesto. If they didn't die in the mine, they died when they were fired upon for asking for the most basic of human rights: manageable hours, time off, basic human needs such as water breaks, Ernesto! And when they asked for this, and for safety measures, they were murdered, and it was Father…"

"Our father did not call the order, Karla! The massacre took place on another mine, not at Father's mine."

"If you want to keep thinking he didn't have anything to do with the orders that killed thousands of unarmed protesters, women, and children, then continue being naïve. Miners from all over northern Chile were killed that day. They were never allowed to protest or speak up…all they did was work and they did that until they died."

"A site can only be nominated by someone in its own country unless, of course, a committee member makes a nomination, and I know how you feel, but that place represents much more."

"Stop. Stop. Stop," she said. "That place represents nothing but a slice of hell. That place should not be protected, should not be cherished, and there is no heritage there other than the heritage of suffering. Think about our father. I know that's where he is."

Her breath became labored and I tried to interject, to calm her down, to tell her how much I loved her, but nothing worked. She was already too upset. We hung up the call and shortly after that, my sister went missing. I waited a few months, but then I went ahead, wrote the report, and made the official nomination and the Humberstone and Santa Laura Saltpeter Works were accepted as a UNESCO World Heritage Site.

The Humberstone and Santa Laura Saltpeter Works are two that have managed to survive in the desert. Together, they are a unique testimony of the saltpeter industry. They meet the requirement of authenticity because they are an outstanding example of the saltpeter era. The essential features of their

authenticity lie in their productive and economic functions. The
design, structures, materials, and overall architecture with the
social and cultural aspects of these places adds to their value.

An envelope arrived one day from Chile announcing a large celebration to welcome the new member of UNESCO. Dignitaries, current and former miners of other locations, descendants of miners of Humberstone and Santa Laura as well as the press would be onsite. I had become overwhelmed in emerging prospects and time had escaped me. It's true that I was the one who had made the nomination for the location in my country, but I long suspected that I would never get on a plane again. Scheduling conflicts coupled with the fact that I was the Chilean who had made the nomination for the Chilean site that was accepted into our cadre of protected sites, made it so that I was the likely, and ultimately only, representative that was able to make the trip.

I had met with a doctor a few days before my flight. He had prescribed me some anti-anxiety medication for the trip. Upon take off, I only remember thinking of my wife and daughter and desperately feeling a pang of dread for leaving them for the country I had left many years before. I took the medication the doctor provided and forced my eyes closed.

At the airport, a driver, scheduled through the UN, was stationed at the departure gate. My name was handwritten on a large piece of cardboard in black marker.

"Mr. Santiago," He folded up the sign when I gave him a nod. "My name is Ivan Roman. How was your flight?"

"I slept the entire flight."

Ivan was a wide man. He looked more like a bodyguard than a taxi driver. He wore a dark, buttoned shirt and black slacks. "Good. Good. Feel free to sleep the whole drive if you want. Tonight's going to be a busy night for you. There are a lot of people waiting to see you."

Ivan reached for my briefcase, but I pulled away.

"No, just the suitcase will be fine. I can keep my case with me up front in the car. You're familiar with the event tonight?"

Ivan lifted my suitcase. "Yes, many people will be there. It has been talked about for quite some time."

Outside I filled my lungs with the air that gave me life. Here in Chile, the smells were sweet but mixed with intense heat and a sliver of ocean air. Once inside the automobile, Ivan pulled on his seatbelt, slapped his large hands on the steering wheel, and said, "To Humberstone and Santa Laura then…"

"Not the hotel first?" I asked surprised.

Ivan pulled out a small slip of paper from his back pocket and read the writing to himself. As he did, he shook his head. "Apologies sir, but this says that the celebration is in a few hours and so I thought you wanted to go straight there. There is a hotel close by, of course. That is where I was instructed to take you after the festivities this evening."

"Very well," I said.

I do not know why I was fearful then. Perhaps it was my internal alarm telling me that something was off. First came the invitation, then my wife and co-worker's insistence that I come to Chile, and then that oddly uneventful flight I slept completely through. Of course, I assume now that most flights should be uneventful, but still—it felt too quick, too easy for Chile to call me back. I had left as a young man, desperate to take on the world, and now here I am, an elderly man fearful of my own country.

A few minutes outside of the airport, the intensity of the Atacama Desert began to seep in through the car's vents. The blast of the air conditioner felt merely like a powerful fan blowing warm air back in my face.

"Millions will come visit the saltpeter mines now with this new honor," Ivan said proudly.

"That was the intent," I said, looking out of the window as the land became paler and paler, the buildings became fewer and eventually there were no buildings at all.

Humberstone had closed in 1960 because demand had dwindled considerably. Ivan did not mention if his father was a miner or even how he knew about the mines. I supposed he must live near them.

"Do you live near the old mines then?"

"You could say that. I guess you could say I spent some time there," he said as he turned on the radio.

The saltpeter worker was the personification of what in Chile is called the "social issue"; i.e. the ongoing debate concerning living and working conditions in working class districts. The life of the saltpeter worker was arduous. The options open for a worker beyond the saltpeter system were few. In the Works themselves, the majority of the workers had no possessions whatsoever: neither the tools, for which they had to pay a part of their salaries when they began their jobs, nor the furniture (scarce: even the beds were made of old drums and sheets of metal); less still the houses where they lived or their food they ate. Even their clothes were provided by the Works, so that they looked alike. Not only were the Works abysmally neglectful of their workers' safety on the job, they did not give them the money they owed them for their work; the salary consisted of tokens they were handed weekly. These tokens, made of metal or high-density plastic, were issued by the Works themselves and could be exchanged for products in the General Store, owned by the owners of the Works, with prices and stocks also fixed by the Works themselves, which assured the owners they would be profitable.

All of the workers worked around the clock, split up into shifts so as not to bring the Works to a halt. The administrators placed a lot of value on brute force and resistance to tiredness.

The drive wound us through lonely stretches of road that have lived in my mind since I was a boy. The lonely Atacama desert stretched before us, and it all seemed so eerily still and quiet, like a watercolor painting.

The land here seemed to have died way before man began to creep across its surface. And why would anyone ever want to come out here? How did anyone even come to think of exploring a landscape that, in my mind, is what the surface of Mars must look like? It was more difficult for me to comprehend how people could make a life out here, working in this dry air and blistering sun. What became of the people who worked here for so long?

The harshness of the environment, the lack of an impartial authority, and the difficulty of life in general introduced violence; a violence that involved inter-personal relations as well as those with the authorities. The saltpeter owner, through his administrators—the real representatives of the owner of the

Works—organized with an iron fist. That objective converted the administrator into police and judge, who handed out punishment with total impunity. The saltpeter worker could not turn to the Chilean Government. The Chilean state left law and order among the workers in the hands of the saltpeter Works.

"Corpses," Ivan said as he pointed in the direction of a withered wooden shack.

Confused, I asked him to clarify. "What do you mean?

Another structure came into view, this time a rusted, rectangular building. Its frame was dusted with a layer of sand.

Ivan pointed toward the windshield. "All of this, you see, is a cemetery, and this land is the grave for over a hundred mining towns. Here, this land was once home to people who worked here, had children here, where their children were schooled, where they worshipped…"

"And where many died," I concluded before he did. I didn't want to hear about the hard life these people lived. I just wanted to come and celebrate the work that was done while they were here and the buildings that remained.

"Indeed, this is where they died, where they all died; miners, their wives, and their children. The life of a miner. It's not just the corpses of the buildings that remain in this place. The cemeteries are all here, and so here is where they remain. All of them."

As we approached the compound, I saw nothing to indicate anyone was there, or had been for some time.

I could feel my mouth drop as we pulled into the town. "Where is everyone?" I demanded.

Ivan parked on a patch of land at the main entrance.

I unhooked my seat belt, pushed open the car door, and approached a large sign that read: Oficina Salitrera Santiago Humberstone. A map of the complex indicated each of the buildings that still remained.

"This is the entrance," I said to Ivan. "So where is everyone? There must have been some mistake. There should be people here." I pulled out my cell phone, but unsurprisingly, there was no signal.

Between two buildings a hundred yards away I thought I glimpsed a shadow. I listened for a moment, but there was nothing. We were miles from the closest city. I had not seen a car pass us for miles. There were no animals I had spotted on this drive. Not so much as a bird flying overhead could be seen. The wind did not even stir. It was silent, completely silent. It was dead. I stood still, peering down between the buildings, down the road, but there was nothing. This was a true ghost town, dried out, faded, and crumbling.

Just then, the engine started. As I walked toward the car I looked to Ivan. He opened the driver side door and stood there. His chin shook and his lips trembled. His skin looked even paler than just a few moments before.

"To the hotel then? I am too old to be standing out in this dreadful heat."

"I'm sorry."

"No worry at all. I'll just make a call to the office to see if this event has been rescheduled." I lifted the handle to the passenger-side door, but it was locked.

"I'm sorry. I must return to my rest at Santa Clara." Ivan said. He dropped back into the driver seat and put the car in drive.

"Ivan," I slammed my palm on the passenger window. "Open the door."

Sitting behind the steering wheel calmly he looked at me, and for the first time I noticed his gray eyes. They were the color of ash. "I'm sorry," he mouthed.

The car spun quickly, and as it did Ivan lowered his window a few inches and slipped out what looked like an envelope. He then hit the gas, and as he did, I threw my briefcase at the car. The case crashed to the floor and lay there.

The car just kept accelerating. It charged down the long, empty road, moving further and further away from me until it was a speck and then it became one with where the horizon met the mountains. I stood there for some time, in a daze of denial, but ultimately I accepted my fate.

The saltpeter workers expressed themselves in terms of rebelliousness and solidarity when faced with the harsh life and conditions surrounding them; they demanded being listened to and looked after by the owners of the Works, by the administrators, and by the Chilean Government; they formed unions and they organized themselves.

There was no spiritual or religious support in the Works. The workers instead channeled their religiousness into certain devotions, particularly their devotion to the Virgin of La Tirana.

When I finally moved, my legs were cramped from standing still so long. I lumbered over and bent down to pick up my briefcase. It was then that I remembered the envelope. It lay just a few feet from me, gleaming and white against the sand.

I sat on the ground, took the envelope in my hands, and saw that it had been addressed to me, Ernesto, written in my sister's delicate hand.

Inside a single slip of paper read: "We have been waiting for you."
They were here. All of them.

I walked with purpose now. The sun had turned a golden orange
now as it began to set. On the other side of the sky, shades of pinks,
blues, and purples began to wash across the heavens. As in my dream,
I walked between buildings, and they stood empty, doors open, the
floors covered in dust. The living quarters were abandoned, rusted
bedsprings and a few collapsing cabinets remained. The main square
was desolate, the carob and tamarugo trees stood alone, dried, burned,
and neglected by the hot desert wind. A face looked back out at me
from the schoolhouse window, a small boy, with a gaunt face. His black
eyes were lost somewhere else.

"You, child." I called.

I stepped into the school, the one where only the smallest of
children attended as older children worked in the mines. There was no
response to my call.

Broken glass crunched underfoot as I walked through the small
hallway. I turned and moved into a classroom. There, wooden desks
were broken and tossed about. An old ruler lay against a chalkboard
and a pencil sat on one lone desk beside a window. I took a seat there
and removed the notepad from my briefcase and the pen I write to you
now.

For a moment, I wondered what if I would have been the son of a
miner? What if I would have worked in the mines, hunched in the dark
for hours in a suffocated space? My eyes watering from the smoke and
the fumes, my cough growing incessant, my thirst uncontrollable, but
the need to keep moving was mandatory?

To risk your sight, your limbs, your life for just a few dollars—this
was their purgatory.

Many people had died. Many children had died too, and I knew because I saw it with my own eyes. For so long, I had lived with the torture of seeing men carted from the mines, their lifeless shells covered in the blood of the mine. I saw this. I ignored this, but there was nothing I could do, so I had said nothing. I just left. All I did was leave. My grandfather grew rich from these lives, as had my father. I, however, found myself back here, sobbing, asking for forgiveness for not doing something, but it was all too late. I was a coward. I sobbed in that classroom more than I ever had in all of my life.

What seemed like hours passed and the only light cast was that of the moon and the stars overhead. It was time to leave. I tucked the notepad and pen into my pocket. I left the school and walked past the empty energy house, its windows covered in the dust of decades, the old foundry workshop, and the foundry whose wooden structure seemed so brittle it looked as though it would disintegrate with my touch.

I walked beyond, past the town, a few hundred yards east. I saw them there, rising from the ground; wooden crosses. A mist hung over the cemetery where hundreds of miners were buried, many with their families. I imagined them to be uneasy there in their graves, laid to rest in a place that forbade them from having any true comfort.

The iron gates surrounding the cemetery were merely cosmetic, even then. The black, metal archway over the main entrance read simply "Cemetery." They were buried here in plain, wooden coffins. Walking among them now, I could see that even in death, there were corners cut. Many remains were exposed to the night sky. The desert wind had blown away much of some graves, exposing rotting, wooden coffins. Others were splintered and broken, as if someone from above had kicked to get to the dead. Grave robbers were likely surprised to find there was nothing to take from these people. What little they had was already taken by the mine. Pockets of unearthed graves lined the land. Hallowed eyes looked to the heavens. Even in death, they prayed for escape from this place. Shreds of clothing were strewn about the cemetery. Most here were buried in the same clothes, their miners' uniform of dark pants and dark shirts.

As I continued through the maze of battered wood, bones, and skulls resting in the sand, I came upon a freshly prepared grave. The word "Karla" was written across the painted white wooden cross. Beside her was another grave for "Raul Santiago," and beside that one was "Esther Santiago." I knelt next to them. I should have known they had all come back here, to the hell my family had curated. I paused a moment, noticing an empty space beside my sister's resting spot. It was a freshly dug grave. Besides the hole there was a plain wooden coffin and a white cross with the word "Ernesto" written across it.

I heard footsteps approach. I looked to my side and found the little boy from the schoolhouse standing beside me. I stood up and turned around to see them. The old lady from that airplane was right—they were all here waiting for me. The town had come alive.

There were no longer desiccated bones strewn about the ground. What stood before me now were the inhabitants of Humberstone, their ghosts, in the flesh as they had lived decades ago. Hundreds of them stood there silent.

Together, they slowly proceeded to walk toward me. I took out my pad and paper once more and began to write.

To my wife, I am sorry.

I looked up again and now they were circling me.

To my daughter, I love you.

Now their shadows blocked out the moon. I was surrounded. The young boy tugged on my jacket and then pointed to my grave. The mass of dead kept coming. I was lifted by my legs by dozens of hands, carried off, and dropped in my coffin. The lid was shut, nails were hammered.

"I'm sorry!" I shouted as I felt myself being lowered into the earth. Thumps of dirt falling onto the coffin sounded like the beating drums from the Chilean folklore music of my youth.

"I'm sorry!" I shouted again, but they continued to dig, and dig, and dig.

28

LA SANDIA

THE WATERMELON

endors begin setting up their booths beneath the last sprinkling of stars. They drop their bundles gently on the ground. Since the days of the ancient, they have come here, surrounded by the verdant mountains and valleys. In modern times came the red-tiled roofs and the cobblestone streets. As daylight spreads through the sky, bundles are unwrapped, their products are gently hung in booths, and quickly the colors of all the products along the vendor stalls are charged with life, practicing their beckoning energy for potential owners. There are dresses and pants, hats and shoes, belts and socks, curtains and bedsheets, clocks and mirrors, and so many other wonderful things, and of course there are all sorts of foods that can be found in the market.

The little girl comes walking into the market each day with her basket. She comes alone. Vendors who have been working here for years do not know who her parents are, nor even from what town she comes from. The little girl dresses in traditional attire, a traje, a textile dress. The pattern of the textile indicates which village and group one belongs to. Yet, the little girl's brilliant pink, purple, and blue stripe dress cannot be tied to any local group in the area by any of the vendors. She is thin and barefoot. As she walks down the path, she passes a cacophony of chatter from varying Guatemalan dialects. Holding her basket closely to her chest, she passes sellers of pottery, herbs, fresh mountain produce, chickens, and pigs. An old woman calls out to the young child from behind a table of watermelons, oranges, and bunches of bananas. The old woman was the only one to call out to the little girl today. Some days no one sees her. Some days everyone sees her. Today, it was just the old woman.

Rising gently from her wooden chair, the old woman goes over to the row of watermelons. She had just sliced a large one, cutting it first into round circles and halves. It was the best watermelon she had that day and had hoped to make more from selling it in pieces than selling it whole. Taking a napkin in hand first, the old woman picked up the largest watermelon slice, and held it out for the little girl.

The watermelon slice was bright pink, its rind the magical green of dreams. The little girl looked first to her basket and removed the sheet that covered its contents. Within were dozens and dozens of teeny wooden dolls, no longer than a sewing needle, no wider than a pencil. The girl carefully handpicked six dolls and laid the miniatures on her palm. Thin cotton-colored string was wrapped around each, delicately stylizing pants, a shirt, and some with dresses. The exposed wood was dotted with two black dots for the eyes, and a line of red for the mouth.

More cotton string was strung about their head for hair. The little girl then dug into her satchel and retrieved a painted yellow box. She lifted the dolls closely to her lips and whispered her little girl whispers to them. She then brought the six dolls closely to her ear and nodded. Then she placed the dolls in the wooden box with great care.

"When you have a worry, tell that worry to one of the dolls and place it under your pillow. The doll will cure your worry for you in the night."

The old woman took the box into her hands. "But I don't want to buy this."

The little girl smiled. "I don't sell the dolls. I give them to those people who have the most worry. These dolls chose you."

The old lady opened the box and inspected the dolls, each were brilliantly dressed and gave her comfort right then.

"You only have six dolls, so no more than six worries per night," the little girl said.

The old lady sighed. "My only worry is to die in the night."

"Tell a doll your worry, and if you are meant to die in the night you will, but you will do so without worry."

The little girl took the watermelon slice thankfully and continued walking through the market.

29

EL TAMBOR

THE DRUM

I only ever drink rum.

I like the way it sits on the tip of my tongue, as if there's something I'm about to say, or need to say. Or perhaps it's because there's something my body, the very fabric of my DNA is aching for me to speak?

Even on my wedding day, as people toasted and champagne flowed around me, I sipped on rum.

There is Jamaican rum, which is rich and can include sticky-fermented notes, bold spices and a hefty touch of molasses. There's balanced Barbadian rum, that incorporates notes of oak. There are other Caribbean rums, those from the Dominican Republic, St. Lucia, the Bahamas, Grenada, St. Martin, Bonaire, St. Croix, and more. Yet, for me, what tastes like home is Puerto Rican rum.

OUR HONEYMOON WAS QUICK, mostly because we could not afford to take many days off. We had to get back fast, returning to our lives where we would continue to work to live. Leo surprised me with a trip to Puerto Rico.

I had not visited Puerto Rico since I was a young teen. I could not say I had particularly fond memories of the place. Perhaps because as soon as my parents and I would arrive we would leave the airport and drive inland to visit with my Uncle Manny, my mother's brother, and his family. I remember asking my parents why it was we didn't visit the beaches and they would just give each other a glance and then one of them would say "There's no time for that."

What they meant was that there was no time for me to go to the beach. In the mornings when I would wake and get ready in the bathroom, I would find a light layer of sand on the bottom of the tub from whomever had showered previously. My parents would say they went out early in the morning to try to catch fish, but they never returned with any fish. They did always return covered in grains of sand.

After I would get ready for the day, I would find my parents seated at the kitchen table with my Uncle Manny and documents spread before them as they sipped coffee. They would grow silent, and exchange looks when I would enter the room, as if I was disturbing some long, buried secret.

It was on one of those unsuccessful fishing trips from which my parents never returned. They risked going out during a hurricane warning. The small boat they were on was found capsized near the Puente de Piedera, a natural stone bridge just outside of our town in Cabo Rojo, not far from Los Morrillos Lighthouse.

Over the years I often thought about those childhood trips and wondered what it was my parents were doing out there on the water each morning. Soon after my parents died so did my Uncle Manny. There was no one left to provide any real answers.

I was raised by my father's side of the family who were neither Puerto Rico nor who could explain to me why it was my parents insisted on being on a small boat during dangerous weather.

My mother was good on the open water, growing up around boats and boating her entire life, but there aren't many people that are good on a small vessel during a hurricane.

On those childhood trips, we did not visit any of the key Puerto Rican tourist sites, El Observatorio de Arecibo which was used in the Search for Extraterrestrial Intelligence, or SETI program. We didn't visit the nearby Cueva del Indio, a cave surrounded by dramatic cliffs with preserved pre-Columbian petroglyphs carved on the wall. We failed to ever visit Rio Camuy Cave, a cave system spanning 268 acres thought by some to be one of the largest cave systems in the world with cathedral high ceilings and magnificent stalagmites and stalactites. Also missed was Ponce's historic center, the Plaza Las Delicias, and the black and red horizonal striped Old Ponce Fire Station. We didn't even visit any of the beaches, like Luquillo known for its palm-lined stretch of golden sand, and clear and tranquil beaches. There was also no Rincon Beach that attracted suffers and humpback whales.

What I had wished we had seen so many years ago was Old San Juan and the Castillo San Felipe del Morro, the island's top tourist destination. El Morro, is an impressive fortress that juts out on a peninsula that sits high over the Atlantic Ocean. Its position in the harbor meant that this massive, intimidating site was the first structure to be seen by approaching ships coming from the east. Between El

Morro and the Castillo San Cristóbal, the city of Old San Juan was surrounded by 25 feet high and 18 feet thick stone walls, making San Juan once nearly impregnable to invaders.

WE LANDED AND DROVE our rental car straight to Old San Juan. We walked the cobblestone streets and window shopped at darling little stores on the first floors of pastel pink, yellow and green buildings. We drank piña coladas made with Bacardi Gold rum, distilled in one of the largest distilleries in the world in Cataño here on the island.

It was then time to stroll down Norzagary Street toward the main destination for the evening. As we walked, I felt a tug in my chest.

I stood beside the San Juan Historic National site sign. I smiled as Leo took a photo with his phone, but still, I could not shake the feeling that I was being pulled forward.

The fort was an impressive, looming structure. The parts of the stone walls that were exposed were faded by sea salt and sun, and the other surfaces were covered in moss and mold. We entered this labyrinthine world by stairs, and as soon as we did, I felt a door close within me. A new chapter had begun.

El Morro is made up of six staggered levels that include barracks, passageway's, storerooms and dungeons. The massive fortification was built by the Spanish in 1539 as ordered by King Charles V of Spain as a defense against England's Sir Francis Drake who was known for his naval aggression. The structure built was likely the best response at that time, a fierce castle on a rock aimed to deter intruders, which it very often did.

We visited the museum inside and walked through an exhibit with photographs and artifacts. We then started a private guided tour my husband had arranged. Our guide, Felipe, led us along the ramparts, where inactive cannons faced the ocean. It was that first gust of wind, while standing outside, where I felt a surge of electricity that has yet to leave me.

Leo and I each stepped inside a domed garita, or sentry box, one of the iconic symbols of Puerto Rico. I looked out from the slit carved into the stone. I imagined many soldiers manned this spot for hours, hundreds of years ago, watching for potential invading ships.

"Hundreds of cruise ships arrive to this port each day, and for many of them, they are greeted by this grand structure," our tour guide Felipe said.

Leo held up his phone and snapped a picture of me that I was not yet prepared to pose for, and then I sensed it. I felt hot breath on my cheek and the whispered words of a woman: "Fifteen men on a dead man's chest."

I didn't scream, but I looked into Leo's eyes. Blood rushed into my ears, or was that water?

Leo slipped his phone into his back pocket and reached for my hand. "Alida, are you alright?"

"Yes," I stepped out of the dome. "Maybe it's jetlag," I lied.

We walked over to one of the inoperable cannons when I asked Felipe "Is this place haunted?"

Felipe clasped his hands together. "There are some ghost stories for El Morro. One of them says that the ghost of a soldier is often seen still standing guard in this location, looking out for any enemy ships."

"Obviously," Leo laughed.

I raised my fingers to my lips to silence him. He covered his mouth with his hand and winked at me. I knew he felt ghost stories were silly, but I still found them fascinating, the idea that someone long dead could have some agency in the physical world.

"A woman in white is often seen here, too," Felipe started and then Leo interrupted.

"Every town has got a woman in white," Leo said sounding not impressed. "We have one too in our city."

Felipe continued "People have reported strange noises being heard here, of soldiers marching up and down. Sometimes they say they hear the blast of cannon fire, and very often people have reported seeing ghost ships approaching."

I turn back to the narrow garita. The position where a guard once kept watch was bathed in darkness, and not even the full moon rising above offered it much light. It was in that moment I could taste fresh rum on my lips.

"The ghost ships are sometimes thought to be those belonging to our famous Puerto Rican pirate, Roberto Cofresí," the tour guide said, and it was as if canons fired all around me.

"Cofresí?" I asked startled.

Leo wrapped an arm around my waist and squeezed. "That explains it all. You're a pirate, Alida."

Felipe raised an eyebrow. "Your surname's Cofresí?" He gave a silent applause. "Well, welcome home."

"Wait," I laughed because it sounded ridiculous, like a children's story. "Pirates of the Caribbean?"

"Of course, where do you think the most fantastic pirates roamed, but here? Robert Louis Stevenson was influenced by many real stories when he wrote *Treasure Island*. He even mentioned real pirates such as William Kidd and Blackbeard. There's no way to know for sure, but why wouldn't he or other writers or artists be influenced by Cofresí who was legendary even during his day? Pillaging large Spanish ships and taking hold of their silver and gold and goods? He was infamous for taunting authorities and evading capture for years.

Cofresí was the last of the real pirates of the Caribbean, born June 12,1791 after the Golden Age of Piracy, and he was probably the most legendary. He was born into wealth, but the economy shifted during Spain's control of the island. He eventually went on to man a small fishing boat, transporting fruits and vegetables. He spent a lot of time talking to a lot of the older sailors, perhaps picking up on ideas of being free from Spanish control.

Cofresí became frustrated with Spain's rule over Puerto Rico and wanted independence for the colonies. He eventually acquired a larger boat, a six-gun sloop named Anne. He added a crew of fifteen men and he and his crew would intercept Spanish ships leaving the Caribbean with supplies and money."

"Fifteen men…" I said and another gust of wind blew.

I could feel the blood run down from my face. I knew then I had not imagined those words.

"Yes, like the song from *Treasure Island*," Felipe said:
Fifteen men on the dead man's chest—
…Yo-ho-ho, and a bottle of rum!
Drink and the devil had done for the rest—
…Yo-ho-ho, and a bottle of rum!

THE THREE OF US were gathered around a cannon now that pointed toward the ocean. Night had completely fallen.

Felipe continued his account of the legendary pirate. "Cofresí was known to take much of this wealth and share it with islanders. But soon the United States became so fed up with him an international call was put out for help to stop him.

The U.S.S Grampus was placed out at sea one day for bait, and Cofresí took it. He boarded the Grampus, and an assault began that killed five of his men and severely injured Cofresí who fled back to his ship, Anne. He was eventually captured off the coast of Puerto Rico with his remining crew. He was brought here to El Morro where he was tried by a Spanish court."

I found myself leaning against the stone wall now. The words whispered in my ear still ringing.

"Cofresí was then executed here, with his remaining ten men, on March 25, 1825. He was 25 years old," Felipe said.

The numbers didn't lie. Five of Cofresí's men died in the assault on sea and ten were executed on land.

Fifteen men on a dead man's chest, I thought.

Cofresí had gotten his crew of fifteen men killed, as well as himself. Were those the same fifteen men referenced in that legendary pirate song?

Leo asked, "So do people see his ghost here?"

"Not here, but people have reported to have seen his ghost in caves and coves throughout the island. They say he appears first outlined with fire."

"Why in caves or coves, and not here?" I asked.

Felipe winked "Because he's protecting his buried treasure. Cofresí is one of few pirates to have hinted at having buried his treasure while he was alive. Maybe that entire idea came from him, who knows? But it's thought thousands of Spanish coins he stole were never found."

Leo smiled "I guess we're going looking for buried treasure," he joked.

"Maybe not," Felipe said. "The U.S.S. Grampus was eventually shipwrecked. People say it was the ghost of Cofresí, that he's cursed all of those who contributed to his death. It's also been said that anyone that has gotten too close to his treasure has gone missing, being dragged by the spirits of dead pirates to Davy Jones' Locker."

"What's that?" I asked.

Felipe pointed out toward the sea. "That's what they say of anyone attempting to take cursed buried treasure. That once a person arrives at the location where the treasure is buried, with the intent of taking it, they are dragged by the ghosts of long-dead pirates to the bottom of the ocean. Pirates call that place Davy Jones' Locker."

"I never understood that," Leo said. "What's the point of burying goods and gold if no one can access it. They're dead. Why would their ghosts care?"

Felipe rubbed the back of his head. "I've thought of that too. Maybe they want the right person to get the treasure."

Leo pulled out his cell phone, taking more pictures. "Like whom?"

Felipe shrugged. "Who knows? Another pirate? A relative?"

As Leo and the tour guide proceeded to walk, talking about the best way for us to make it back to our hotel in the Rio Grande I looked out at the Atlantic Ocean. I closed my eyes and raised my arms out. I relished in the cool breeze that came rolling off the sea. When I opened my eyes, I saw several lights sparkling out in the distance.

"I see some cruises coming in," I directed Felipe's attention out toward the water. I thought I heard the sound of a drum, and singing, but those words, it couldn't be…

He strained to look. "I don't see anything."

When I looked back into what seemed like infinite darkness, the lights were gone. There was only the reflection of the full moon shining down on the water's surface.

"Maybe it was a ghost ship," Leo said.

LATER THAT NIGHT, LEO and I sat outside on the beachfront of our hotel. We had more drinks and listened to the sound of waves crashing. I looked over to him to ask him what he thought of the ghost stories, but he had been lulled to sleep by the song of the ocean.

I took another sip of my rum and looked out over the dark water, hoping to see those ghostly lights from shadowy ships manned by the dead, but there was nothing.

That night, when I fell asleep I dreamed I was sinking.

IN THE MORNING, WE visited all of the tourist locations I had longed to visit. We drove up winding mountain roads. I heard the co-kee song of the Puerto Rican tree frog and we danced to live salsa music.

No matter what we saw or what we heard nothing could undo the excitement I felt when I heard that name, Roberto Cofresí, or that longing I experienced in wanting to see the ghost lights once again.

LIFE IS A PROCESSION of steady events, all revolving around work and the expectations to build and maintain a life. Leo and I returned to work. Leo worked for Chicago's Streets and Sanitation department, patching up pothole covered streets, and I did what my mother did until she was taken by the ocean one day, I drove a Chicago River Taxi.

Most people think of public transportation and defer to images of subway cars or elevated trains and buses. I transported thousands of passengers each year along routes on the river.

I didn't mind the long hours, because I enjoyed being out on the water.

A boat is always in motion, swaying with the current and wind. Unlike a car, with a boat the momentum will always be moving you. There are no breaks on a boat. You're either going under power, or with the current pushing you along. Or, you're having to forcefully put your boat in reverse to go backwards. Even with a perfectly set compass, you will be pushed off course just a little because of the wind or the current or both. You will always have to compensate and correct to stay on course.

And even when anchored and tied to a marina, you're still being moved around by the wind.

WE HAD CHILDREN AND raised them as best we could with the money we made. They moved on to their loves and lives and Leo and I continued working to save up for a life where we could sleep in and move slowly.

I remained silent about my dreams, plagued by the sight of ghost ships with their billowing masts in the twilight.

With each sleep the floating vessels drew closer until one night I dreamt I was swimming in the great ocean and the great and narrow ship was just above me. I could practically touch the rotting and worn wooden boards that constructed its hull. I could finally hear its frayed flags flapping in the wind, and I could see the crew that gathered on the deck above to peer down on me.

The figures stood still. Their gaunt faces. Their eyes wide and focused on me. Gray skin hung from their bodies. Patches of missing flesh revealed black bones. The tops of their heads held strips of black and greasy hair. Machetes and daggers were strapped on their hips. One man was missing a leg. One woman was missing an arm, and all of them were smiling at me, smiles that were most fierce, gruesome and grim.

I WORKED MY THIRTY YEARS plus, and the week before I was set to retire Leo told me he was going to take a nap before dinner, from which he never woke.

My present to him for our retirement was going to be a small house and used boat I had purchased in Cabo Rojo, the small town on the southwestern side of the island where I was from.

I sold all that I could and readied for a life alone. My children asked me to stay, but they were all adults now and our relationship had been relegated to five-minute check-ins on the phone. I raised them to care for themselves and they had done a fantastic job.

The night before I boarded a plane, in my dream I had finally made it on board the ghost ship.

On either side of me was a line of rotting and wasting men and women, standing at attention. A cabin door stood just a few feet before me and inside candles flickered. A dark figure stood at the threshold, its back to me.

I felt a cold, slimy hand take mine. I turned and a woman in a white silk gown, all wasted with moss growing out of her eye sockets said, "He's got fifteen dead men on his chest."

And I felt the anguish and the guilt that this marauder of the seas once felt; a tyrant, but also a revolutionary. A criminal, yet a Robin Hood.

Some men and women haunt houses. Others haunt the sea, and beckon those of us—members of their lineage to them. A family reunion. And perhaps that's what this was, I thought. Or, perhaps it was all in my head. I wondered why it was my parents would go on excursions in the morning on fishing boats to return with no fish. I wondered why it was my uncle died shortly after my parents went missing. Were they all in search of something that was meant to remain long hidden? Who knows?

I MOVED INTO THE PASTEL blue one bedroom house easily. I only brought one bag with me. An old woman didn't need much. I would let my hair grow long and gray and welcome the wrinkles that would deepen in the sun as I navigated my small boat.

She was everything I ever wanted, a 1978 Pearson 365. She was worn and faded around the edges, like I was, but she had hope, as did I. She had a new main sail, solar power panels, and a newer engine. We would explore the island together.

I spent days practicing my freedom which expanded beyond a road or a river. Unlike the water taxi, I now had the open ocean and the option to go as fast as I could. I named the boat Leo Rum, and it kept me company, as well as a small dog I found wandering my house one morning. She kept visiting each sunrise. I named her Soledad and she's been my expedition partner ever since.

I spent years exploring new beaches and caves and coves, circling the island and visiting the nearby islands of Vieques and Culebra. I knew I was delaying what I was meant to explore, but I felt as if I had time.

When I felt ready, I soon isolated my explorations close to home in Cabo Rojo. I spent a lot of time around Bahía de Boqueron moving north to Canal Norte. One day, I found myself in Laguna Guaniquilla, struck by the huge, jagged rocks that looked like they could have been plucked from the moon and set here on this island paradise.

In that moment I turned behind me, wanting so much to tell Leo to look at the wonderful site, but fell silent realizing as always that he was gone. I anchored the ship and walked up a beautiful boardwalk. I found myself on a flat hill and took a seat on a smooth rock. Soledad nuzzled close to me, and I rubbed her head.

I took a deep breath and spoke to Leo. "I do miss you. This was supposed to be our adventure." I sat quiet for a few minutes and when it was time to leave I pulled out my phone and revised the map so I could get a sense of how to navigate back home.

Then, I saw the name on my map I had been avoiding, Cueva del Pirata Cofresí.

Perhaps it was the sign I was waiting for. I looked down to Soledad and rubbed her orange and white coat. "There's one more stop we need to make."

I ANCHORED AND WALKED ALONG a collection of mangroves. Soledad walked happily beside me. I thought about my parents and how much I missed them. I thought about my children and how beautiful they all were and how proud of them I was. But most of all, I thought about Leo and how lonely I was without him, and how my life had shifted so much over the years.

And that was life, wasn't it? One day you wake up and your past is all a memory. One day you wake up and you look at a picture of yourself decades before and you're unable to recognize that person, and that is fine, because there's always another adventure.

I climbed up the limestone rocks and Soledad followed steadily, her tail wagging. I pushed past branches and found the opening into the cave that I only needed to step down into. It was small inside, and the walls were smooth. The dirt floor was packed tightly, probably from all of the visitors over the years. It looked like a gallery with other small coves for entry, and I knew that this was the place. I knelt and wrapped my arms around Soledad and gave her a kiss on the top of her head.

I thought about legends and how very often the person that is a legend has a family. So, what becomes of them and their legacies? Are those children and grandchildren and great-grandchildren, and beyond, connected to the magic and the curse of their legendary ancestor somehow?

I stood up and wondered if this is where my parents came all of those years before and did not return. I wondered, perhaps, if the misstep in finding secrets hidden so long ago was that one needed to come alone, not intending to take anything, but just intending to see and to know.

And that is all I wanted, I just wanted to know.

"I'm here, finally," I said, tasting rum on the tip of my tongue.

I looked to the ground, and it glowed, covered in silver reales, Spanish coins.

I wondered if a parade of long, dead pirates would appear and drag me down to Davy Jones' Locker.

I wondered if my great-great-great-great grandfather would welcome me.

And, as I saw that golden red and yellow and orange fiery outline of my ancestor appear I wondered…

30

EL CAMARON

THE SHRIMP

Jesús Malverde: Nothing is confirmed, not even this.

He was either a railroad worker, construction worker, or some kind of worker.

He stole from the rich and gave to the poor in the Mexican state of Sinaloa.

He was shot, or hanged, by law enforcement on May 3, 1909.

Dates. Weeks. Months. Years. May vary.

A shrine was built to honor him near a railway track in Culiacán, Mexico.

He may or may not be buried at the shrine.

He has been prayed to by some.

He has been ignored by others.

He has answered prayers, some think.

He grants miracles, some say.

He is left offerings of candles, money, food, photographs, and shrimp in jars of formaldehyde.

He is venerated today by the poor who want to believe.

He is venerated today by the rich who need to believe.

He is venerated most by those who are forced to believe.

He is a bandit saint.

31

LAS JARAS

THE ARROWS

A sign at the entrance in Japanese reads: "Please reconsider." There are more of these signs nailed to the ancient trees throughout the forest.

It is quiet here, eerily so. The air is crisp, clean, but when the wind stirs, you catch the heavy scent of moss and earth. The only cars parked in the parking lot at this early hour are those who have come to volunteer. This is not the prime destination in the area, so there will still be time before the tourists arrive to get the bulk of the work done. Some who come here are indeed just tourists, but others come to the Aokigahara forest with other intentions.

Most cars on the road are driving further ahead. Hiking gear, such as heavy-duty shoes, fleece sweaters, knives and rope, and assortments of pretzels and energy bars are packed carefully in those car trunks that pass. Rucksacks can be seen secured to many automobile roofs that wind down the highway to Mount Fuji. The people in most of those cars are not likely candidates for this forest. However, it is unpredictable to determine who will change their mind. This forest is successful in attracting the attention it needs.

People come from all over the world to hike and to climb up paths of Mount Fuji. This is for all to test their physical strength, their patience, and their determination. This is all done in order to reach the summit, the ultimate prize.

Rafael made this journey alone, to prove that he could do something on his own. Life in Brazil, was, well…life. He would wake in the morning, shower, dress, and commute to work where he sat behind a desk doing things like sending emails, answering a phone, then writing code for a computer program he pretended to understand. When work ended, he would commute back home, change into jeans and a T-shirt, and again get on a computer where he would send emails or read things or look for people who had similar interests as him, though there were very few interests he had. Rafael was thirty-nine and he lived and functioned very much alone.

One evening, he received an instant message from someone named Misaki_99.

"Hi," they said.

"Hello, how are you?" he responded.

They went along this way, saying things and asking questions all into the night. They would chat for hours. They would chat mostly while Misaki was at work and Rafael should have been asleep. Misaki was Japanese American, she told him. She lived and worked outside of Osaka, teaching English at a high school. Rafael was a Brazilian of Japanese descent. There were thousands like him in Brazil, Japanese

Brazilians. They were the largest group of Japanese outside of Japan in the world. Yet, regardless of his country's reputation for amazing sun and sand, beautiful people, and vibrant culture, he still felt very much alone.

One night she called him. Work had been another episode of boredom and frustration, but regardless of all of the gloom, once he heard her voice, it all was washed away; the sadness and the suffering.

Suddenly she told him, "If you don't live life now, then you never will."

ON THE JET BRIDGE after landing, he called her. There was no answer. In his hotel room, he called her again, and again there was no answer. Perhaps she was waiting for him at the mountain, he thought. That is where she said they should meet for the first time.

"It's one of the three holy mountains of Japan," she said. "Meeting there, well, it will make it all the more special."

The other two were Mount Tate and Mount Haku. While reading on the plane, Rafael learned that Mount Fuji's name was speculated to mean a variety of things. Some said it meant wealth or abundance, others said it meant a man with status. Some said that the name meant fire, while others said it meant an old woman.

Rafael tried Misaki's phone one more time before he got into the rental car. This time he left a message.

"Hi," he said awkwardly. He could feel the smile stretching across his face. "I, um, have tried you a few times but um. I'll just head out now over there. Just call me whenever you get this. If not, I'll see you there. I can't wait to finally meet you in person and well, yeah...I'll see you soon." He hung up and regretted everything he had said, thinking he could have said it better. He wondered if she would think him silly. Worse, he wondered if she was even going to be at the mountain. Either way, he was here, and so he was going to go drive out, hike through the evening, as most climbers did there, in order to reach the summit as the sun rose.

AT ONE POINT YABUSAME rituals were held here. Yabusame was a highly skilled form of archery on horseback. This practice was designed in order to entertain the variety of gods that are believed to watch over Japan. The archer would gallop down a track, bring back his bow, and shout "darkness and light," as he released. A loud thump would ring out as the arrow struck a wooden board.

Today, very little noise can be found in these woods. Not even wildlife makes this place their home. There are no birds that fly or flutter overhead. Small furry critters do not want anything that any of these trees produce. Even the animals sense that this is a place of torment and so take their activities elsewhere.

This morning's group of volunteers is comprised of old and new members. In years past, there have been rumors as to what happens to some of the members who disappear, but no one speaks of those things. Recurring members still come. The leader has been doing this for years. During the briefing, all members listen carefully to the plan. As soon as the sun rises, they will start their search. The leader said, "Stay with the group at all times," it seemed after every sentence. One of the new volunteers laughed and said, "We get it. We'll stay with the group."

The leader, a man with the perpetual look of anger on his face, responded with, "That's what you say now, but in there, things change."

Assignments were handed out. A few people were charged to carry the equipment, knives and large bags and small bags and markers for making notes on the bags. Two were designated to collect. One person was assigned as back-up collector if the main two could no longer perform their duties. A medic was also in the group and his task for the morning and afternoon was obvious, so no one said anything to him. A communications director would manage connections with the outside world, in the dreaded case they got lost. A driver, the only person who would be in a vehicle, would follow the volunteers on foot closely. The truck to be used for the collections. Everyone else was there to scan and to provide support.

The entire time, Mount Fuji towered over them. It was the highest mountain in Japan with a cone so symmetrical and perfect, even from here it seemed unreal. Its snow-covered top is featured in photographs and prints in every tourist shop nearby, and from here it looked just like a postcard. It was an astounding natural beauty. To climb its peak was a dream for so many, and so the terrors here at the foot of the mountain seemed in stark contrast.

RAFAEL WAS NOW MAKING his descent. He had tried Misaki's phone again at the summit and this time there was an answer. The person on the other line told him that he had the wrong number. Reviewing the number Rafael was confused. This was the same telephone number that had been programmed into his phone for as long as he knew Misaki, which had been months. He had even spoken to her as he boarded the plane in São Paulo. How could this be the wrong telephone number? It just could not be the wrong telephone number. He dialed again. The phone rang once and the bitter man answered again with, "I told you, stop calling. You have the wrong number."

"I'm sorry, sir, but I assure you this was my girlfriend Misaki's number…"

"Misaki? She's dead. She's been dead for years. When will you people just stop and leave an old man alone?"

He slammed the phone and Rafael was left there standing, alone again.

THE GROUP OF TWENTY did one final round of checks. When the leader asked if there were any questions, a woman stepped forward. She seemed so young to be a police officer. "Sir," she spoke up. "Do we have an idea of how many we are searching for? Is there a specific count?"

The commander looked around him to the rest of the law enforcement volunteers. The veterans knew the answer to that question easily, but these new volunteers still did not understand.

"We search as long as there is light. Whatever we find is what we find." He didn't want to go into details right then about how each year the numbers increased and how the international media had run with this story. It was an honor this country did not want to hold and so they stopped publicizing the figure a few years back. Still, the commander knew that with each year, more could be found.

Inside, the mass of trees drowned out much of the sunlight. Walking in pairs, they stepped over twisted roots that curled and lay in the most treacherous of places. It was easy to slip and to fall here. None of the volunteers spoke as they followed the leader who inspected each tree and each formation of rocks carefully. He seemed to know where he was going and proved so each time he pointed out a strip of blue tape across a tree trunk. A volunteer would quickly step in and replace the tape with a fresh strip for next year's search.

A sense of dread floated above the group as they made their way further inside the forest. The change was apparent in their faces. This was a particular sort of concentration, one which involved knowing oneself and not sinking into the midst of depression in this strange, wooded place. Their senses were heightened as they looked forward, high above them in the trees, behind them around dark corners, and to their sides at imposing boulders. Each tree looked the same. Each patch of grass, fallen branch, and bunch of leaves looked like the other. The air grew heavier the more they walked. Cluttered, tangled, and ghastly vines and dark shadows inhabited every inch of space here it seemed. There was a dizzying reluctance to want to continue moving. Many of them felt the heaviness in their chests and feet, but they kept moving, following their leader. The view never changed. There was nothing but dark greens, browns, and grays.

The energies here were imbalanced.

Suddenly, the leader raised his hand, and as people came to a quiet halt there was the snapping of twigs beneath their feet.

"Listen," he said.

Something was creaking overhead.

Creak. Creak. Creak. Creak.

Slowly, their faces turned upward to see a long dead corpse swinging from a tree. A noose around their neck. The remains had on a gray, weatherworn suit. No one moved. No one spoke until the leader commanded to cut them down. Swiftly, each of the members stepped into their designated roles. The leader shone a flashlight on the man's chest. A handwritten note was visible.

"Hurry up and cut him down," he shouted.

One person climbed up the tree. With a knife in hand, they cut the rope and the body fell to the forest floor. Brittle bones cracked. Two volunteers approached, with blue plastic gloved hands. One unfolded a body bag. The other rolled over the body. The flesh, what little remained, was pockmarked. Muscles and tendons could be seen around the eyes and cheeks. As the body was rolled over pieces of skin from the dead man's hand stuck to the forest ground and peeled away.

The medic gave his opinion. "Three months."

For a quarter of a year, the lifeless suited man swung there on the tree branch.

The body was bagged, and the commander started his count: "One." And they continued on their way to collect more bodies.

Another first-year volunteer ran ahead and asked the leader, "How many more do you expect?"

"Last year we located 245," he said, marching ahead with determination. There was no time to talk of what they had done before. There was very little time at all. They needed to collect the bodies of the suicides from the past year as quickly as they could. Staying here after dark was not an option. Returning a consecutive day was not an option. This task took a mental, physical, and spiritual toll. To keep the team safe this needed to be done quickly.

The veterans from years past spoke very little as they gathered another seventy-six bodies over the course of four hours. The smells of earth and moss and rotting trees were sweet compared to the putrid smell of decaying flesh. Some of the newer members cried as the varying states of decomposition challenged all of their horrors thought possible. People were found in unsightly conditions. A woman laid across the grass in her wedding dress; she had slit her own throat. Two teenage boys in their high school uniforms died from their carefully calculated murder suicide, with a handgun they had found in one of their fathers' drawers, per a discovered note. Then there was an American tourist found dead at the base of a tree. He didn't seem like he had come here with the intent to kill himself. He looked as though he had gotten lost here and starved to death.

Many of the bodies were found with identification—wallets and ID cards in their shirts, pockets, or purses. A few had left notes while many had left ripped and torn pictures of themselves strewn about the ground where they last took a breath.

Many in Japan believe the mountain calls people here. This is where the lonely come and, tragically, this is where the lonely are brought and disillusioned by the ghosts and the demons that live within the trunks of the trees, the leaves, and vines. This place, this land, is purgatory for the unsettled.

Another one hundred and fourteen bodies were collected throughout the next few hours. The leader walks along as though he is a commander in a war zone. He reminds his team repetitively to stay close, to not look at anything too long, and to not stray away because no one would come looking for them.

The experienced watch the new members carefully. It is even difficult for them to ignore the whispers that are carried through the wind from tree to tree. Some of them feel picks and pokes at their shoulders or sides, but there is no one standing that close. Every so often a person will halt momentarily, their eyes closed tightly as they force the voices from their heads.

The forest knows they all plan to leave, and this infuriates it. The malevolent energy accumulated from the years of hopeless, desperate souls who turned finally to suicide torments all life that enters here.

The ghosts and demons of this place do not want the living to cross out of the woods and back into the parking lot, to their life. It pierces their minds and allows the hidden memories of loss, guilt, and failure to seep through. Some crumple and cry. Others go cold, but ultimately, they all continue on together as they came.

They pass another sign. This one reads: "Please consult the police before you decide to die!" An elderly man's body was later found a few yards away. He, too, had hanged himself.

A beeping goes off and the leader checks his watch. It is time to head back.

"Aren't there more?" A new patrolman asks.

With a straight face the leader says, "Of course there are. There are likely dozens more from this year we didn't get and the year before and before that, but I wouldn't stay here after dark, or I would be one of them."

With that they start to head back following the blue tape. The bodies have been stacked in the back of the truck. With each step they take it is as if there is a tear, a rip in the forest. They are taking the forest's offerings with them.

Just a few hundred feet from the entrance they come upon a man. He is seated cross-legged against a tree. He is in hiking gear, utility pants, a fleece shirt, and heavy boots. His head is slumped forward. The leader calls out to him, but there is nothing. No movement.

As they approach, he sees the chunks of bloodied brain matter sprayed against the tree. The gun had fallen out of his hand and now rests right below the man's knee. A trickle of blood runs from his mouth. The leader approaches and finds torn photographs on the man's lap as well as a cell phone. The picture is that of a beautiful woman. The leader has seen that face before. That smile was seared into his mind many years ago when he had discovered her here, at this very spot. She was the first suicide he had ever found. He places the photograph back on the man's lap. Two men approach with a black body bag.

The group leaves the forest.

Many will return to continue on with a duty very few care to do. Next year the leader will find another man here, in the very same spot, and likely with a similar story. Others will visit for other reasons. It is difficult to tell who will lose themselves in the wood; losing their minds, blood, and life. Though it will continue to happen. It continues even now. Bodies sway gently from trees. A single gunshot echoes through the land, followed by the thump of a desperate, lonely soul crashing to the ground.

It happened again just now.

32

EL MUSICO

THE MUSICIAN

We don't listen to the words
maybe we'll focus on their meaning
lulled by plucked sounds, a chorus
a revolution of rhythms

tucked between melodies we refuse
to concentrate on the murmurs of
suffering tucked within the tones
words pitched with pain

and so, we dance, stories recounted
of agony and death, and there's
twirling as we laugh at choked back

cries, a lesson, a moral, a story

a song written as elegy, eulogy
a tribute and warning, music as
mockery, and we'll ignore the
screams, as the sounds grow louder

33

LA ARAÑA

THE SPIDER

My mother pushed me down the stairs.

It was a Saturday morning, the morning of my sixteenth birthday. My father wasn't home. He was out, seeking refuge from my mother who was having one of her moments. My dad was also a victim of her violent outbursts, so there was very little he could do, he said. When I was much younger, after one of my mother's episodes, my father crept into my room at night to check the bruises on my face. He told me I didn't have to go to school the next morning. He apologized for her because she never would. He told me that night, "Just do whatever she asks of you."

I landed on my back on the cement floor of our basement. I think I was more disappointed that I didn't break my neck from the fall. I just wanted it all to end. I heard something smashing and crashing off somewhere in the house. I assumed she was now in my bedroom. My mother liked to do that, break my things when she was mad at me and throw them away. Yet, here I lay on the basement floor. I could have broken something. She had not even checked to see if I was still alive at the bottom of the stairs.

Screaming and shouting ensued. Her cries of "¡Dios mío! My God, why did you give me such a wicked, terrible daughter?" pierced my ears.

Her cries continued. I could hear her sobbing and telling herself how she had always wanted a daughter but didn't understand why God damned her with the one she got.

My crime for all of this: A boy called me at home. My mother answered. Growing up in a strict Catholic household, with an abusive mother, I could expect beatings for anything really. One day my mother found my diary and in it I had listed out the names of boys in my class I thought were cute. My mother slapped me with my diary and called me a whore.

When I reached the kitchen, I saw the phone broken in bits in the trash as well as my stereo. She came right at me from the hallway, pulled me by my shirt, then dragged me to the living room, while slapping me with her other hand.

In the darkened room, she dropped me on the floor in front of a wooden sideboard. There, on top of a white, lace tablecloth stood a three-foot statue of Jesus. It was the same statue my parents said they found in the basement of their first home in Chicago in the 1950s, an old brownstone on Mozart Avenue in Logan Square.

My mother would kneel in front of that statue every night, her hands folded in front of her chest in prayer. On most days, flickering white or red candles broke through the darkness with golden shadows.

"Now, pray."

She pointed to the carpet, wanting me to get on my knees in front of the altar.

I didn't want to pray. I wanted her dead. Jesus dead. Well, the Jesus statue out of my face, that is. I didn't want anything to do with living in that house anymore.

I didn't move. I just stood there.

"Pray," she demanded.

Her strikes came brutally. I fell on the floor and she continued to hit me.

"Pray," she screamed as she slapped me now clear across my cheek again, and again, and again, and again, and again.

Rage took over. I pushed her off of me. I kicked at her. I screamed. I cried. I pulled at my hair and ripped out chunks of dark strands. "Get the fuck away from me. Don't touch me! Don't ever touch me again or I'll kill you," I cried.

"You're possessed by the devil," she snapped. "¡Diabla! ¡El Diablo te tiene!"

"Yes, the devil has me, and he can have me for as long as he wants. Now, get the hell away from me before I show you what hell looks like!"

The slapping stopped. She staggered away from me. Her face frozen. Her eyes wide. Finally, she was fearful of me. She ran into her room and slammed her door. I heard the lock turn.

In the living room alone, I watched the flame atop a single white candle dance. It was as though it was laughing at me. That evening, I awoke at 3:33 a.m. to laughter. The laughter was coming from inside my room. I pulled the sheets up over my eyes and forced myself back to sleep. "It's just a dream," I told myself.

The next night, the same thing occurred. The cold laugh, bounced along the four walls, encircling me, and, just as it began to draw closer, it faded. I pulled the sheets over my head and told myself it was likely the television in my parent's room.

In time, my mother's beatings stopped. It just took me pulling a knife on her once to make her completely stop. Unsurprisingly, she called our priest over one day to talk to me. I slammed my bedroom door in his face. There was nothing he needed to tell me about good and evil that I didn't already know.

As the years drew on, I continued to wake up at 3:33 a.m. here and there. Some nights I would hear laughter, and other nights I would hear full-length conversations taking place. There were always distinct voices, but with the way the words ran right into each other, it was difficult to decipher what exactly was being said.

Not too long ago I learned that supernatural enthusiasts claim that the devil mocks that hour, waking would be followers, or taunting those he could never really hold. It's the time when demons play. It's the anti-hour.

The last thirteen nights leading up to tonight, I have awakened consistently at 3:33 a.m. Each night, the tone of the evening has been distinct.

The first night, I gasped for air, coming out of my sleep as if I were emerging from watery depths. I whispered over to my husband, "Are you awake"? He didn't answer.

The second night, I awoke to find myself seated on our bed, my arms crossed, looking down at my husband as he slept.

The third night I decided to record whatever thought came into my mind when I woke. When I did, I could only write the words, "I'm too scared to write anything."

The fourth night I looked down at the foot of our bed. The dark there seemed even darker and full of shape. When I thought I had finally made out a figure there, I suddenly fell asleep.

The fifth night, I woke up screaming, convinced a warm breath was blowing in my ear.

The sixth night, that's when the slaps, and the claw marks on my arms began.

Other nights brought their own cruelties.

My husband was able to sleep through the nights comfortably and each morning, I would tell him what had happened the night before. At first, he didn't believe me. I wouldn't believe anyone either. He told me to continue with the exercise of trying to write down whatever it was that came into my head when I woke up in the middle of the night. His assumption was that I was so stressed I would wake myself up each night terrified.

That night I woke and reached for my cell phone. The time mocked me, 3:33 a.m.

The next morning bite marks covered my hand.

Last night, 3:33 came. Instantly, I looked at the foot of my bed. I put pencil to paper, mindful of the shadow that slowly took shape inches away. The words flowed, quickly. After a minute I had written a full page in handwriting not my own. I won't go into detail as to what it said. All I can say is that there is nothing I can do anymore.

34

EL SOLDADO

THE SOLDIER

The newspapers for all of Ciudad Juárez were delivered early to him first thing before the sun rose over the hundreds of maquiladoras. These formidable stone islands of manufacturing, whose owners weren't even based in Mexico, were staffed by cheap labor—people who would assemble products for export to El Norte, the mythical land of opportunity, of salvation. For every new factory opening another one hundred women it seemed were laid to rest in a headline bolded with: *Beautiful girl found, beaten, tortured, raped, and killed.*

Their bodies were often discarded alongside desolate roads. Every so often, a new mass grave was uncovered somewhere in the desert, their soft faces blanketed by the rough grains of sand. He would check off each of these articles, if no names, dates, or even a hint of something traceable was present. Their stories, like their bodies, soon faded somewhere into his memory.

They were all memories.

Memories of poor, young, beautiful girls, and they were almost always employed in the maquiladoras, women who stood for long hours, assembling bits of plastic, or steel, in non-air-conditioned concrete rooms, and they stood there, toiling for meager wages hoping that today wasn't going to be the day that they were approached by a male manager who would stand too close, brush his hand accidentally across a breast, and then give a verbal warning to work faster, or be fired if his advance was received with a sneer. This was how they lived their days. Their nights, standing outside waiting for buses or rides alone in the Juárez night were the most excruciating of moments, and if they had to walk home, they prayed a Virgen Maria over and over and over in their head, asking the good mother that their face would not be the next to appear beside a headline.

He reached the last newspaper and yet again there was that lovely face framed by long hair on the cover. A droplet of dried blood rested on the corner of her red mouth. Her long lashes rested on her swollen, bruised cheeks. She had been painfully put to sleep.

His advisors stood by, patiently waiting for his final confirming nod. It was only after he, the owner of no less than a third of the factories in town, and half of the illegal routes into El Norte, signed off on all the major newspapers in the city that the papers went into full production and deliveries were made. He took a long drag from a cigar and then a sip from a gold-rimmed whisky glass, the word *Invisibility* inscribed across the surface.

"And now gentleman, coming to the stage for one final night, let's hear it for Princesa."

Standing backstage, she looked at herself one last time in that full length mirror. Today, Princesa opted for a long, black halter gown, with a slit that ran from each hip down to her ankles, emphasizing her toned legs and her six-inch, clear, strappy rhinestone heels. *Just one more night,* she told herself, and she would have made enough money to escape Juárez alone. *One more night,* she mouthed to herself and then she stepped onto the stage. The most illuminated spot in the darkened club was the bar situated center and across from the main stage. Pausing for a moment, she could feel the shadowed faces of men watching her, their growing impatience sickening. She focused, looking ahead to the mirrored bar, but was startled for a moment when she met eyes with a single soldier sitting there, staring.

She dropped her eyes to the shiny, black stage floor, ignoring everyone around her. This was the only tolerable part of her job. Up here, on this dark stage, and in this black place lighted only by the soft silver, golds, and sparkling diamond stage lights, she was away from the private room and the searching hands of yet another stranger who would dig his face into her breasts, often burning her skin with his rough stubble, stamping her senses with the sour scent of beer shocking her mind back into the reality that she was here, and needed to get out.

After tonight, this would all be over. She slowly danced her way to the pole center stage. Princesa made the mistake of looking back towards the bar, the soldier's eyes hauntingly transfixed. *The Mexican military were the worst,* she thought to herself. They were paid poorly and expected it her patriotic duty to grind even harder, but what duty? The soldiers here were as corrupt as the criminals.

She closed her eyes, pressed her cheek against the cold surface of the metal poll, raised her hand above her head and let her body melt down to the ground.

"Again, gentleman if you want a private dance with Princesa, in our VIP room number twelve, tonight is your last night before she leaves us. And don't worry, my friends, because if you can't get to our lovely Princesa, we've got eleven more beautiful ladies waiting for you every night here at Invisibility."

She stood up again, closed her eyes, and raised her hands over her head, letting them then slowly glide down her long black hair until she reached the zipper at her side, dropping her gown. There were the typical howls, moans, shouts, and claps. The soldier raised his glass, took a drink and then turned toward the bar.

"So where's she going?" the soldier asked the bartender.

"She won't say. The girl's worked here every night for the past few months and can I tell you this? None of us know her real name. None of us know what she does during the day."

"Un vaso de vino, mami!?" A man at the end of the bar called, slamming his fist down on the surface.

"A glass of wine? It'll put you to sleep," the bartender said as she poured a shot of Patrón and handed it to the man. "From me, it'll keep you awake."

The music pulsed in the background. Cigarette and cigar smoke mixed and mingled in a cloud. The bartender nodded once toward the stage, then set her elbows on the bar. Her voice was now a whisper. "There is a rumor. It's just a rumor that lives only within these walls that she's the eldest daughter of El Rey."

The soldier's mind rushed with ideas of possibility, which the bartender quickly saw. "But hell, no one will want to confess that to him. Who's going to approach El Rey and say, 'mira, your eldest daughter is a dancer by night.'"

"Why'd she be dancing here if she was the daughter of El Rey?"

"Maybe she just wants out of Juárez. What young girl doesn't with a serial killer, hell, killers, running around these damned streets?"

He spun his chair around, facing the stage, and he watched her dance. She was at the edge of the stage now, naked and propped on her knees. Her fingers glided down her neck, her breasts, her stomach, and her thighs.

As soon as the bartender stepped away to pour another shot of Patrón to the gentleman earlier in need of wine, the soldier took out his cell phone. He rested his hand on his left knee, the whisky glass still in hand. At that moment Princesa closed her eyes. Quickly, with his free hand, he focused the phone's camera to the stage and turned off its flash. There was just enough light to capture clearly the club's name inscribed across the gold rim glass and Princesa on the stage in the background.

It had been years since he had gotten a promotion and had been looking for something, anything, that would get him a raise, but nothing was working. El Rey's people had come calling once, but he had denied their initial offer. Now, he wondered, what they would offer him for providing this compelling piece of information. What would it be worth to them? He snapped the picture, typed the text, attached the photo, and hit send.

El Diario de Juárez
By Jesús Malverde
September 24, 2010
Two Dead Outside Club

The bodies of a man and a woman were found outside of the Invisibility Gentleman's Club at the corner of Magdalena and Cristo Rey at 3:33 p.m. Witnesses at the club last night believe that the woman was a dancer, and that the man was a soldier, who spent the evening at the bar drinking. Unconfirmed reports state that the woman had been beaten and tortured—with her limbs having been cut off. The man's remains were located nearby. Both were decapitated. Police say they have no leads but are investigating.

"Sir," an advisor finally broke the silence. "The factories will soon be opening, and people will be wondering where their newspapers are. Is it okay to give the publishers the approval to print, even with the actions you ordered to be taken against your daughter last night?"

El Rey took another long drag of his cigar, taking one final look at the image of his daughter's face in the newspaper, and nodded yes.

35

LA ESTRELLA

THE STAR

"They have to be closed by now. Look at the time," Sandra said as she tapped the clock on the dashboard of their rented SUV.

"No, I think we're good," Lucy said as another car passed them at the entrance.

Sandra folded her arms across her chest. "See, a second car. I told you. I think they're closed already."

"It'll be fine either way, I'm sure. I just need to get a few more pictures for our honeymoon album," Lucy countered.

She drove into a large clearing that opened to an industrial park of abandoned buildings that dotted the landscape. Steering the SUV slowly onto the empty gravel parking lot, she parked the car facing the complex. Most of the buildings were worn and dilapidated, with faded paint and shattered windows.

"I was told at that rest stop that the museum would be opened another thirty minutes," she said as she reached for the camera in the back seat.

A sign with bold, black lettering hung over a single-level yellow building that looked more like a motel than a museum. "That's it," she said proudly. "The Museo Tecnologico Minero. Let me see if there's anyone there." She took the camera, hung it around her neck, opened the car door, and ran off.

Sandra opened the passenger door and looked out toward the hills. The air was still up here in the heavily forested mountains of Michoacán. The grounds were damp as rains had just passed these parts, but instead of the earthy smell of lush green trees and earth, a stinging metallic scent hung in the air. The smell was unnerving.

Lucy's two knocks against the door to the museum echoed through the trees. She paused, but there was no answer. Sandra could see that the lights inside were out, but that didn't stop Lucy from knocking a second time and peeking through the windows.

A breeze through the mountain carried with it an irony, biting scent. Sandra became nauseous, sick, and being alone up here felt wrong, almost as if they were trespassing on these damned grounds of rusting metal and restless ghosts.

"Lucy, really, it's getting dark, and we still have another two hours to Mexico City," she shouted. Her eyes were fixed on the setting orange sun as it cast its last few moments of light over the hills.

A tingling sensation began in her fingertips, intensifying through to her wrists, forearms and then disappearing into her shoulders. Her heartbeat quickened, and her breathing became forced and haggard, as if she had just finished a sprint. *I'm just tired. It's from being in the car so long*, she reassured herself. Stepping out of the car, she stretched out her legs and they responded with painful cramping.

"It's an abandoned mine. I'm sure it'll be here for another few years. Can't we just come back another time?"

"It's not just any mine, Mina Dos Estrellas is historic," Lucy said as she stepped away from the museum's door and snapped a picture of the sign. "Did you know they once had the highest silver production of any mine in the world?" She turned to take a picture of Sandra, but she waved her away.

"You okay?"

"Yes. I'm just exhausted. Can we go?" She slid back onto the passenger seat and rubbed her wrists. The tingling returned.

"Come on. Just five minutes," he pleaded. "There's no one here and look," she pointed to an opened metal gate, "they've left a door open. It's like they want people to walk through here after hours."

"I highly doubt that."

"Come on," she said as she pulled on Sandra's hand.

WALKING DOWN A NARROW passage among the empty administration buildings, the clicking from Lucy's camera was the only sound besides their footsteps. The pain in her limbs had faded, but now her vision had become blurred. Sandra rubbed her eyes, unsure if the haziness was due to her exhaustion or the growing loss of daylight.

"Why did the plant close?" she asked, rubbing her eyes forcefully until her normal sight returned. Nearby she could make out the side of the mountain and the entrance to the main tunnel.

"People around here have a lot of strange beliefs about this land." She brought the lens up to a window and took several hurried shots. Pulling the camera away, she brought the image up on the viewfinder and explained how the ancient machinery they were looking at was a collection of processing mills, refining stations, and purification plants.

"What kind of beliefs?" Her throat tightened and she coughed a few times. She waved her off when she came closer. "I'm fine. It's just a scratch in my throat."

"Just that the land was disturbed by the mining of gold and silver, and that the Nahuals didn't like it."

"Nahuals?" She laughed. "Werewolves? They closed this place because people believed werewolves lived out here? Those silly Aztec legends they teach us in school!"

"Nahuals aren't werewolves. The Aztecs believed Nahuals were people, sorcerers with the power to transform into predatory night animals; wolves, pumas..." she paused and shrugged. "So yeah, werewolves would fall in there I guess." She held up the camera and took a picture.

They continued walking.

"The people here believed that a powerful Nahual lived, and possibly still lives there, in that mountain. So, when the mine came in, they think he was angered because the land was being destroyed. Almost as soon as the mine opened, accidents started happening. First some miners lost limbs in freak accidents in machinery. Then, as they were drilling tunnels through the mountain, some men, when they would break through the rock, would slip and plummet to their death inside a cavern. Those men were never recovered. Then there was a wave of suicides. Finally, a massive storm came in, flooded the tunnels, and killed hundreds of miners, and that's what finally shut this place down."

The left side of Sandra's head, right above her temple, began to throb and then a dull ache grew. Her hand reached for the spot, and Lucy went to her. Again, she waved her off. "It's just a migraine starting, I think." She sniffed around her a few times and then shouted, "Ugh, it's just that…that smell…it's everywhere."

"Okay, just a few more minutes."

"Shouldn't we go before someone comes up here and kicks us out?" she said.

"No one comes up here at night. The villagers think that the land here is charged," she said as she looked at another image.

"Charged? What do you mean, people think the land is charged?"

"They think some people get sick when they sense a Nahaul's presence. They also think some people, depending on their birth date, can shift up here…because they are weaker Nahauls that need the power of this land to shift. Either way, people just fear coming up here because they think they'll either get sick from sensing a Nahual or that they'll turn into one."

The sun was no longer visible. It had descended beyond the trees, beyond the great mountains. Her headache intensified. The all-consuming throbbing, pounding, pulsating pain took over and then darkness fell over her.

COLD DROPLETS OF WATER fell gently from above onto her forehead. She opened her eyes and saw the morning sun breaking through the trees. Droplets of water continued to fall on her face, dripping from the leaves overhead. Her body was stiff and numb. Shivering she looked down to her feet and found herself naked, lying at the mouth of the immense tunnel where just a few feet away into the abandoned mine was an eerie blackness.

As feeling returned to her limbs, they grew hotter, tingling with the sensation of the pebbles and rocks she lay atop of. Lifting a hand to her head, a smear of red caught her eye. She pulled it away quickly and sat up. Her bones cracked painfully. Looking herself over, her arms and legs were covered in rocks, dirt, and blood. Her lips trembled, and as she opened her mouth to scream, an irony taste registered on her lips. It was blood. She leaned over and spat on the floor and screamed. On the ground next to her were her wife's battered camera and her bloodied shredded clothes.

A cold, maniacal laugh roared from within the tunnel, and she looked to see two red eyes looking back at her, then as suddenly as they appeared, they were gone.

36

EL CAZO

THE SAUCEPAN

L orena Glecéau rinsed her hands in the kitchen sink, and as she dried them with fresh paper towels, she looked out over the Andean mountains that surrounded her vacation home. She would miss the cool, damp air this early in the morning, but it was time to leave Aguas Calientes and get back to her medical practice. She was the most prominent and most in-demand plastic surgeon in all of Miami. She was beautiful, a beauty that was painfully unnatural because no one could settle on just a single glance of Lorena's long hair, smooth skin, and bright sparkling eyes for just a moment. She was enchanting, and her clients wanted to be like her.

Peru had been good to her. The benefits of her time here had clearly been visible. She moved better, felt better, and looked exquisite in the designer suit she had put on for her first-class flight back home.

The people here were, of course, the secret ingredient to her beauty regiment. Peru was indeed a magical place, especially up high within the mountains. The Inca called the mountains their Apu— their gods. Although, the indigenous people up here were vehemently superstitious. They were wary of outsiders from America, having claimed the white man couldn't be trusted because he could be a pishtaco, a murderer known for killing Andean peasants to sell the fat from corpses for profit. Yet, even though Lorena was an American, the people here trusted her, and went out of their way to treat her as one of their own, an adopted child of Peru.

Lorena's mother was Romanian, her father was Peruvian and Italian, but she lived continuously in Peru up until the age of thirteen. Regardless of her parent's mixed backgrounds, Lorena always considered herself a Latina. Yes, she had been frightened by her mother's gruesome retellings of Romanian legends and tales such as that of Countess Elizabeth Báthory de Ecsed, the blood countess who adopted the grisliest of beauty treatments, bathing herself in the virgin blood of peasant girls to maintain her youth.

Lorena was also enthralled by her father's detailed knowledge of renaissance art, of the beauty and the purity within Botticelli's *Venus* and the strength and form of Michelangelo's *David*. Her varying background gave her insight into two worlds, one of nightmare and one of fairy tale. So, she fittingly went into the business of crafting and creating beauty—a business philosophy she also had to live.

Lorena felt and saw the spiritual purity up here each day, in the soft, smooth faces of the local indigenous peoples. Even after her family had left Peru permanently, she and her mother would still return each year to Aguas Calientes. Lorena's mother insisted on time in the mountain air. *It purified the skin*, she would say, keeping it bright, young, and healthy. Before Lorena's mother died, she had shared with her daughter the secret to her lineless, firm, youthful looking skin. Standing here, at age sixty, Lorena had the skin of a twenty-five-year-old, thanks to her mother's Romanian secret.

"Señora Glecéau." There was a soft rap on the door below, followed by that sweet, youthful, nervous giggle of schoolgirls. Lorena opened a drawer filled with sharpened knives and pulled one out. With the knife still in hand she reached for a large, white porcelain bowl and a ladle, which she set in the bowl. She set the bowl on the center of the wooden kitchen table.

There was the stamping of feet moving quickly up the stairs. Lorena touched the tips of her fingers to her forehead, cheeks, and then neckline. She felt excited, feverish. It felt like this each time.

"Rebecca, I'm here," Lorena said as her lip curled into a smile.

The giggling and stamping feet stopped.

"Señora," a young girl stood in the doorway. Her hair was cut in a sharp, short bob. She wore the uniform of a private school student—a navy blue jumper, white polo, and black Mary Janes with white socks. Rebecca couldn't have been more than fourteen-years-old. "I'm sorry we are so late. The train…" She motioned to the stairway.

"That's fine, Rebecca." Lorena leaned against the kitchen table, the knife still in her hand, the blade pointing downward. "Can you make sure all of my clothes are packed and, please, be careful with my satin blouses."

"Yes, Señora," Rebecca lowered her eyes and dragged the school bag behind her.

"Wait, please, properly introduce me to your…friend."

Rebecca stepped back into the stairway and yanked on the arm of another person, pulling and tugging until another girl stepped into the kitchen.

All Lorena could see was the girl's smooth skin. It was flawless.

"Are you hungry?" Lorena asked the girl.

The girl stood in the doorway, trembling.

"It's OK, lovely. Please sit." Lorena motioned over to a chair in front of her. On the kitchen table there was a spread of fresh sweet breads, which the girl took hold of and began eating.

"I'm glad you like those. I baked those especially for you," Lorena said, moving over to the door and locking it.

Rebecca was standing in the doorway of Lorena's bedroom, watching, and waiting for praise. "Thank you, Rebecca, this will do just fine until I return. Now, go and make sure I'm all packed."

Lorena placed her hands on the new girls' shoulders.

"Do you know who I am?"

The girl dropped the sweet bread on the table.

"Pishtaco," the little girl said, tears began to fill her eyes.

"No, don't cry." Lorena took the girl's chin in her hand and moved her face up to meet her own. She pulled a handkerchief from her breast pocket and dabbed the girl's cheeks.

"I'm so much more than that. I'm not interested in just selling your fat. I want your blood." Lorena kissed the girl's forehead and flung her hand behind the girl's head, violently pulling on her hair to arch her neck upward. Lorena slit across the girl's throat, and a river of blood sprayed forward. Lorena allowed the dark, warm liquid to stream into the porcelain bowl.

"Rebecca, please help me with my bath."

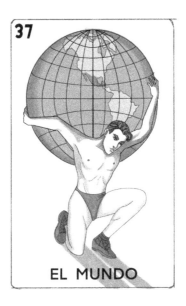

37

EL MUNDO

THE WORLD

've never had so many people in my botanica at once. And, I believe most of you have never been in a botanica before either. In my store I sell herbs for use in rituals and spells, folk medicine, amulets, statues, oils, incense, and products with magical properties. Oh, and yes, I sell spell candles.

I read palms for $20 and tarot cards for $40.
Also, I can communicate with the dead. That's more complicated, but it can be done, for the right price.

But all that doesn't matter because you seem more interested in the candles. Just a warning, if you take a candle home with you, and some of you will take a candle home with you, let it burn through and do not extinguish its flame.

What happens if you turn it off before the wax has been melted away? Well, your spell will fail and if someone is casting a counter spell on you, then theirs will succeed. So just be certain that this is what you want to do.

Now, to the candles—
Each candle has been dressed with a special blend of herbs and oils. So, each color represents a specific spell.

The white candle is for enlightenment, cleansing, and clairvoyance. It can bring you great spiritual strength and peace. I would recommend white if you are entering a phase in your life where you need an extra blessing, such as a new marriage. Or white is also suitable if you need to clear your conscience from something wicked you have done.

The blue candle is used to bring harmony, wisdom, and joy. But blue is also used in healing. Is your health failing? The blue candle can help.

The green candle is used for luck and money spells. If you are a poor gambler you will quickly find yourself winning. Are you on the verge of losing your job? This will ensure that you keep it, and you will probably also get a promotion. Green will grant you the abundance you seek.

Red...well are you in need of love, lust, passion, and power? Then take the red candle home with you and light it. It will make you the desire of each and every person you wish.

Black...we all have people in our lives that have wronged us. But do you have someone who you absolutely despise? Has someone scarred you to a point where you are blinded with rage at the mere thought of them? Do you want revenge? Or, can I ask you this? Have you found the rotted corpses of chickens at your doorstep? Then maybe someone has cursed you, and if so, it's time for the black candle. The black candle will banish all negative energies from your life. And if the spell is strong enough, this person who caused you so much distress may also be banished from the world of the living.

So, think it over. Think about what you want, what you need. Think about what will make your world that much more perfect because we can probably get you there with just a little bit of magic.

38

LA PERSONA INDIGINOSA

THE NATIVE AMERICAN

I was born on the prairies where the wind blew free and there was nothing to break the light of the sun. I was born where there were no enclosures. – Geronimo

A mother went walking through the forest with her little girl, little boy, and her newborn baby cradled in her arms.

As they walked deeper and deeper into the forest, they heard a rumble and a grumble. The little boy and little girl clutched on to their mother's dress. She looked warmly down at them and told them not to fear, that the forest makes many noises.

Just then, a large brown bear emerged from the dark. His claws were sharp, and his teeth dripped with drool for he was very hungry. He told the family that they would be eaten. The mother stepped forward and said that she was old and that her children would be better served as desert and so she should be devoured first. As the bear approached her, she threw the young baby into her daughter's arms and told her children to run.

They did.

As they ran, they heard their mother's last cries.

The three children were now lost. As they came upon a mountain, an old man emerged as if from the air. He had a long, gray pointed beard and long gray robes.

"Come," he said to the children.

The children shook with fright but the old man gave them a reassuring smile and they saw kindness in his eyes and so they followed. They ducked under a large rock and came to a wide, ancient door in the mountain. It opened for the old man without him even laying his hand upon it. A torch on the rock wall illuminated a short hallway that led to another ancient door, and then another, and another, and finally another. As this fourth door opened, a brilliant emerald green sky shone down over a marvelous blue land.

This was the old man's country, this country with the glorious green sky and brilliant blue land.

This is such a strange place, the children thought, but they saw that all of the many people in this land were happy people and all gray people like the old man.

"Come here!" Many of the gray people said to the children. There were hugs and smiles and handshakes.

"Come on. Follow me," said the Gray One again to the children, and the crowd of gray people parted, and the children followed the Gray One to a large open pasture where long yellow tables were set with all of the finest foods of this land under a great golden canopy.

For four days and four nights, the children ate the most delicious of foods. There were orange strawberries and purple oranges and violet peaches. Everything was very good and very special. The gray ones danced and sang and told the children many great stories of the blue sky and the green lands and the vast oceans and the wild animals of what was once their land.

After the four days, the ceremony ended. The Gray One came to the children and said, "Come on. We will go over there, where those little mountains lie across that silver lake."

As they rowed through the silver lake, they spotted colossal flying fish and teeny, tiny schools of swimming lions. Once inside the little mountains, the children saw flour and sugar and meat and coffee, much of the food from their own world.

They walked until they approached a large room. Inside this large room, they saw the large brown bear. He was tied up with chains.

"This is the bear that caused you great harm. Because of this great harm he will be tied up here for the rest of his life."

The children were more sad than scared as they remembered their mother and her beauty and courage.

The Gray One and the children rowed back across the silver lake. Now the sky was crimson, and the land was yellow. At the ceremony grounds, all of the gray ones had gathered.

The Gray One asked the children, "What would you like to do? You may go back home, or you may remain here."

The brother and sister looked at each other and the sister hugged the little baby softly.

"We would like to go back to our land and our relatives," the little boy said.

With tears in his eyes, the Gray One smiled. "I will show you the way back to your country."

They traveled back through the great ancient doors and through the dark forest together. The children came upon the spot where their mother was killed, and where her blood was spilled, a tree with rubies as leaves had grown.

The Gray One knelt and told the children, "Many things have changed in your country. There has been much sadness and much loss for your people. Much more sadness and much more loss will come, but you are strong people, and this is your country. When you are sad and miss your mother, you can come back here to this tree and speak to her for she will listen, but know that she is in every tree and in every mountain and in every lake, as am I. We are the Old Ones and we lived in this land too many, many moons ago. We hunted the buffalo, and we lived outside with the sun and the rain and the snow because this was our land. We now live in a new country because we are now Gray. When you are ready you will come visit us again, but remember, this is your country always."

39

EL NOPAL

THE CACTUS

L ines dug in the earth. The whale. The spaceman. The monkey. The dog. The condor. The hummingbird. The parrot. The lizard. The huarango tree. The trapezium. These are the principal figures seen from the sky. Lines dug deep into the earth by hand.

On foot, they are merely lines where dirt was pushed aside. The red, iron oxide pebbles brushed away, by hands, we can only assume, as no note was left, no instructions written to indicate the forms drawn across the landscape. And what is it that extends football field distances? The light-colored earth beneath the dry, cracked desert floor, and it is gleaming with meaning unknown. Several hundred concentric circles and patterns are carved on the Nazca plateau of the city of Ica, and these marks were put here hundreds of years before the conquistadors arrived.

The Nazca people, of the dry southern coast of Peru left behind a desert picture book of mystery, of geoglyphs. And who was the viewer of these images that could only be seen from high above? Were they messages for their gods? For celestial beings hanging in the sky?

The Nazca honored nature and the environment and worshipped their gods, from the killer whale, to the enigmatic spotted cat, the serpent, and even the mythical anthropomorphic. The gods brought agricultural wealth, advancements for irrigation, talent and skill for the production of pottery and textiles, but sometimes, as gods do, a holy human hand was needed for communication.

The shamans would speak to the land; heal its wounds by taking the extractions of the San Pedro cactus. Vision induced, they would praise their gods asking them for strength, for food, for water, and the waters did come. El Niño came, rushing and flooding, destroying and killing. The waters washed across the land, killing people, but leaving behind their imprints.

Centuries swept across the desert floor until flight exposed the drawings from above of great animals and figures. Excavations began finding them, many of them. Nazca bundled up in cloth. Limbs separated. Heads were missing, and in their place was a lone jar with the depiction of a head on it. Eventually some heads were found, with holes carved through foreheads. Assumptions were made. Were ropes strewn through these holes to hang the heads as decorative trophies? Prizes of war? Or, prices of sacrifice?

The Nazca are all gone, but their lines remain and are a reminder of a time when they were used for something that we still do not understand. Planetary alignments, stars, and galaxies look down on them.

Today, in the early morning hours, visitors pay to board light Cessna aircrafts. They fly over the shapes and figures, fully viewing what could only then and now be seen from high above—lines and shapes meant observed from beyond.

Whispers remain of continued sacrifices, as every few years tourist planes tumble out of the sky, bodies falling into a heap of flesh, blood, and bones.

Perhaps the ground still hears the echoes of a shaman song asking for rain and a bountiful harvest. Perhaps the gods above whisper still demanding their offerings.

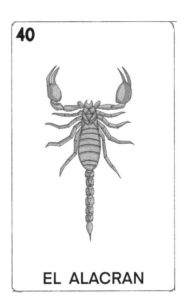

40

EL ALACRAN

THE SCORPION

"Matthew, take that mask off. It's too hot," the young mother said, looking over her shoulder. The train car charged out of the subway station.

Next stop, California, the mechanical voice announced.

Matthew ignored his mother. Instead, he continued walking his toy action figures along her seatback.

The mother pulled the baby's stroller in further from the aisle. She bounced the wide-eyed baby on her lap as she looked through her phone.

"Mom." Matthew leaned forward, the silver mask of El Santo still fitted securely over his face.

"Ay Matthew, I don't know why your father buys you those things," she said as she bounced the baby on her knee.

"I'm El Santo!" the boy exclaimed as he crashed both of the masked wrestling action figures together. One was wearing a blue mask and the other a silver mask like him. "I'm hungry," he said.

"We'll be at your dad's house soon. You'll get something there."

The boy sat back in his seat. The train cars opened, and more people boarded. A man in a suit smiled when he saw Matthew and pointed at his head. "Nice mask." Matthew ignored the man and kept playing.

Next stop, Western Avenue.

No one sat next to the little boy. He was now on his knees looking out of the window. "Mom, there's park over there. Let's go!"

"No, Matthew," she said.

Western Avenue came and more people boarded. In the aisle across from Matthew, a young woman and a little girl sat. The little girl whispered loudly to her mom that she liked the mask. Again, Matthew ignored them. Looking out of the window, Matthew tapped on the glass and alerted his mother, "Mom, look at that dog! He's so big. Can I have a dog? We can be partners and he can eat the bad guys when I'm done beating them up!"

"Matthew, por favor, sit down already." The mom leaned back and made as if to take the boy's toys away.

"No!"

"Then sit down or I'm going to tell your father."

The baby began to cry, and Matthew walked around to where his mother sat. He tickled his little sister's feet and she responded with coos and smiles. Just then, the mother's cell phone rang.

"I'm on my way," she said to the caller and she kept talking about things that mothers talk about; being tired, having a mountain of chores at home, but still needing to tend to her children.

"Mom!" Matthew squealed. "There's a spider outside the window!"

"Spiders are good luck. Just ignore it," she said, breaking mid-sentence of her conversation and then picking back up with ease.

The train lurched over the elevated tracks and the mother kept bouncing the baby. Matthew now had set his toys on the empty seat beside him and concentrated on all of the things outside of the window; cars whizzing by, bicyclists cutting through sidewalks and streets, and people standing at bus stops or walking from store to store on this sunny afternoon.

Then Matthew screamed, "Mom!"

His mother turned around and gave him that "Stop disturbing me and be quiet or I will tell your father" look and returned to her call.

Matthew pressed his face to the glass and said softly, "Mom, there's a demon outside."

Division, this is Division.

The train's doors opened and several more people boarded, including a young woman in a white spring dress, flip-flops, and sunglasses. She stopped in front of the aisle seat that was empty beside Matthew.

"Can I sit here?"

Matthew scooped the two wrestlers out of the seat. The woman said thank you and told Matthew how she liked his mask. "I've seen one like that before, a long time ago."

"Really?" Matthew ran his fingers down the cheeks of the silvery fabric. "My dad bought me this one."

Matthew's mother turned around, looked, smiled, and continued with her phone call and bouncing the little girl on her knee.

"My dad bought me one when I was maybe your age," the young woman said. She was pretty, with wavy light brown hair that fell past her shoulders.

Matthew glanced back out of the window and the woman asked, "What are you looking at?"

"Demons," the little boy responded.

"Matthew…" his mom said. Her voice sharp.

The young woman laughed. "It's alright."

The mother returned to her cell phone.

"How old are you?" the young woman asked.

"Me?" he said, while still looking out of the window. "I'm forty-five and sixty-three-eight."

The boy's mother slid the phone away from her ear. "He's five."

"Five," the woman exclaimed. "Well, you're very young to be a wrestler. What's your wrestling name?"

"El Santo!" the little boy announced his name theatrically as any ringleader might.

"That's a good name," the girl said. "My mask was red and so my name was La alacrán Roja, the Red Scorpion. Is that your mom?" the girl asked.

Matthew nodded. "Yes, and my little sister. I'm going to see my dad now!"

"I had a mom once," the young woman said. "I loved her very, very, very much, but sometimes she would take very long to take me to go see my dad and so do you know what I did to her?"

The boy shrugged and shook his head.

"One night, I put my red mask on after she fell asleep in her room. I went into the bathroom where she kept her needles and her medicine. So, I filled up one of the needles with her medicine and went into her bedroom. There, I stabbed the needle in neck, and she kicked and kicked."

Matthew gasped. "You stabbed her in the neck?"

"Yes, and then I then slammed my elbow into her back, the very tip, as hard as I could right there in the center of her back and I heard a loud crack."

The boy's mother, still on the telephone turned around.

"I then flipped her over, slit her neck, and I watched her bleed all over the sheets. I cut off each of her fingers and threw them against the wall. Then I opened her chest and ripped out her heart and I took a bite."

"You ate her heart? All of it?"

The woman nodded. "I sure did."

The mother dropped her phone and shouted, "Are you crazy? Get away from my son right now!"

The young woman smiled and stood up. "I didn't scare you, did I Matthew?"

"I didn't tell you my name," Matthew said. "You really ate her heart?"

"Yes, and all of her too."

"Get the hell out of here before I press the panic button," the mother said.

Just then the train descended underground.

Chicago Avenue. This is Chicago Avenue.

The woman in the white dress departed and as the doors closed behind her, Matthew told his mother, "Mom, she was the demon."

"No, Matt, she was just some crazy lady."

Matthew looked down and, on the empty seat beside him, was a red Lucha Libre mask.

41

LA ROSA

THE ROSE

Our little princess was birthed of beauty and misfortune
baptized in a brook flowing with thieves' blood
darling reveled through her father's decayed kingdom
mounds of human skulls, femurs, spines, and rib cages
all delicate and dancing, the undulations, motions
black balloons that catch on blackened fingerbones
lined her garden path, in winter sparkling snowy banks
deep spotted in crimson, pained, screams echo across
ravines, an endless void, stretched across treetops strewn
and flapping in the wind, human skins as prayer flags
dried husks of billions, their movements marked, their
great applause, the adulation of death for dying
never moving, forever stagnant and festering, mildew

a plea, a beg for help, but she danced as they moaned
biting through tough hearts, ripe stars, rotted apple cores
slicing tense necks of lovers who blinked too loudly
fewer people draw near, for each word uttered is met
with a battle blade, and he, her father, Mictlantechutil
forgives, forgets, and he feels a pinch of regret, for his
rose is life from death of death, and he assures her that
pain is their greatest existence, their oxygen is suffering
she nods, and one day as he sleeps, she creeps into his room
biting down on his ancient neck of rotting skin, piercing
through black-tubed arteries full of sand and squirming terminates
she dined on his stewed tongue for dinner, and slurped his
boiled eyes for dessert, for she is Mictecacihuatl, goddess of the
underworld, consuming their shadows in her castle of despair
anguish is her morning call, and when the sun breaks through
red clouds, she adds a rose petal to her elixir, and toasts to
great suffering, unending, a full view to humanity's damnation
they will all meet her here soon

LA CALAVERA

THE SKULL

Madeline followed her parents' rules. All of their rules. She attended ballet classes every morning before school, practiced piano two hours a day after school, right after her homework, and read when she had leisure time—if there ever was leisure time. Madeline's leisurely reading list was one of classical literature, selected by her mother, of course. She did things the way her mother expected, and deviated very little from those expectations, even though it brought her misery.

She was also respectful to her aunts and uncles who visited frequently with her cousins, who would boast about whatever it was going on in their lives, which Madeline didn't really care about. All the while, Madeline fantasized about murdering each and every one of them.

There was one aunt Madeline wished would visit more. The only aunt on her father's side was a peculiar woman, and the friction between Aunt Esther and Madeline's mother was clearly evident. Madeline's mother was a refined, but quiet women, who liked things done her way and that certain way did not care for the dark and grim, the things that Madeline enjoyed.

It was Aunt Esther who bought Madeline the books her mother would never purchase for her. At first there was *The Castle of Otranto*, then *Dracula* and *Frankenstein*. One evening it was *Wuthering Heights*, the next *The Complete Works of Edgar Allan Poe*. That night, Madeline strolled through Prince Prospero's abbey, but left his masquerade ball with a red-robed gentleman who left her at the steps of the house of the curious Roderick Usher. That night, Madeline fell in love with Edgar Allan Poe.

Madeline met a man, Thomas, and completed her studies with exceptional record, and moved through life doing the things that her mother encouraged and expected. One night at the dinner table and seated with her family Madeline's mind split. Across from her, her mother's head sunk to her chest, black blood poured from her mouth into her yellow squash soup. Madeline's father, seated beside her mother, picked up a butter knife and drove it straight into his esophagus. Thomas picked up two salad forks and rammed them simultaneously into each of his eyes.

Madeline broke into laughter.

"Madeline," her mother snapped. "Are you alright?"

Of course, she wasn't alright. Not with having spent her entire life aiming to please her mother.

TIME WENT BY AS it does, too much time. Routine set in, but at night the monsters crawled. In her welcomed nightmares, creatures would lurch across the screen of her mind as she dreamed, and this brought her joy. As years past the monsters in her dreams led her to a green gate, but never beyond. And so, that dream remained fixed, a green gate and nothing beyond, until one day...

IT WAS A DRIZZLY cool day, and the steel gray sky overhead swallowed the sun. Madeline opened her umbrella and stood at the bottom of her front steps for a moment. There was no doubt where she was going—she was going to go find those green bars from her dreams.

Her black rain boots splashed in puddles as she walked away from the home that was never really a home. There was a humming sound that buzzed in her ears as she walked. With each step closer to the busy intersection the noise intensified, growing clearer and clearer until she knew that sound. It was her mother's voice, taunting, nagging, ridiculing.

Madeline rode the bus for the first time alone in a long time. She walked to Lincoln Park Zoo in the rain, and she didn't mind being one of only a handful of people there. She looked at the bats and snakes but was saddened when she didn't get to see the Andean bear, as he was sleeping. Before she left, she strolled over to the Kovler Lion House at the heart of the zoo. A beautiful, black-spotted, golden jaguar eyed her carefully as she approached. On the "About this animal" placard next to the animal's home, it read: "A secretive, nocturnal species, jaguars are difficult to study in the wild." She laughed to herself, approached the plexiglass, ran her fingers across the surface, and whispered, "I know. I know"

The Clark Street bus left her at Harold Washington Library Center. There, she researched historical photographs of the city. *Those green bars are here somewhere*, she said to herself. She would know that entrance as soon as she spotted it; the simple bars with two gray stone posts on either side of a pair of gates that opened inward. These weren't iron bars in front of a school, or a church, or even a grand house—that much she could tell. After one final keyword search, "cemetery," she had her answer.

Madeline got back on the bus. The rain began to fall harder, streaming across the windows. Just then, her phone rang. She lowered her window and tossed her phone outside.

They were almost there.

Once they pulled up to Byron Street, Madeline pushed through the doors and walked down to Irving Park Road.

He was waiting for her at the gate.

Standing directly in the middle of the two posts, he stood there with a black umbrella doing a poor job of shielding his pressed black suit from the rain. Regardless, he stood there.

Madeline asked who the man was and he answered: "Death."

Madeline looked beyond the man, beyond the rain, and saw the tombstones and mausoleums, grand obelisks and statuary. Here she was—at the park of the dead, with her invitation to enter.

A soft mist hovered over the grass. Dark shadows danced and swayed around trees and bushes, and way beyond—way deep beyond into the darkness—she felt she was being watched, not by one set of eyes but by thousands. The cemetery held its breath. The sound of shuffling approached. The man in the suit did not look behind as Madeline peered over his shoulder.

The black parade was approaching, a funeral procession. A mass of people dressed in black, waving flags from places she's never known and will never go.

She looked down and noticed that she still stood on the public city grounds, on the sidewalk. She was still connected to this world. Yet, there, just past those gates, was another world, one with dreadful promises and sweet secrets; perhaps of the living dead, or wolves that searched hungrily for scraps of bones to gnaw on the night of a full moon.

"We've been waiting for you, Madeline," Death said.

He handed her a small black envelope.

Madeline opened it carefully. Inside was a black, die cut silver trimmed invitation. As she looked closer, she realized it was not an invitation, but a funeral card with her name and today's date.

Without saying another word, Madeline entered the cemetery grounds and didn't look back.

LA CAMPANA

THE BELL

There's rustling above.

My eyes open. It is dark. I am hungry. Starving. Ravenous.

Had it always been dark? This dark?

Were my eyes closed before or have they now just opened, lids rolling back and blackness rolling in? There has always been blackness; that I am sure of somehow. Some kind of blackness in all of my time. Much time has gone by.

I think I am awake. It's difficult to really tell as I am enveloped by a darkness that knows no limits and sees no end. I am here and the night is around me, with me, and in me.

The rustling above continues.

My stomach painfully twists and turns. The hunger continues. I am so hungry I could eat a horse. No, I could eat a man.

I am not certain when I had my last meal or even a drink of water. The moon to me is a memory so far back that I can no longer see it, just recall it as being a faint recollection of something beautiful before terror fell.

My mouth is so dry that as I struggle to move my tongue out of my mouth to moisten my lips, the movement causes my blistered lips to crack sending warm liquid rolling down my chin. I can't raise my hands to dab the blood. My body is laid flat against a hard surface. My palms are faced down and I can feel the planks of wood beneath me. The planks of wood just barely brush against my chest. I am confined. I am trapped. I am waiting for the alarm.

The bottoms of my feet rest not against the planks of this wooden coffin, but on a hard, metal surface. I curl my toe and tap against the object and hear a small ping as my nail taps against the cold, hard material. It is there, something precious to be protected.

The rustling overhead becomes louder. It is coming closer.

I look around but still see black. The blackness has penetrated my eyes, polluted my blood, gnawed on my flesh, and embedded itself so deep into my bones that it is now soaking within the softness of my marrow. I fear I am becoming mad. Perhaps I am already mad.

Bells clang outside!

The bells!

Oh, how I've missed the jangling, and the clanging, and the tintinnabulation of those church bells.

I remember now.

I remember it all now.

The bells of Catedral de San Gervasio. Oh, the cathedral and Padre de Vega. That night I can see it now, clearly. He led me up the twisting, curving stone path, a lit torch in hand to see the bells—the very same bells the Spanish had installed just two hundred years before in 1543. The father was coughing violently. His health had been failing and we were all worried that he wouldn't be able to survive the harsh trip by boat to Spain, let alone the days leading up to it.

"Father, you should rest here more days with us."

"I cannot, my son. The Lord calls me, and I must leave in two weeks." He coughed into a white handkerchief. The shadows in the stone stairway danced as the torch in his hand shook.

I was honored that our beloved priest was taking me to see the treasured bells before he departed for his new post. We were all going to miss our Padre de Vega. We all loved him and our cathedral, and so we gave all the money we could for years to help preserve the cherrywood pews and the gilded and saint-filled altar. We the poor gave more than any others because it was for our church.

As we both emerged outside from the stairway, under the moonlit sky Padre de Vega motioned me over to a chest beside one of the bells. The rains were coming in that night. I could smell the electricity in the moist air. Droplets of water began to fall, and when he opened the chest, I stood aback, shocked and confused by the hundreds of thousands of gleaming gold coins within.

"Have you ever seen such a thing?" he asked.

"I have not, father."

"Such wealth should be cared for. You agree, yes?"

I nodded. Not knowing then what I had agreed to.

"And so, I need to ensure that this is very well protected in the days before I leave with it to Spain."

"Father, I am confused, but this is the church's money."

Padre de Vega approached me with a knife in his hand "But it is too late, my son. You have already agreed to protect my treasure." He began to recite Latin and raised the sharp blade.

Then, night fell.

THE BELLS! THEY GROW louder!

Above me, there is now knocking, scratching, and pounding. I hear a peculiar piercing melodic tune and then a voice.

"Hey Eric, yeah, it's Grant. I found it. It took me two years, a shit load of GPS and metal detecting equipment, but hell, it's true. I'm sick of ocean recoveries… Yeah, I'm just going to break through now. I've got a couple of guys here with me. It's dark as hell but we've got enough light and gear to pull this baby through…I know…hell, this treasure has been sitting here for hundreds of years…that stupid priest died right in that church, stabbed to death the night he was supposed to make off with it. Oh well, our gain that the story has stayed around for so long…alright…call you later."

I hear the wooden boards being cracked and ripped open. Pieces of wood puncture my rotted flesh. I push myself out and dig my teeth into the fatty neck of the thief attempting to steal the gold. I have been entombed to protect it until Padre de Vega returns.

44

EL CANTARITO

THE WATER PITCHER

ome will never be found, and how could they be? Carlos Fuentes thought as his horse followed the faint tracks along this familiar route. *Their desiccated corpses will only collapse into the desert sand and become new mounds where snakes will turn to for rest.*

He rode past a familiar mound where an anonymous woman and child were found last week blistered, burnt, and dead from the flaming desert sun. On that mission, he was with other members from the Border Patrol. A few of the men were so devastated by the find that they buried the child's stuffed bear in the sand and said several words of prayer.

The desert is unforgiving and always takes its sacrifice.

As the horse's hooves kicked up a new cloud of dust, something scurried into the grass. The horse jerked and snorted.

"Just a rat," he said.

There was a faint cough nearby and he pulled on the reigns. "Who's there? ¿Adonde estás?"

There was silence.

He scanned the brush, listening, feeling the dry air, and waiting to sense movement. He dismounted, crouched down, and saw a tan work boot caked in sand. There lay the last member of the group he had found earlier that morning.

Hours had passed by.

The sun's warmth intensified, raging an unforgiving wave of heat that blasted this empty land. Considering the condition of the last group of illegal immigrants he found trying to cross into the United States, he doubted this man would be alive much longer.

The afternoon sun hung at its highest point in the sky. Its searing rays were maddening. Water, if not consumed in vast quantities out here, meant the difference between life and death. Carlos knew that, his horse knew that, and he was sure the man lying out and dehydrating on the ground knew that.

He knelt next to the old man. The sleeves of his jacket were covered in sand. His wrinkled, leathery face was a burnt orange. The man's dry, cracked lips were swollen, blistered, and bloodied.

The old man must have been about seventy, Carlos thought. *It's insanity to risk your life for a trip to a country where you have never been.*

Lying there, out in the open, it was clear that the old man didn't even have the strength to settle under a tree not twenty yards for shade. Carlos grabbed the old man gently by the shoulders of his jean jacket and pulled, dragging the dying man under the nearby tree. The tree's leaves and branches were so meager that little shade was offered. The old man groaned. His eyelids pulled back. Cloudy, vacant eyes losing themselves in death looked out.

Carlos patted the old man's torn and faded jeans pockets, but there was nothing. *They never carry anything with them on this journey*, he thought.

Once they set out, they must walk, and walk with as few distractions as possible. So, they never carry wallets, let alone any type of identification cards, or cell phones. All they have in this world are the clothes they wear to cross and whatever small piece of luck is light enough to tuck inside of their shoe, or boot, or in the back pocket of their jeans. Sometimes they wear a rosario around their neck, but common are the prayer cards in their back pockets.

As Carlos dug into the old man's front pocket he felt a worn, thin piece of plastic and pulled out a prayer card of La Virgen de Guadalupe. He put the card back into the man's pocket and patted him on the chest gently.

The old man's left hand jerked up. He pointed at Carlos's nameplate. "I'm Agent Fuentes."

The old man smiled with relief and let his arm drop to his side.

The horse stirred. It was time for water. Carlos looked around the tree, found a warm jug of water, and sneered. Human rights activists had taken to leaving water jugs in various parts throughout the desert. They neither supported nor opposed illegal immigration; they just wanted to minimize needless deaths.

Carlos walked over to his horse, unscrewed the cap of the jug, and let the water fall slowly over the animal's snout until its tongue slid out. It licked at the stream, splashing droplets onto the ground.

The old man had turned his head and watched. Carlos covered the jug, removed a blade from his back pocket, and slashed at the plastic, letting the remaining water pour out. The thirsty ground quickly drank each drop and dried over once again.

Mounting his horse, he turned the animal around, facing the direction from which they came. As the horse's hooves clicked against the dirt, there was a pained groan from the tree.

There must be something desperately sad in those last gasps of breath, straining for moisture, knowing that your family and friends will never know that your grave became this rugged, barren, desert, he thought.

EL VENADO

THE DEER

think about them sometimes, my sisters. Although I suspect they are as busy giving care as I am. That is what we do after all, protect. It's been quite some time since I have visited with my sisters, and I suppose that is a good thing. The less frequently we see each other, the less torment whirls in the air. They are all so beautiful. We all are identical with long gray hair that falls below our shoulders. Our dresses are white with trails of crystals along the bodice. We are the daughters of Skull, his crystal daughters.

I couldn't tell you where each of them lives. That is part of the mystery. We must be kept separate because that is what the world commands. Although, I suspect one can be found in the jungles of the Yucatán, another in the deserts of Egypt, one surely sits on a bench in Rome, another likely walks besides the great shadows in the woods of

Russia, one walks solemnly through the pathways of Jerusalem, one must surely sit in a temple in Thailand, while another roams the far-reaching corners of the world. The others are certainly in locations where even my deep suspicions are unable to touch.

When we meet again, the thirteen of us, then things will change. It will indeed happen one day soon, but not today.

Today I will do as I have been charged to do, sit here and care. I can step away sometimes but must remain close by. My requirement is likely much different than my sisters. Perhaps they guard ancient openings to caves, or secret passages in long abandoned buildings, or perhaps they even guard magnificent architectural objects that are out in the open. Essentially, what we do is all the same—guarding prophecies.

My one requirement is to stay here and remain close to their hearts. There are a few hundred of them. Sometimes I sit quietly with my eyes closed on a warm patch of green golden grass and feel their hearts beating. They are unlike anything I have ever sensed before. They are gentle, yet powerful. I surprised one at the creek today as he bent his heart-shaped nose and dipped his tongue into the water. When he sensed me, he stood straight up on his delicate four legs, stretched his neck high, and perked his ears upward. His coat was a ghostly white, like the others. I approached with my arms out so he knew I would do him no harm. When I got close, I carefully stroked the space between his deep brown eyes and kissed him where his antlers would soon grow. Then he ran along. I giggled to myself because the beauty of the white deer is something that brings me so much joy. I love them as a mother would love her own children. I watch them for hours each day, playing with one another in the woods, carefully emerging out into the open expanses, and peacefully grazing.

The only building nearby is the former Seneca Army Depot that sits on acres of this fenced off land. During World War II, I would float through the facility and see rows and rows packed with munitions. Ammunitions would enter for disposal and as many would leave for use. Cargo planes would land and take off, and I wondered each time they did if one of my sisters knew of these horrors. It's strange to think that the land that stored devices of death was the same land that birthed animals that guaranteed life. Decades later the military left, abandoning their storage. For a time, I could go to the empty warehouse and sit in peace with my thoughts, thinking of my sisters or sobbing over the deaths I, too, have caused.

My only job was to care for my white deer miracles.

"Albinos?" I once heard the hunters say as they raised their rifles, but my darling white deer are not albinos.

From cars along the highway, I could sense small children calling out to their parents that unicorns were frolicking between abandoned bunkers. My joys were not unicorns. My loves are the white deer of Seneca.

Their prophesy told that as long as a pair of white deer were seen together that people would come together, that humans would continue to exist. If these animals faded into the darkness, then theirs would be one of the firsts in the destruction of us, the thirteen protectors who rule over the scaffolds of life.

THE HUNTER COULD NOT see me standing there in front of him as he raised his rifle.

The blast.

Then echoes.

The bloodstained purity that toppled to the ground. The hunter was now an impure thing. Standing there, shaking with his rifle, he fell to his knees and pleaded that I let him live.

I couldn't.

That was not part of the prophecy either.

I drove my hand into his flesh, and I tore his still beating heart from his body. I leaned into him so that he could see clearly. I sunk my teeth into the warm muscle. Blood splashed across his cheek and ran down my chin. Choking back my own tears, I devoured his heart.

Death to those that threaten the prophecy, as I am a protector.

46

EL SOL

THE SUN

He's not that bad. He really isn't. He's just got this little mischievous spirit, and well, we can all blame his mother for that.

We all know how the story goes. He shows up at her doorstep after seven years without any money because he had lost all of his earnings rather carelessly. His mother became enraged and forbade him from ever entering her house again. So, he wandered alone in the woods until he wound up here, in this tiny little town atop the San Luis Mountains. Around here, some people call him the Dueño del Sol, the owner of the sun. He really prefers the nights, by the way. The Germans would consider him some sort of elf, but we would never call him that around here.

Many people around here still fear him, but I don't now and I never did. Even as a young girl, I could hear him whistling out there in the forest, mimicking nocturnal birdsong. I longed to meet him so that I could give him a hug. I suffered for his suffering. He did give up everything, and around here, even a few dollars in your pocket can make you feel like a millionaire—but him, he had nothing, just his knapsack that people would say he filled with coffee beans, sweet potatoes, and bananas he would steal from nearby farms.

I'm sorry if this all sounds so silly. I'm nervous, but it's all true. And yes, we're just not used to reporters around here. Concepción is such a small city, and even then, I don't think large cities in Paraguay have seen many reporters come in from America, let alone one that is writing an article for the *Guinness World Record* book.

Are you sure you wouldn't rather come inside and sit down? I don't mind doing the interview out here, but I guess…I just don't want him seeing a stranger standing at my doorstep. No, this isn't his house. He lives in the forest and at times will sleep in an abandoned house…but he does, in a way, consider this his house because of my condition.

So, the story of how the Pombero and I met—which is why you came this far—to hear about his legend. I had watched how my grandmother would leave him offerings of cigars, rum, and honey right here on this very door step every night so the Pombero would protect our house…really so he would move his mischief elsewhere. Then, after my grandmother died, my mother took over. Then after she died, I started leaving the offerings myself. In all of those years, my grandmother and mother had never encountered him.

It was on the morning after me leaving the first offering when I met him. I opened the door and there he stood, with a freshly plucked daisy in his small, furry right hand. He held it out to me. There were those big brown eyes, filled with love, and that wide, silly, gap-toothed grin. He wore a pair of blue jeans; he must have stolen them from a clothesline from a household with a child. He wore his trademark big, wide, dusty Stetson that flopped down over his ears. His large, hairy feet were bare, and he looked like he hadn't ever taken a shower. He smelled of earth and roots and dead things and live things, but oh, that smile. I reached out for the flower and he gave me a tight hug. He only comes up to my knees by the way. After that, he pulled away, scooped up his offerings and walked off into the woods. After that day, I would see him each morning, and each morning he stood there with a fresh picked daisy for me to pluck from his fingers. He continued to leave our livestock and farm alone. Like before, he would entertain himself with his familiar trickery, driving those who refused to leave him offerings mad.

About the animals...well, he's not too fond of horses because, you know the story. Even if he sees a rider on horseback he'll get wildly upset and chuck a stone at the horse's head. Cows, he hates. Every chance he gets, he'll unlock a gate and let the cows out onto the dirt road—probably in hopes that some ill fate will befall them. Sometimes, if you look up that hill, you'll see Don Luis's cows up there, bewildered and roaming around. When you see that, you'll know that the Pombero is somewhere snickering behind a tree because of his misdeed. Again, he's not evil at all, just a trickster. He does the same with the pigs, lets them out, and with goose eggs, well, if it's not a stone he's throwing at a horse's head, then it's a goose egg he's hurling. Now, with the gold, well, people around here don't really have any gold. We're not sure how he'll react if he sees a lump of gold. Maybe he'll really go mad, and we wouldn't want that. He's been around so long...well, we really don't know how long, but from what Padre Alberto says, the Germans have had stories about similar little men for, well—hundreds of years.

I guess now you want to know about that other part of the legend. It's true you know, absolutely, completely true…about him having the power to impregnate a woman with a single touch of his hand to her belly. Just look at me, I'm due next month.

47

LA CORONA

THE CROWN

King of Spain	Sinaloa Cartel
King of Castile	Los Zetas Cartel
King of León	Juárez Cartel
King of Aragon	La Familia Cartel
King of the Two Sicilies	Tijuana Cartel
King of Jerusalem	Knights Templar
King of Navarre	Beltrán-Leyva Cartel
King of Granada	Los Negros
King of Toledo	Gulf Cartel
King of Seville	Medellín Cartel
King of Valencia	Black Eagles
King of Galicia	Colima Cartel
King of Sardinia	Norte del Valle Cartel

King of Córdoba

King of Corsica

King of Menorca

King of Murcia

King of Jaén

King of the Algarves

King of Algeciras

King of Gibraltar

King of the Canary Islands

Guadalajara Cartel

South Pacific Cartel

Sonora Cartel

Cali Cartel

North Coast Cartel

Oaxaca Cartel

Blandón Organization

Gomez Organization

Paulino Organization

LA CHALUPA

THE CANOE

've always been uncomfortable around plush animals. Unnaturally colored animals stuffed with cotton, staring back at me with blank, black eyes always sent a wave of terror through me. The discomfort was greater around dolls. I know you're going to tell me that you felt the same as a child or even now. It's different with me. I learned it long ago when I was seven years old, standing in the sand, the lake water lapping against my feet, and screams echoing from all corners of the world. All that seemed as real to me there on that beach as the doll that had washed up, bumping against my toes. I threw all of my toys away that night.

My mother had to work a second job. After she finished teaching her kindergarten class, she would work nights at the local department store. She had no choice, really. After my father had drowned, there was no one that could help besides my Grandmother Gladys, who would watch me while my mother was at work.

Occasionally, Mom would come home with a present for me: a Barbie or some silly talking bear or chubby-faced Cabbage Patch Kid. It was likely all part of my therapy, slowly trying to reincorporate childhood devices into my life, but I didn't want them. Each time she would enter the house with a plastic bag, pulling out the newest doll from that particular season, I would cringe. My skin would crawl.

When they were in the box, it wasn't so bad. There was that separation at least, some kind of barrier, and that made it easy when I removed them from the house. Yet, when they were just bare, without any packaging or plastic wrapping, and I had to touch their cold plastic skin, I felt wrong. I know what you're going to say, that it was probably my imagination, but it was not my imagination. Each and every time I had to touch a doll, I felt a sickening flash of evil charge right threw me.

I didn't want to upset my mother any further. So, each time she arrived home with a new gift, I would pretend, as best I could under that state of fear, to be thrilled. After the first few toys went missing, she grew suspicious.

I tried to wait a few days before making the disposals. The Barbie dolls were easiest to play off. I just told my mother I left those few in my locker at school. The Cabbage Patch and stuffed animals, I told her, I had let some friends borrow. The American Girl doll, I told her, was ripped out of my arms by a bully. I know she knew I was lying because I didn't have any friends and bullies were too scared to even come near me. No one wanted to come near me after that day on the beach.

I would wait for her to fall asleep. I would then gather my courage, rush into my darkened room, and face the closet door. With my bedroom door open, the hallway light slicing through the darkness, I would put my hand on the doorknob and pause, listening for breath, listening for whispers, or their demonic little instructions. Inhaling deeply and blocking out all of the noise in my head, I would open the door, reach in and grab the doll by the arm, or grasp the box, and rush out of my room quietly towards the back door. All the time mindful not to look into those plastic eyes. If I looked in their eyes, I knew I would be lost.

Under the motion detector spotlight in the backyard, I would rip open the box and tear the doll's head from its body. I would pop off its arms and then its legs. My mother kept her gardening tools on the back porch, so I would grab the spade and use that as my shovel. I would never bury the pieces for one doll all together. I would bury the head one place, the torso in another place, and finally the limbs all separately in their own graves.

She found them one day as she was making room to plant more tomatoes in the garden. At first she was furious, but quickly her anger shifted to concern that I was no longer coping with my father's death. A series of psychiatrists diagnosed me with having an intense fear of dolls, and later added automatonophobia—the fear of all human figures.

Years of anti-anxiety medications, talk therapy, and cognitive-behavioral treatments helped me push away what I had seen and heard as a child. I'm sure I imagined it all. Like my psychiatrist said, when my father died all that was left was a doll. So, I imagined that the byproduct of death was a small, human figure. It made sense. Wanting to fully understand my adolescent delirium led me to a career in psychology, with a keen interest in the exploration of the unexplained. Shaking my debilitating fears made me believe that I, too, could free someone from their mental restraints. That is, of course, what I believed until I came here.

IT WAS EASY TO locate the crew amidst the dozens of colorfully painted, flower-covered canopied boats on the dock. Most of the people milling about were locals, or the few tourists this time a year trying to find a bargain priced boat tour. The temperatures had reached sweltering in Mexico City, and here, just thirty minutes away at the entrance of the ancient Aztec canals of Lake Xochimilco, the humidity made even breathing unbearable.

Stepping onto the small boat, the only ones on board were my five team members and the boat's captain. As I unhooked my rucksack, the captain waved his hands and told me in Spanish not to worry. He helped me slip off my bag and set it down next to the rest of the equipment.

"You're late, Lourdes."

"You're very perceptive, Jason," I said, taking a seat on one of the empty wooden benches to the very rear. I wanted them to know I was mad.

"It's just one day. I don't see what your problem is," he said.

The boat's captain untied us from the dock. The others on the boat were in their own world, pretending to ignore us while not really ignoring us.

I slipped on my sunglasses. "See, my problem is you haven't even told me anything about this case. I don't know what's so important to rush down to Mexico after my class. I should be back home grading my Psych 101 student papers instead of venturing off on some mysterious whirlwind weekend."

"It'll be worth it. You'll see. Like I said over the phone. This place is just two hours by boat. We'll be there just one night and then back home." Jason hugged my shoulders and gave the captain a nod. He knelt down, his hands squeezing my shoulder softly. "You'll be fine with the boat, right?"

"I have no choice."

He gave me a hug and went off to speak to the rest of the team.

Looking out toward the river, knowing that we would be surrounded by water on all sides was enough to make my heart race. I took deep breaths, trying to quell the anxiety I knew would be present this entire trip. I hated boats. I hated bodies of water. I hated the possibility of drowning.

"Let's head out, Diego."

With that, Diego pushed off the dock with a long, wooden pole and we began moving through the canals of Lake Xochimilco, the Venice of Mexico.

Something all psychologists will never tell you is that they went into this field to escape their own demons. All psychologists were terrorized by something at some point, which made them question their own realities. You can escape from your mind working in this field. You become so preoccupied with other peoples' conditions and behaviors that you are not allotted the time to question what rests beyond the doors in your own mind.

Jason is the one who brought all of this together and who continues to bring us five together, all academics, all PhDs in respectable fields: biology, geophysics, anthropology, divinity, and psychology. University of Chicago continues to fund our efforts maybe because of the cross-departmental collaboration or maybe because they find the pursuits of this group comprised of alumni and faculty so outrageous that they are entertained with our findings. Either way, what we do is slightly different than what the amateur paranormal investigative group does. Our backgrounds are all scientific. Our interests are also all based in the present. So instead of tackling the typical decades or even centuries-old haunts that are on the scheduled stops of ghost tours, we search sites of suffering so fresh that blood splattering can still be seen on the walls.

We investigate locations where suicides, murders, and massacres have occurred recently, within days ideally. We are especially interested in researching locations where the cause of death was attributed to paranormal activity not previously investigated. Ultimately, we are interested in knowing the ingredients that lead to a physical space being later deemed haunted.

The group didn't disturb me as I sat quietly in back, watching as we slowly navigated the waters. We moved gently past chinampas, small rectangle-shaped islands all along the canals.

"The people before us," Diego said, waving his hand toward the land, "they made all of these little farms. That one is mine." He pointed to a tiny cornstalk-covered patch of land. "That one over there, they grow cucumbers, and that one over there, they grow beans."

Victor, the theologian, was talking to Mike, the anthropologist, about the native beliefs of this land, mostly about Niñopa, a child-like image that was found in the sixteenth century around these parts. "Niñopa is a hybrid of Spanish and Nahuatl. That means *child of this place*. The locals here say that it goes about at night, visiting people, and checking on their crops."

"This is what they believe," Victor said handing a photo over to Mike. I stood up, and leaned in to get a closer look at the picture in

Mike's hand. It was of a porcelain figurine that looked a lot like Baby Jesus.

"They believe in it, especially because the people who care for the Niñopa figure. The statue's caretakers say that some mornings that they find the figure's feet covered in mud. It's been said that tiny little feet print, that matching the statue, have been found miles from here."

"And people live all throughout these islands?" Julie, the geophysicist, asked as she turned on her GPS. Jason went over to check on its settings.

"Yes, many people live there," Diego answered.

"And where we are going," I said, "someone lives there also?"

The pockets of conversations faded, and their eyes flashed over to me.

"You all know where we're going, don't you? I'm the only one who doesn't know?"

"Lourdes," Victor said, approaching me with his hands up as if surrendering. "We figured if you knew where we were going, you wouldn't come with us, and we really need you here for this one."

"Where are we going, Victor?"

He let out a strained breath.

"You're going to be a damn priest. Don't you keep this from me, Victor."

"Theologian is different than a priest," Julie countered.

"Shut up," I said. "Fine then. Mike, tell me, where are we going?"

Mike was now opening a case on the floor of the boat and inspecting the Moultries, the self-firing infrared cameras we set up at night around our camp's perimeters. "Talk to Jason. I said I wouldn't get into it, and I'm not getting into it."

"Tell me now or I swear to…" My voice echoed through the treetops. The sound of water rippling behind us was punctuated by a splash.

Julie ran to the edge of the boat and leaned over. "Dammit! I missed one! An axolotl! They're an endangered salamander that only exists in these waters and are brilliant for their regenerative ability," she said.

Mike snapped the case closed and both he and Victor followed to inspect.

"Okay," Mike said, sounding rather confused.

"They don't just regenerate cells after an injury. From what their evolution tells us about them, well, they evolved backward; first living on land and moving to the water, but that's not just it," Julie said, removing her camera from the strap across her shoulder. "If removed, they can completely regrow limbs."

Jason handed Mike the GPS, then dug into his green khaki pockets, and pulled out a rubber band. He pulled his shoulder-length hair into a ponytail and approached me.

"Look, you're the only psychologist with the brain, behavioral, and cognition experience in this field…" He rubbed his red and brown goatee.

Navigating down a smaller tributary, the boat rocked, nearly sending us crashing to the water. Holding on to the side, I looked ahead.

"¡Estamos aquí!" Diego shouted. "This is Isla de Muñecas."

I could only attribute what I was seeing to a delusion. I turned back to face Jason. He took both my hands in his.

There, just a few feet in front of me, they dangled and swayed on strings spreads across the length of the tiny island. Some were propped up on spikes, hooks, and tree trunks. They were beckoning me to their island grave. The creeping, sickening attack to my senses was just beginning.

"I can't do this," I whispered before collapsing.

"AYE, QUE MUÑECA. QUE muñeca tan bella." Those words pulled me from my sleep. I awoke, on a dirt floor. Sitting over me was an elderly man with leathery skin. Holding my right hand in both of his, he smiled. "Que muñeca tan linda."

I screamed, pulled my hand back from his, and kicked myself away. I bumped into a bowl and it rattled. It was full of pennies and Mexican coins. In front of that was a table with chocolate bars, handwritten notes, rosaries, and crosses fashioned out of palm leaves. Standing before it all was a three-foot plastic doll in a dusty, pink taffeta dress. Her arms reached out. I screamed again.

"Lourdes, it's okay." Jason came running in and picked me up off the floor. "It's alright."

"Where the hell have you brought me!? This is sick!"

"It's the Island of the Dolls. You're safe. I'm here. We're all here."

It took a moment for my eyes to adjust to the dimly lit room. Once they did, the gruesome reality came into view. Four dingy white walls lined with figures of all shapes and sizes surrounded me. Some of their flesh coloring had turned a dusty black, likely from being burned purposefully. Others were grungy, their flowered, rose-colored, frilly dresses stained with mud and grime. Many were nude and many more were missing limbs, eyeballs, and or even heads. Flies crawled across their bodies. Tiny spiders wove webs in their tangled hair. Each and every wall was covered with battered dolls. Many looked as though they had been here for decades. A few were fresh, their smiling faces unaware of the toll time would eventually take on their forms.

Above I heard creaking and settling, and I looked up to see more dolls hanging from the ceiling.

"¿Muñeca, adonde estas las muñeca?"

"Don't call me that! I'm not your doll."

The man kept asking me the same question over and over, until his voice became a whimper.

"I don't know where she is! I don't know where your doll is."

Jason hugged me tightly. "It's okay, Lourdes. No one is here. See?" We circled the room, but the old man was still there. He was standing now, quiet, looking out the window. His hands were clasped together.

Mike leaned in the doorway. "You should've told her about this, Jason. You're a damn psychologist yourself."

"She was cured a long time ago!"

"Apparently not."

The old man waved to get my attention. He pointed to a Barbie in roller skates, who had been completely covered in a spider web. "Una ofrenda a los espíritus."

"An offering to the spirits?" I tried to break free from Jason's hold.

"There's no one here, Lourdes." He shook me.

I felt my mind cracking, splitting open, and taking me back to that beach. That day. My father had taken me and my twin sister Rachel to the lake. My mother had let us each take our new talking baby dolls with us. Each held fifty pre-recorded phrases and was capable of bouncing, dancing, and laughing. When they were asleep, their eyes closed. When you told them to wake up, their eyes opened.

With our dolls set to sleep mode, we splashed in the water carefully, so as not to get them wet. Suddenly, Rachel submerged herself. I then was pulled under and violently yanked and spun around. When water had begun to fill my nose, ears, and mouth, I found myself dripping wet, standing on the sand, watching as my father went in after my sister. Both were never found. The only thing that did emerge from the lake was my doll, washing up on the shore, her eyes open as she bumped against my toes.

"Will you play with me?" she said.

The doll told me other things that night, besides what was on her prerecorded list. She played back to me Rachel's panicked, gurgling cries before she drowned, and the doll told me it would do the same to me unless I appeased their souls, souls of lost children from before and always. I silenced that doll's menacing words after I tore it apart.

"Offerings to the spirits?" I repeated the old man's words in English. "What is he talking about?"

"The souls talk to you, too, like they talk to my uncle. You see him? Yes?"

A short man made his way past Mike and into the room. He knelt beside me. "I'm Anastasio. The nephew of the man who lived alone on this island. Where is he? Do you see him?"

I looked back to the window and the old man was gone.

"He told you about the offering, yes?"

I nodded.

The man addressed Jason. "We were very clear to your university that if you wanted to investigate this place before my uncle's funeral, you could do so freely as long as you brought with you an offering. Traditional offerings of candy and candles are customary to our dead. My uncle also made it mandatory that anyone visiting his land bring with them a doll to appease the spirit of the little girl who made this place her home."

Julie entered, her camera clicking as she moved. "Fine. Is there anywhere we can get a doll around here?"

"It's too late, miss. It is also insulting to me, the spirit of my uncle, and this land that you have not followed the most basic of rules. You can't just think you can leave and come back. The spirits know what you have done. That you have been careless. That you have not acknowledged their presence."

"Can't leave anyway," Victor interrupted, popping his head in from the other side of the window. "The boat just left and won't be back until early morning.

There was a large splash outside and then a scream.

"Did anyone hear that?"

Jason released his hold.

"Help! Please!" A young girl screamed.

I ran out of the shack and was instantly attacked by them, all of them. They were propped up on stakes amongst the tall blades of grass. They were present in the hundreds of trees that covered the island. Each and every tree in the vicinity was decorated with grimy, ghastly dolls. They hung from every branch, were tied to every tree, and were all bounded together on this floating garden.

"Help me, Lourdes! Help me!" the girl cried.

I followed the voice as I ran past rotting faces of little girls attached to tree limbs, some consumed so by the wildlife that their once smooth, clean faces were spotted by moss and mold. The sun, orange and gold, began to set in the sky, streaming shadows of lifeless little people all along my path. Pink plastic decay hung from the trees like leaves everywhere. Hundreds and hundreds of clear, glass, plastic, and button eyes followed. For those that were eyeless, their empty sockets peered back at me. *Don't look in their eyes*, I reminded myself. *Just don't look in their eyes.*

I could feel them, watching me as I stepped on the dock. As soon as I looked down, I spotted her. She was right there, right in the murky river water below. The skirt of her white dress flowing around her, her long reddish-brown hair rippled and swayed as she tried to break free from that watery coffin. The gleaming pale white arms broke the water's surface, and, as I reached for her hand, I was pulled back.

"Lourdes! We've been looking for you for hours, which is insane because it doesn't take long to circle this small island." Victor said. "Didn't you hear us calling you? Lourdes? Where have you been?"

"No. I've been here the whole time. Looking at the water."

"What are you doing with that?"

In my arms, I was cradling the torso of a nude, burned baby doll. Her white, little dress was drenched. A wave of ripples disturbed the calm river and up emerged a doll's head bobbing in the water. Her matted reddish-brown curls were tangled with twigs, and her empty eyes looked at both of us.

"Come on, Lourdes, it's time for the interview." Victor pulled the doll out of my hands and dropped it on the ground. He led me away with one hand as he made the sign of the cross with the other. "Dios mío, this place is so freaking weird."

Outside, over the cedar structure, the word "Museo" hung over the door. "And this is the strangest museum I've ever been to," Victor said. "I hate knowing that we're the only ones on this damn patch of land."

Inside, Anastasio was telling Jason that the dolls in here were his uncle's most precious. "Many have been here for decades," he said.

"This here is the shrine to my uncle and the one beside his is for the spirit of the dead girl who, really, this whole island is dedicated to.

My uncle left his wife and children many years ago. He came way out here because he wanted to live a life of solitude, but as soon as he got here, he heard the voice of a little girl. He never really told us what she told him on that first visit, but he decided then that this was going to be his home. The little girl's spirit told him she wanted dolls. She instructed him to decorate the entire island with dolls because they would protect him and the rest of this place from evil spirits. These dolls became his friends, his protectors."

"Where did he get these dolls?" Julie asked. She was manning the video camera stationed a few feet away.

"Many of them he would find floating in the water. He thought they were drowned little girls and he would bring them here, wash and clean them, and hang them up. Others he would get when he would go into town, and many were given to him by locals who would trade him dolls for the fruits and vegetables he grew here."

"Where's Mike?" I asked, realizing that he was not in the room for the interview.

"He finished setting up the cameras so he's grilling up some corn Anastasio picked for us," Victor said.

I continued recording the conversation while taking notes, observing any peculiarities in tone or body language. My job was to establish a baseline psychological reading of the person being interviewed; had they themselves experienced strange phenomena, did they believe the location was previously haunted or had the potential to be deemed haunted, and what were their ultimate plans with the physical space.

Jason asked the questions while Victor swept the area taking temperature readings.

"Can you explain again how your uncle died?" Jason asked.

"That morning we were preparing to go fishing and he mentioned to me how the spirits in the water kept calling to him. It was something he had told me about before, these mermaids that tempted him into their world. We went fishing together, sitting right there on the dock, and he told me again how he heard the voices of the mermaids, beckoning him. He told me not to worry, that he would ignore them. I left to water the crops, and when I returned, I found him face down floating in the water. It was the same place the little girl drowned half a century before."

AFTER THE INTERVIEW, WE ate outside under the stars. The smells of rotting plastic were impossible to ignore, even with the sweet smell of roasting corn and warm tortillas, frijoles and fresh made salsa. But still, we ate happily knowing that we would be gone in the morning.

During our meal, Anastasio told us how the island would remain without a resident because he himself could not live there because of his own experience. "As you see, at night all you can see is their shapes, their forms, and shadows. It is difficult to see their faces and that is what frightens me—their faces. During the day, that is most bizarre, as their heads turn straight up and look to you. But tonight, you will hear them. Everyone hears them."

"What do they tell you to do?" I asked.

Anastasio took a bite of tortilla and shoved a spoonful of frijoles in his mouth. He chewed, swallowed, and pushed away his cleaned plate. "They tell you to bring them more offerings."

Anastasio left us to our work. He would spend the night on the other side of the island. The base camp became the gardening shed outside of the museum. Our equipment of digital recorders, electromagnetic devices, and laptops sat alongside gardening tools, spades, shovels, machetes, and watering buckets.

This was Don Julian's land. The land that gave him love, guidance, comfort, and food. The water is what took his life, but now they were all connected, the land, the river, the dolls, and now Don Julian. Our investigation of the island turned up little in terms of movement, sounds, or anything that we could quickly note as out of the ordinary. Yet, this whole island itself was a little out of the ordinary.

It was almost time to wrap up our investigation and all that was needed was the final, most terrifying part of our visit; quiet time. This is where we spent time isolated in the supposedly most charged location of the physical space. While there were encounters at the dock, considering it had been the location of not one, but two deaths, Jason surmised that the museum was the most active spot, as that is where most people spent time and, especially, that is where I thought I had seen Don Julian—the most recently deceased.

"Who's going first?" Julie asked.

Jason looked to me.

"What am I supposed to do?"

"What do you mean, what are you supposed to do? Just do what you have always done. Go in there. Take a seat and listen. We need to especially record your experiences. Don Julian heard a voice that told him to do something, which he did by decorating this island with these dolls. As a little girl, you experienced very similar phenomena. You heard dolls talking to you, blaming you for the drowning of your sister and your father."

"I'm not going to listen to this any further. How dare you bring me out here for this to make me some part of this experiment!"

"Isn't it true though, Lourdes? You know it's true. We are just trying to do what we have always done—try to understand people."

I took a seat on the floor. Julie checked to make sure the camera was recording, and Victor did another check of the audio equipment.

"Thanks, Lourdes," Jason said. "We'll be right outside."

"Just…leave the door open please," I said.

Sitting on the dirt floor, legs crossed, I closed my eyes and took a deep breath. I listened outside. There was the buzzing of insects, the breeze through the trees, the rattling together of plastic bodies and their plastic shoes, and then the rustling of taffeta dresses. The buzzing intensified. A cool wind blew, carrying the scent of the river, and bringing with it hushed words, murmurs of conversations, bits of sweet childish laughter. My heart raced, sweat rolled down my cheeks. The whispers became rhythmic, singsong, a child's lullaby.

I am imagining this, I told myself. Just like I had imagined it all as a little girl.

They giggled now.

There was the crackling of a walkie-talkie. It was Jason's voice. "Lourdes, are you all right in there?" He sounded distant and afraid. "Lourdes, we're seeing someone in the room with you."

Was that even Jason's voice? I wasn't going to be fooled again. I was just going to sit here, on the soft soil.

"Lourdes! Open your eyes! Do you see what we're seeing?"

Those tempting voices. They weren't real. All that was real was this, right here, sitting, and feeling the breeze, the wind through my hair, the dirt beneath my palms as I pushed myself up. They weren't going to trick me again.

"Lourdes." Tiny fingers tugged on my pant leg. "Come play with us, Lourdes."

The voices when I was a little girl, the destruction of my dolls that led to the destruction of my childhood, were just part of some psychosis triggered on by a traumatic experience. That's what it was, yes, that's all it was.

"Lourdes, where is our offering? What have you brought us to play with?"

There was no such thing as the animation of inanimate objects. Dead, vengeful souls could not possess the bodies of plastic and cotton. There was no possibility that a doll could be sentient, that any human figurine could become sentient. There was no possibility that an object can control a human being!

"Lourdes, will you play with us?"

I opened my eyes, and finally I looked into her cold, plastic eyes. That doll, that pretty, little doll. "Yes," I told her. "I will play with you." She reached for my hand, and we walked out of the door.

"OH MY GOD! DIOS santo! What have you done to them? What have you done to them?"

The sunlight burned down on me. I tried to shield it from my eyes with my arm. Then I saw it. Caked and dried dirt and blood covered my sleeves. I looked down and found myself sitting outside in Don Julian's garden, my green khaki pants stained red. On the ground beside me was a bloodied machete, and the heads, torsos, arms, and legs of my team members all piled together. All like doll parts. I stood up and looked back across the field to see the multitude of freshly dug graves.

49

EL PINO

THE PINE TREE

LUCKY BLACK CAT IS A MAGICAL NEEDS SUPPLIER. OUR STORE IS LOCATED IN LOS ANGELES, CALIFORNIA. FOR YOUR CONVENIENCE, WE ALSO HAVE AN ONLINE STORE FROM WHERE YOU CAN HAVE YOUR MAGICAL SUPPLIES SHIPPED ANYWHERE IN THE U.S. OR THE WORLD.

WE CARRY A FULL LINE OF HANDMADE SPIRITUAL SUPPLIES INCLUDING OILS, INCENSE, POWDERS, CANDLES, HERBS, MOJO BAGS, SPIRITUAL SOAPS, AND BOOKS. WE IMPORT AND DISTRIBUTE FOLKLORIC, MAGICAL, OCCULT, HERBAL, AND SPIRITUAL SUPPLIES FROM ASIA, LATIN AMERICA,

AND THE MIDDLE EAST. WE ALSO MAKE SPELL KITS FOR THOSE WHO WOULD LIKE TO CAST A LOVE SPELL, MONEY SPELL, OR PROTECTION SPELL USING AFRICAN AMERICAN HOODOO, PAGAN MAGIC, OR OTHER WITCHCRAFT TRADITIONS.

Rey balled up the white slip of paper. He had a headache from reading that all-cap, bolded print. He tossed the crumpled mass over his shoulder, and it hit the wall and fell to the floor with a soft thud.

He felt ill.

His hands were clammy, shaky, and moist, but he continued digging through the white wastebasket in Lydia's pristine, pine smelling bedroom. She was so organized and detailed—almost too organized. He knew she would know instantly that he had been in here without her. If anything were out of place in her large, all white room with that cherrywood four-poster bed covered in white 1,200-thread count sheets, she would know. Her white vanity was without a speck of dust as was her white nightstand. Digging through the wastebasket, he wondered if he could find anything in here that would rival what he had found in her walk-in closet.

His girlfriend of over a year was downstairs making him a cup of coffee, but he no longer trusted her or the coffee. Rey changed quickly after meeting Lydia, and at first he thought it was good, almost too good. She was successful, and absolutely stunning. Lydia was enchanting and smart, with a doctorate in folklore. At first, the doctorate in folklore seemed a little odd, but she was a professor at Miami State University, and she loved discussing everything with him, from food to sports, and yes, the occasional superstitious and folkloric beliefs, but that was fine because she was beautiful.

After a few dates, he found himself thinking about her. Well, it was really more like obsessing over her, wondering where she was in the world, what she was doing, and wondering if she was thinking about him. The thoughts became intense, then they turned into lust and desire, and quickly it became love. He was changing. Rey, who would lose interest in a woman after a second date had fallen hard.

A few months went by, and things began to change again. Lydia now called less and less and made even less of an attempt to see him. He felt like he was suffocating when a day passed and he didn't see her. Sometimes he would sit outside of her office in his car. Other times he would go to the gym where she worked out hoping to bump into her, and sometimes he would sleep outside, beneath her window—in peace that she was so close. He couldn't understand why she didn't feel the same for him because he loved her so, so much and would do anything for her. He even quit his job at the law firm just to make sure he had enough time to sit around his house and think about her.

With the wastebasket pressed to his chest and his legs sprawled out, he continued searching, frantically, until he found another important-looking document crumpled up. He heard her light footsteps on the stairs, and that sweet, dear voice call, "Café, dear..." He ignored her call, unfolded the paper with his now cramping fingers, and read.

SOME PEOPLE WHO PRACTICE MAGIC BELIEVE THAT SELLING SPELL KITS IS A BAD IDEA, AND THAT NO OCCULT SPECIALIST SHOULD SELL SPELL KITS BECAUSE THEN ANYONE COULD CAST A SPELL. WE AT LUCKY BLACK CAT BELIEVE THAT

IF THE INGREDIENTS AND THE MAGIC SPELLS
CONTAINED IN THE SPELL KITS ARE CREATED WITH
TRADITIONAL HOODOO ROOTWORK THEN IT IS A
GREAT IDEA TO OFFER THIS SERVICE.

OFTEN WE ARE ASKED, "DO SPELL KITS REALLY
WORK?"

IT IS OUR EXPERIENCE THAT SPIRITUALLY GIFTED
PEOPLE WITH NO PREVIOUS MAGICAL EXPERIENCE
CAN ACTUALLY PUT MORE ENERGY INTO
THEIR CEREMONIAL RITES THAN EXPERIENCED
PRACTITIONERS. THIS IS ESPECIALLY THE CASE IF
THE PURPOSE OF THE SPELL KIT IS TO WORK LOVE,
MONEY, PROTECTION, AND SOMETIMES EVEN
BANISHING SPELLS.

The word "Banishing" had been circled in red pencil. Lydia once
joked that her grandmother and mother practiced magic and had
passed the traditions on to her.

IF YOU HAVE NEVER TRIED TO CAST A LOVE SPELL OR
MONEY SPELL BEFORE, OR PERFORMED A CLEANSING
SPELL, UNJINXING SPELL, OR PROTECTION SPELL,
OR EVEN TO BANISH NEGATIVITY THINK OF LUCKY
BLACK CAT SPELL KITS AS A WAY TO TEST YOUR
OWN POWERS OF MAGIC.

"Oh Rey, you should really get off of the floor, dear," Lydia said, leaning against the doorframe. She wore a curve-hugging heather gray skirt suit. Red lipstick stained the rim of the white porcelain cup she held with her manicured hands. She took another sip from the mug and smiled. "What are you looking for, dear?"

"You did this to me? I know you did." He dug frantically into the wastebasket until he found a copy of a receipt that said, "Commanding spell kit." In the description column it read:

FOR THE POWER TO COMMAND OTHERS

"You put a spell on me," he cried. Saliva ran down the side of his mouth. "Command, me…" His thoughts were becoming jumbled, a mix of images, words, letters, and emotions. "To do…"

"To die, Rey. I've been commanding you to die. It was fun, it really was, while it lasted, but I guess I just made that love spell a little too strong, and honestly, I've been trying to be rid of you for months. You've broken into my house every night this week and every night I find you asleep in my bed. I don't even know how the hell you've gotten past the security system each time. It's just not cool anymore, Rey. I've tried breaking up, ignoring you, or just being downright cruel so you would leave me alone, but you don't.

I admit, I got a little *too* greedy there in the beginning and just kept lighting love candle after love candle because I liked you, and I really wanted you to like me, well, love me. But I'm bored now, Rey. You bore me. I figure it's just easier than killing you myself."

Rey could feel his eyelids drooping. He fell sideways on the carpeted floor and looked into Lydia's walk-in closet. A small table in there was lit with nine thin, black candles, each down to a nub.

"I've slowly been commanding your body to die, and from the looks of it…" She stepped over Rey and into the closet. One by one, the candles flickered out.

She clapped her hands and said, "the spell is set."

50

EL PESCADO

THE FISH

Much like the creature reported to inhabit Loch Ness in the Scottish Highlands, a similar cryptid has been reported to live in the Nahuel Huapi Lake in Patagonia, Argentina. Sightings of the Argentine lake creature dubbed the Nahuelito began around 1922 when the press began showing interest.

Accounts have stated that the creature is serpentine and has an enormous hump. Similar to sightings at Loch Ness, photographic evidence has been provided to local cryptozoologists for interpretation. Most of the images appear hazy or grainy, capturing the horizon in the background, waves in the foreground, and in the center, a shadowy figure emerging from the lake. What appears is an animal similar to the early Jurassic plesiosaur.

Throughout the decades, sightings continued to stream into local authorities. Then, on April 17, 2008, local newspaper *El Cordillerano* announced that an anonymous package had been delivered. In the bundle were two striking photographs and a note. The two photographs, dated just two days previously at 9 a.m., show from several feet away, a long, winding, serpent-like figure with a small head sitting atop of the water.

The accompanying note said: "It is not a twisted tree trunk. It is not a wave. Nahuelito has shown his face. I'm not giving out my personal information in order to avoid future headaches."

51

LA PALMA

THE PALM TREE

There are objects so precious that they will themselves into hiding, safe from the greed-fueled hands of man. There is the chalice used by Jesus Christ at the Last Supper, safeguarded first by Saint Peter, later passed to successor popes, and eventually falling into the care of Saint Lawrence, who then passed it on to a Spanish soldier, Proselius, where it was to travel to Spain. Eventually, the exchange became muddled, confused—lost forever. There are objects that may occasionally emerge from hiding, to be imbued once again with power—and for these objects, this is what makes their horror possible.

These people have been butchering each other for centuries. Do these politicians really think that a bunch of soldiers are going to stop these people over there from fighting?" The barrel-chested man shouted to a small dust-covered computer, set on an equally dusty glass shelf.

Everything in this small shop was covered in a thin layer of age. The customer breathed in the perfume of ancient mold and mildew. Running his fingers along the spines of cracked and worn books, he could feel the energy from each pulse through his fingertips.

Even from this aisle, marked Wiccan/Pagan, Felix got in a full view of the massive man sitting in front of a glass-encased bookshelf full of carefully arranged antique, worn, and frayed leather-bound tomes. From here, he knew what was behind those cases were not copies. He could spot the calf binding of a 1633 copy of *Delrio*, the seventeenth century witch hunter manual. There was also an edition of the works of powerful magician Agrippa on occult philosophy, and other manuals on exorcism, demonology, and mysticism. While those texts would throw any common collector into a frenzy with the knowledge they possessed, in Felix's opinion, those were just quaint texts.

He had not traveled here to Faro in Portugal for just a philosophical text or some meager book of spells.

"Estudante?" the shopkeeper asked. He was sitting on a red wooden stool behind the counter. Felix couldn't see the image, since the computer screen was facing away from where he stood. From the clear, rapid Portuguese, he could detect a news reporter's voice detailing the news-breaking slaughter of a small village.

"Sim," he lied yes. It had been a few years since he had completed his Doctorate of Theology, but he could still pass for a college student.

"You know what these people do?" The shopkeeper motioned to the screen. "Hate and kill people for just existing."

"That's terrible," Felix said, focusing only on the wooden case behind the attendant, where volumes of true value were kept.

The attendant shouted something obscene at the television and waved a fist connected to a bulging forearm. Then he turned, and his small black eyes finally fell on Felix for the first time.

"There's no one to protect us, anyone. We think law enforcement will protect us, other countries, the United Nations, there's nothing and no one really here to protect anyone." He took a deep breath. "What can I help you find?" The shopkeeper finally asked.

Felix slipped off his blue backpack and set it on the floor with a thud.

"*El Libro de San Cipriano*. The original."

The attendant's face twisted into a look of confusion. The silence between them was thicker than the layer of grime that covered the windows. The shopkeeper stood up slowly, tapping once on the computer to silence the news report. The large man looked out toward the door, perhaps to make sure Felix was alone. Then he looked up to the ceiling, directly above the computer, and there a security camera played silent witness.

Leaning forward, both hands planted on the glass counter filled with books opened to yellowed texts in Latin, Spanish, Portuguese, and Hebrew, the shopkeeper growled through his teeth, "That book does not exist. Also, I don't appreciate amateurs coming into my shop."

"Let's just say this textbook of magic did exist, one of the most powerful grimoires ever written..."

"You wouldn't even have the money to buy it if it *did* exist."

Felix lifted the backpack from the floor and set it on the counter carefully. Peeling back the zipper, and bunches of bounded hundred-dollar bills spilled out.

The attendant took a single stack of bills, flipped through the notes and then dropped it on the counter. For a moment, they stood there in silence, the attendant staring at the bills and Felix staring back at the attendant. In that moment of silence, it was as if the shopkeeper was consulting his silent partners, the thousands of books that stood on heavy cedar bookshelves from floor to ceiling, or that sat stacked in corners by the dozens. There were first edition books only located here, their existence unknown outside, except, of course, to a select few. There were books here written in blood, in black ink, and baptized in fire. There were books here bound in the skin of donkeys and goats, bears and human flesh. This was The Occult Bookstore, the first occult bookstore, and the most celebrated for hundreds of years.

"The book contains prayers to call forth guardian angels, mysteries of witchcraft, ways to capture little devils, explanations on the hidden powers behind love and hate, ways to make a pact with the devil, and more. Most who open it die within moments because their physical selves cannot comprehend the magic that lies within…and so, sir, how will you be using the book?"

Before Felix could open his mouth, the attendant knelt, tapped an unseen compartment in the display case, and produced a plain, brown, leather-bound book. There was no cover text or lettering, not even an image.

Felix quickly grabbed the book, shoved it into his bag and said, "That's my business."

The door chimed as Felix rushed outside. The attendant watched patiently as the glass door closed.

He looked around his silent kingdom of paper and leather, blood and ink. Shuffling back to the stool, he took a seat and then roared with laughter. The pages of his books flipped and fluttered, rejoicing; his children jubilant. All of the books, all containing passages and incantations he was forever bound to protect, moved and breathed, and they all laughed.

"The grand-grimoire always comes back home to its guardian.

Always.

I shall see it back after your death."

52

LA MACETA

THE FLOWERPOT

The sickening, overwhelming sadness would strike at the same time each night after 3:00 a.m. Soledad would wake in bed. Her body would be covered in a thin layer of sweat. Her cotton, pink nightdress would cling to her skin. Each night, she would grasp the edges of the sheet, pull it up right beneath her eyes, and turn her head slowly in the darkness to the clock. The digital alarm clock on top of her dresser ticked away the minutes that tortured her so.

Limiting herself to one side of the queen-sized bed felt silly sometimes. She could just sleep on the other side of the bed where Raul had slept beside her for thirty-eight years. Yet, she could never manage that. That was Raul's spot, her husband, and sleeping on that side was almost as if acknowledging that she would never see him again, that he would never return. She wanted him to return—for her.

The red, menacing digital figures on the clock looked back at her, taunting, 3:13 a.m now. A wave of panic jolted her body, freezing her there. Her legs stiffened. Her fingers cramped as they clutched the thin sheet of fabric that rested beneath her nose. Something changed in the humid, musky air in her room. There was the smell of something so faint, but so distinct, and it began to fill the room.

She wondered if she had securely locked the door to her flower shop, Flores de Soledad, which adjoined her small living room. She always locked the door to her flower shop. Soledad was obsessive about making sure that door was closed at night because, if it wasn't, then the smell of dead, rotted, or decaying flowers could easily creep into her home. Although this wasn't the smell of death that filled her room; it was something fresh and sweet.

She was just so tired that she wanted it to be all over. Work had been overwhelming. Yes, she had been strong enough to keep up with the order taking, preparing, and watering. Even now, just as the orders piled on for the approaching holiday, Día de Muertos, she worried if she had enough of La Flor de Muerto, the cempazúchitl flower. The marigold was believed by the Aztecs to attract the dead, to bring their souls back home, especially on the day it was believed the line between the living and the dead blurred, el Día de Muertos.

On this day, home altars and cemeteries were covered in the heavily petaled orange flowers. Even days leading up to the Day of the Dead, the petals of the sun-colored marigold could be found down streets, sidewalks, and walkways leading up to homes. The graveyards would soon be lit with the brilliant golden flowers. Their stunning color rivaled that of the setting sun.

Soledad thought of her husband each day, but during this time of year, he would be there, everywhere, in all of the folds of her mind.

When he was stricken with his illness, he had asked her for two favors; the first was to continue living, and by that, he had meant taking up something new, embracing the gifts that life still had to offer her— which she did by purchasing the flower shop. The second was to never set an altar for him because, as he said, it would pain him too much to return to the plane of the living for a few hours only to have to depart when the door was sealed again for another year.

Her floral boutique had grown so popular this year that she disobeyed her husband and did create an altar for him. *It was time*, she thought. The altar was small and simple. Set on a plain wooden table was his picture, a few chocolate bars—his favorites—as well as other mementos, like his camera and a photograph of the two of them at the gardens in Puerto Vallarta. Then, of course, there were the flowers, tons of Day of the Dead marigolds, arranged in vases, scattered over the table, collected into bunches, and set next to the frames.

The scent was now overwhelming.

She placed her hand on Raul's side of the bed. Her heart raced. Her breath quickened. There had just been so much stress lately—the stress from being so very tired, the stress from doing something her husband had clearly instructed her to not do, and the wrenching stress of being so, so very alone.

A door opened and closed somewhere in the house. Soledad held her breath as footsteps approached her door. The footsteps drew closer, slowly, until she could hear the doorknob turn in the darkness.

"Who's there?" she called. No one answered.

The door swung open and there was a dark silhouette of a man standing in the doorframe.

"Who are you? What do you want?" she shouted.

"You called me, Soledad." He entered the room slowly and sat down on the bed. Her body shook with fear. The man lay down with his back to her. She couldn't move, couldn't scream. The man took one of her arms and wrapped it gently around himself. He was ice cold.

"Let's just sleep for now, my love. The journey has made me so tired."

"Raul?"

He patted her hand softly. It was stiff, rigid—cold.

"Yes," he said groggily.

Tears filled her eyes, and she pressed her face against him.

"I am here now. Sleep, my dear. Sleep away this last night in this bed, in this house. In a few hours I will take you with me on the journey to the other world because I can't leave you, not ever again."

53

EL ARPA

THE HARP

Alida Obregon knew when her mother would die. Her mother had told her to look for the sign. "It comes raging through the night, freezing your blood to a level that you will only know again moments before your own death," her mother had told her. "Be careful with glass as it will break and shard and pierce. When it begins to fade, be strong because we come from one of the five greats."

And so it came. The sign her mother had warned her would come. It was the same warning given by her grandmother, great-grandmother, and so on, as far back to that memory of that brilliant green isle where their name was born.

It was supposed to be one evening, her final evening as principal harpist with the Orquesta Sinfónica Nacional before moving on with the New York Philharmonic.

Her mother wasn't there, of course, because of the illness. She had told her mother that she would delay her appointment in America to be with her, to which her mother replied, "I do not need my daughter at my side holding vigil until I die. When I die, you'll know, just as when you die, no matter where you are, your daughter will know. The Aos sí, she will alert you."

Alida held her mother's hand in her own one last time, and they sat there in silence with tears in their eyes. "Mother, how can you still believe in such stories?"

With her eyes closed, Alida's mother said, "Because she announced my mother's death to me. The sound is something you will never forget, it rattles you, disjoints your soul for a second from its body. The five great families have always had our own designated mourners, the women who keen."

"But mother, we are not Irish," Alida said.

"No, but you are a Mexican woman of Irish decent. Your great-great-grandfather fought with the Saint Patrick's Battalion."

Alida rubbed her mother's hand. "I know, Mom…it was just a long time ago, and I don't believe in those things. Just rest, please."

At the Palacio de Bellas Artes, the curtain was drawn. Alida sat in the front of the orchestra, listening to the tuning of violins and cellos.

"The first National Theater of Mexico was actually torn down," the maestro was telling a visiting violinist from France. "They tore it down after the Mexican War of Independence to make this building."

With just the mention of war in the air, it came back to her, her mother's story, her family's story. The Saint Patrick's Battalion was a group of expatriates from Europe, mostly from Ireland, who were brought to the United States to fight with the Americans, but they defected and instead fought with Mexico against the United States.

Many in that battalion were from Ireland. Los Colorados, they were lovingly called because of their red hair. Some were captured, court-martialed as traitors, and sentenced to death. Those who survived settled along coastal towns in the state of Jalisco.

The curtain raised, Alida lowered her head and pressed her body against the wooden frame of her harp. She listened, waiting for the percussions to begin. As they did, her fingers touched the strings, and as she plucked the first string of Alberto Evaristo Ginastera's Harp Concerto, it came.

There was a low moaning groan, which quickly rose to a vibrating screech. The windows in the neoclassical building shook and the sound intensified. She could feel it in her teeth, but she continued to play. Musicians paused. Some stood and ran offstage, frightened by the horrendous noise. The whistling, moaning, painful cry grew, and the windows came crashing in, sending pulverized glass raining down on the audience. As fast as it happened, it stopped. Alida still playing, with tears down her cheeks, knew that was the sign.

The banshee keened and mourned for her mother.

54

LA RANA

THE FROG

Jerry felt hesitant as he followed the old man into the dark room. The cramped, cement room smelled of earth and mold. White, red, and black votive candles outlined a red painted pentagram on the floor. On sinking wooden shelves surrounding the room, there were stacked ragged boxes, which overflowed with dried herbs, chunks of bark, and twisted roots.

It was the first Friday in March. Today the Black Mass would take place at a cave off one of the largest mountaintops in the town of Lake Catemaco. Thus, it was thought in these parts that today was the most powerful day of the year to cast a spell. That is why he was here.

Crossing his arms and standing off to the side, he watched as the old man made his way to an aquarium, its glass covered in a sheet of grime.

"How did you learn to do all of this?"

"You don't learn magic," the old man said with disgust. "It's in the blood. My blood, something people have carried in this town before the damned Hernán Cortés arrived on this land."

Now, visiting a town known for its large population of witches and warlocks was not something he ever thought he would do, but he was here and there was no way to turn back. The money, a large sum, had already been paid.

His original plan was to go to Cancun and have fun, which he did. In Cancun, he drank every night and met beautiful people and fell into each other's desires. But after all of that, he didn't feel satisfied. He wanted and needed more. After learning about this town from a bartender at his hotel, and the upcoming mass, he boarded a bus and made the twenty-two-hour journey.

"Why is the Black Mass held at a cave?"

The old man turned away from the aquarium with a toad in one hand and a hand-stitched doll covered in black cloth in the other. "It is the cave where the devil loiters."

The old man pointed to the center of the pentagram. "Stand there," he said.

Jerry did as instructed. After murmuring some words, the old man put the toad in Jerry's left hand and the doll in Jerry's right hand.

"Now, feed the doll to the toad."

Jerry did as he was told, prying the slimy animal's mouth open, and shoving the doll down its throat. The toad wrestled, writhed, and gagged, but Jerry managed to force the doll into its mouth.

The old man then handed Jerry a rusted, threaded needle. "Now, sew its lips together and when you are done, your partner will die in thirty days."

Jerry took the needle into his hand, smiled, and pierced the animal's lip.

FIFTY-FOUR

"Say it," I hear my Aunt Angie say.

"It's only a game," I say.

"Say it again," she says.

I repeat her words.

I hear her, in that faraway, never where place. It's an echo. A memory. A whisper.

"Remember to find your way back. Stay on the path and go around and around."

I look down and see the Lotería cards in my hand.

Her words reach out to me and pull me through. Those safe words. And so, I repeat as she taught me to: "It's only a game," and then I find myself here, in the small coffee shop I work at, shuffling my deck of Lotería cards. I'm standing behind the counter. In front of me there are two people watching me.

It's only a game.

A card game.

Something simple.

Without stress.

Without worry.

I shuffle.

And they watch as I weave the cards in and out. The flicking and clicking of cardstock might as well be freshly sharpened blades clacking into each other. Or, a knife held overhead.

I look down at my hands, wondering where's the blood and then I wonder why I'm even thinking that.

I'm here.

I'm shuffling.

They are waiting for me to answer their question, which I can't recall and so I ask:

"What was your question again?"

The man, his name is Gael. I remember that now. Gael asks: "What happened to our daughter?'

The anxiety here mounts as each card moves and shifts. Any and every unseen card that moves between my fingers holds the possibility that when presented it could be the one to indicate a tower of destruction. But what the still grieving mother and father before me don't realize is that these cards are more powerful than they'll ever know. Her name is Julia. I remember that as well. Gael and Julia. Two parents grieving the loss of their daughter, not in death, but slipped away into some unnamed place, joined with every other person smiling out from a missing person's poster.

All I know for certain is that tonight we will be presented with some answers.

We all come to a point along the route of our destination where we need a guidepost. Some people come to me. I am that nudge, that reminder, that assurance, perhaps even that omen—or calculation.

Sometimes I tell them awful things, things that will twist inside of their stomachs, clang against their skulls, or squeeze their rib cages so tight as to threaten to splinter bone. This is why I ask everyone at the beginning of each and every reading:

"Would you like me to tell you everything I see, the good and the bad?"

Everyone always agrees to know the bad thing, and I understand why. People want to be prepared for the creeping thing in the distance ready to destroy their lives. Yet, I comfort them all, assuring them that there is no predestination. Our lives are not mapped out by the gods. The fates and fate are a bitter fairy tale and anything and everything can be moved along the board game that is life.

The future is not fixed.

There is no destiny.

No guarantee.

What happens tomorrow, the next month and year, it's all in flux. There's beauty to that constant shifting of possibility. There's madness to it too. We shape the future with our thoughts and actions in the present. Each moment before us can be adjusted, readjusted, and tailored, directing us to the correct way along the forking path. We just need to know the right calculation, the accurate operation, and allow the process to flow, just like a math problem.

The past however cannot be undone, no matter how much we will it to not be so. I know that terribly well.

The cards indicate the past quite clearly, because unlike the future, the past just is. The past is cemented with all of its cruelty and destruction. No matter how gruesome. No matter how painful. What occurred before cannot be changed no matter how much we will it, no matter how much we try to push against logic. Some doors cannot be reopened, and if we spend our lives holding onto the doorknobs of those sealed rooms, we guarantee a sort of living death for ourselves. We must break the pattern of suffering and move on from the awful things in our past that threaten to define our futures, even when we think no future is possible.

I thought that for me for a long time, that no future was possible given the hideous thing in my past, dreams full of screams and a bathtub stacked with dismembered doll parts.

But I found a way to carry on. Or, at least my Aunt Angie found that way for me, and because of her I found that the power was to believe so strongly in something that to manifest it real, no matter how impossible it seemed.

That's how I came to be here.

It's not just wishing something, it's knowing and believing in the reality of that thing. Some people may think my very existence, even standing here should be an impossibility, but in that garden all I could think about were the numbers and Aunt Angie's words. I repeated them, and so here I am.

The numbers kept me calm. The numbers kept me steady. The numbers kept me here.

Often when people come to me, their questions come wrapped in the movements of the past, with hopes towards a prosperous future, all while they stand before me in the present, wanting and waiting. While I cannot grant them all of their answers, I can surely point them along the way. I don't have any psychic abilities, not really. I can't tell them when they'll die, or when their loved ones will die. If I knew that, maybe I wouldn't be here right now. Maybe my reading would have been different.

All I can guarantee is that we all will die, and for some of us, the path to the end is quiet. For others, it's marked by a great suffering.

Still, all I can do is shuffle. All they can do is tell me when to stop. And when those moments are in agreement, I pause and draw. Card by card. An answer to their question, no matter how clear or cloudy. No matter how bright or grim. One reading. That's all I'll offer each person who comes to me.

The process is simple: They question. They pay. And, so we play, Lotería.

The traditional way to play Lotería is that each player will select a game board that includes a random selection of sixteen images. The caller then takes the deck of fifty-four Lotería cards, shuffles, and then announces the card to the players. Sometimes the caller will just state the name of the card "El Bandolin" for example, or sometimes the caller will recite the corresponding verse before announcing the card "Tocando su bandolon, esta mariachi Simon." The players with the corresponding image on their gameboard will then place a game chip over that picture. The caller will then call the next card and they will continue on this way, and the first player to fill their game board will shout "Lotería!" The concept is similar to that of Bingo.

The Lotería cards were thought originated in Italy, taken to Spain, and then to Mexico in the 1700s. The word Lotería translates to Lottery. The images of the cards range from people to things, but each image is believed to hint to various aspects of Mexican history and culture.

What most people don't know is that there's another way to play Lotería, a game of divination with the fifty-four cards.

There's no question to my technique. Julia and Gael stand there silently, watching as the cards move between my hands, slipping back and forth, back and forth. The soft susurration as my fingers slide and place, slide and place, one stack on top of the other. It's soothing in a way, calming, hypnotic, as if the movement of the cards are preparing me for a great transformation. They are here after all to be hypnotized, to enter into another state of consciousness, one in which we are open to receiving messages from someone else, something else, other than the three of us who are standing here in this closed coffee shop.

They both want to believe so bad that I can provide them with the answers they need, and they need to understand that the only reason I can do this is because of the cards, the power lies within those numbers, within the pattern they provide.

I'm just a conduit.

Their eyes remain transfixed on the movement of the cards, not on my face, or my hair or anything else in the room. I use this opportunity to look them over one more time. Each of them ordered the same thing before I closed up shop, black coffee, hot. Each of their white paper coffee cups with brown sleeves remains on the counter untouched. Gael stands with his arms crossed. Julia tries inching towards him, but he doesn't respond. They're hoping for answers to be plucked from the universe. They're hoping that in this little coffee shop, with worn, creaking wooden floors, that they are able to find the comfort that can allow them to continue existing with the awful thing hanging over their lives. They are hoping that I can provide them with the solution to the mystery, but even if they find a solution will they find relief? Sometimes there is no relief from tragedy. We spin tales, folklore, legends, and myths all to process very real human suffering. Threaded within the fibers of each and every folklore, legend and myth there is truth, no matter how sad.

The air conditioner kicks on. I notice the beads of sweat dripping down in streaks from the water pitcher besides us. Julia wipes her brow with a white paper napkin, but still, I shuffle.

A single mystery is an endless rainstorm, a question leading to another and another, a torrent that floods all reason. The terrible thing that punctuated their lives cannot be reversed. Perhaps they'll find answers as to what happened, but they will find no comfort. Death is permanent. This is all arithmetic. It's a pattern. A sequence, and we have to calculate what's been established for us. There's always an answer. We just have to look at what the numbers have provided.

"I didn't know people could use Lotería like this," Julia says.

Gael remains silent. He was the one who called me and asked if I would read for them this evening. He said it was urgent. I agreed, because I have time. We all have time. We just have to carve it out from the weight of our existence.

I eye them and don't say anything, because it's true, Lotería is a game of chance, its position influenced by the randomizing effect—the shuffling of cards. There's not much skill here.

When used in divination, the same principals as the Eurocentric tarot applies, a single person shuffles the cards. Once they feel the shuffling is sufficient, they stop and pull a series of cards from the top of the deck and lay them down flat in front of the querent, the person for whom the reading is taking place. The order of the spread varies. In tarot, there are simple spreads, like a single card, three card, Celtic Cross, horseshoe and so on.

A single card reading often yields a simple yes or no response, a quick answer for a simple question.

With Lotería, I always turn to a three-card spread, with the card on the left representing the past and all of the events that have led the person to where they are today. The card in the center represents the present, including all actions and states of mind. Finally, the card on the right speaks to the future, the current path of the situation. But as we know, all futures can change.

Any path can be diverted. Any path can be adjusted. Our futures are not static. We just need to be in command of the information we have. There is no great beating drum signaling the finality of our course. We are destined for nothing and everything, all the same. All possibilities exist as one.

"Did you play this game when you were little?" Julia says. Her fingers are wrapped around the strap of her purse, twisting and tightening it. She's nervous. She should be.

"Yes," I say, still shuffling. I must have been nine years old the first time I played it. I remember the pictures on the cards terrified me. I was immediately drawn to them, because they are so colorful, but as I flipped through them I grew scared, and not even of the obvious ones that you'd think a child would be afraid of like the El Diablito, or El Alacrán, but I was frightened of cards like El Cotorro, La Chalupa, El Venado, and others. "Something about the images just seemed…" I paused, not wanting to say what I really felt, because my feelings didn't matter in any of this. It didn't matter that these images seemed fixed to a point that did not exist.

"Haunting," Julia offered.

"Sure," I say. There is something curious about the Lotería cards, their numbering system, their design, their history. So much is known, yet so much remains muddled. The pictures are iconic, including that of El Corazon, El Borracho, and La Sirena. These pictures have stepped off of their cards, and into the hands of products and marketing— plastered on T-Shirts painted on restaurant walls and more. The images, and their corresponding numbers, hold power. There's a mystical design here that I cannot explain, but that I accept, because I've seen what the cards can do for me. The cards can be used simply as a game, or with caution to divine.

I wanted to keep this simple. I needed to keep this simple. I never wanted to be seen as anything more than I was, just someone here to analyze the information presented, to note the pattern, find the calculation and present the solution. Beyond that, I could not get wrapped up in their lives, even though I felt like I somehow already was. Julia reaches for Gael's hand, but he rejects it.

My purpose is not in solving other people's puzzles. I already had a great puzzle at home waiting for me that was destined to be my end. My drive, my obsession was in picking apart the clues and presenting the answer. All good mysteries follow a staggering path which we must be committed to walking. All good detectives think of themselves as devoted to the craft of detecting, following the direction of Edgar Allan Poe's C. Auguste Dupin, I suppose. Maybe in some ways I'm like him, that fictional detective obsessing over problems.

"Do you have children?" Julia asks.

"No," I say. I know I'd never have children. Even the possibility of having them had been taken from me. I didn't offer that both of the people standing before me reminded so much of my own parents, my loving father and cold stepmother mother who never wanted me.

I stop shuffling, sensing it was time. "No partner. No kids. Just my job here at the coffee shop. My studies, and math."

"Your Aunt Angie said that," Gael said.

My Aunt Angie was the one who introduced me to Lotería. It was also my Aunt Angie who was very worried about me retreating into the city, into this job, and really into the labyrinth of numbers that consumed, but yet saved, my life.

Aunt Angie believed that I should be careful and cautious. She would tell me things like: "Our stories are always in movement, even when we think they aren't. For we never truly end."

When I was a little girl, it was Aunt Angie who noticed things at home were not right. Of course, she could detect the cruelty threaded within the fibers of her older sister.

"I know your mom can sometimes not be so nice. If you ever need to call me for anything you can."

Growing up, we only had one telephone and that was in the kitchen. It was mounted on the wall and had a long twisty cord. If mom saw me on the phone, she would surely get mad. She got mad about everything else. The safest place in my house was outside in the garden. There we had palm trees and a pine tree, beautiful hanging roses that stretched across a trail of trellises, healing cacti, and more. One day, I discovered a massive flowerpot decorated with bright blue, green, red, and yellow tile, with the markings of fish and arrows in the middle of our garden.

I asked father what would be going in it, and he said a new tree. The next day, when dad was away mom got mad at me for dropping a plate of sliced pears. Her rage flashed behind her eyes, and it was as if that ticking clock had finally stopped.

I rushed out to the garden and hid behind the colorful new planter. My heart pounded in my chest, and I was so scared that I couldn't even close my eyes, so I focused on the colors on the ceramic pot before me, hoping somehow that those shapes could protect me. I started to count because that's all I could do in that moment. I counted the birds, fish, and trees along the surface.

I heard mom murmur under her breath that she was going to kill me and make the flowerpot my grave if I didn't appear right away.

I stayed hiding until dad came home later that night. She would never get mad at me in front of dad. I thought about calling Aunt Angie when dad came home, but I was too scared, and hoped the next day things would get better, but they didn't.

I no longer speak with my parents. The only person I keep in contact with is Aunt Angie. She worries I don't have friends. She worries I don't have a partner. She worries that my entire life has been devoted to these cards, and numbers, and that great problem that waits for me at home each day. I stressed to Aunt Angie that the only reason I was here was because of her, because she told me to hold on to the numbers and to think of the story unfolding when I was in that deep well of worry, and I did. I hold on to that sequence and followed the pattern, and here I am. She says some things can't be explained, but I disagree. Everything can and should be explained. We're a seeking a solution to the problem haunting our life.

Numbers and their synchronicities dotted my life. Me and my parents for example all celebrated birthdays on the fourth of our birth months, March 4th, April 4th, and mine, May 4th. In summer I remember clearly sitting beneath the pine tree in our garden in a hat to further shield my face from the sun, searching for patterns in our garden, because even in nature one can identify the magic of numbers. Even after that awful day with my mother, my curiosity with the power of numbers continued to grow and evolve, moving further into complex math equations, formulas, and now my drive has settled into solving the impossible problem, because in a way, I suppose, my existence here is impossible too.

"My daughter and I used to play this game," Gael said.

I didn't offer anything, because I didn't matter in this, but yes, I would play this game too with my father. We all did. For holidays. When it was too cold to go outside. We would gather the game pieces, and we would sit around the living room table, assign a caller and proceed. I haven't played the game the way it was intended to be played for leisure in many years. I had been cursed, in a way, to utilize the cards in a different way, to tell people about the things unfolding in their past, present, and future. I had become swept up in the cards, and it was because of them I was held together.

I blame my attuned Aunt Angie for spotting it. I remember being very young and her telling me that she saw me trapped in an endless loop. Mother didn't like her sister, but she tolerated Aunt Angie. We rarely visited her house, but when we did I would be enchanted by the sweet and smokey smells of floral incense, mesmerized by the chunks of colorful crystals lining her windowsills, and would be curious by the amber colored bottles full of liquids and dried plants and flowers overflowing in the hutch in her living room. Mother called Aunt Angie a bruja, but Aunt Angie would correct her each and every time and say she was a curandera, a healer.

"My only job is to heal, to seal those fissures where the pain seeps in and out," Aunt Angie would say when mom called her a bruja. And that is exactly what she did for me, and it's because of that why she sends people here so that I can read their Lotería cards, and in a way provide them with healing too. Those of us who can heal are an impossibility ourselves, existing neither here nor there, occupying a space that cannot fully be realized.

Aunt Angie tells them I'm special, that I exist in this in between place, and maybe I do, and maybe that's why I need the solution to this great spiral that consumes my life. I need the solution to this pattern, and I don't know why. I wonder, if I find the solution of the endless repetition then will things end?

"Remember to find your way back. Stay on the path and go around and around."

Aunt Angie would say this to me, especially when I would spend the night with her when she babysat me. Of course, I felt safe with Dad, but I never felt safe around Mom. And if Mom was in the house, I tried to be wherever she wasn't in our home.

"Remember to find your way back. Stay on the path and go around and around."

I thought of Hansel and Gretel, a little brother and a little sister who were discarded away in a dark forest by their father and wicked stepmother. And who then broke off pieces of bread and scattered the bits along their path so that they could find their way back home along the trail. But when they returned to the path, the birds had eaten all of the breadcrumbs, making their return much more difficult because they could not remember the way. What I didn't realize then was that Aunt Angie's words:

"Remember to find your way back. Stay on the path and go around and around," were like those scattered breadcrumbs, a way for me to find my way back here.

"Our daughter's name was Rosa as well," Gael offered.

A striking coincidence. I hadn't asked the daughter's name. I wanted to know as little as possible, but still, Gael offered.

"I'd like to think that she'd grow up to be like you, smart, studying to be an academic," he said. "I would love that very much for my daughter."

Julia said: "It seems like she was just here. Her room is the same as that last day we saw her. It was the day of her nineth birthday. I had laid out a pair of jeans and a blue top with rainbows all down the front for her to wear. When I called to her to come get dressed she didn't answer. I looked everywhere in the house. I moved from room to room, listening for her. Sometimes I would find her, standing and looking out the window, counting the clouds or the birds that flew by. She was always counting. Lost in numbers. Then I looked in the garden. And when I didn't find her there I knew there was something wrong."

Gael finally spoke. "She's been missing for five years now."

There was no comfort that I could provide here. I assumed even this, me standing here, a grown woman with the same name as their missing daughter stirred a series of heavy emotions. I remained silent, as I placed the deck of cards on the counter.

I believed it was all synchronicity, two simultaneous occurring events seemingly related, but having no true connection. What most people assumed to be superstitious or paranormal activity was often just synchronicity. And while these coincidences were interesting and could make one take pause to consider their nature, there really was no truth that there was anything occurring in the natural realm other than just two events happening at the same time. So many possibilities existing together. There are an infinite number of activities unfolding at any given time, so similarities between variables shouldn't surprise any of us, even though it still often did.

I know these parents came to me for the same reason others did. I don't cheat. I don't lie. I'm horrible at both. They came here because they want to trust and believe that I can provide them some relief. I hope I can, but ultimately, the cards will show themselves and their numbers will outline the story.

Still, my brain is forever occupied with my real work, my true work that is ongoing at home, that the truth is my default because it's easier to keep track of than a lie that could twist and tangle into chaos. And I do not like chaos.

We are forced to remember so many facts; dates, numbers, times, events, appointments. It's all numbers. All of this. Me and these parents before me, and even these cards. Yet, I prefer order, design, patterns, and rules. I prefer numbers over people.

Numbers can't hurt you.

People hurt you.

Zero. One. Two. Three. Four. And on and on. Stretched on to infinity, the number of things that we pile on, wrap around us to feel a sense of importance, to feel alive. To grasp on to order, because order gives us calm. Order helps us feel safe. Order helps us to feel alive. The cards know that we're alive, that's what Aunt Angie told me. When Aunt Angie handed me the Lotería cards one night she was babysitting me she told me that the cards and the numbers within would save me from the awful thing in my house. I just needed to:

"Remember to find your way back. Stay on the path and go around and around."

Aunt Angie never really did explain what that meant, and I never did ask her for an explanation. I supposed the true meaning of it all was hanging there somewhere, waiting for me to find it within a pattern. It was just another problem waiting to be solved.

I looked to the stack of cards before us, and all of the pressure was on me now. People wanted to believe in me so much, and in doing this, I wanted to believe in me as well. But I knew all of this was random, all confined to the number of cards in the deck and the amount of times I had shuffled.

As I shuffled I tried to at least keep my thoughts fixed on the people before me, wondering; What is it that they want to know? Most people's questions were predictable:

Who loves me?
I can answer that simply—no one truly.

Is my lover unfaithful?
Of course! None of us really belong to anyone.

Do I have riches coming?
No, you will live the life of a pauper.

When will I die?
You're already dead.

Sometimes people will ask me: "What really matters?"

And I'll respond truthfully: "Numbers matter. The numbers are never false. There's no separating a digit from its very nature. A number will behave according to its rules, or the rules outlined in the formula or problem for which it finds itself."

For us however, for people, we are much more malleable. We bend and take shape, play and form. There's no trusting who we really are and what we really need or aspire to be.

None of us are reliable.

I told Julia and Gael that they could trust me, and so they do for some silly reason. Two people who are suffering and who have nowhere else to go. Police can't provide them solutions. Private detectives they've hired, and paid thousands of dollars to, cannot give them an answer. No one can explain why their daughter Rosa was one day in their house, and why then one day she vanished.

I might not be able to provide them with all of the answers they seek, but me, the cards, their images and their numbers can provide them with something. Myself and the cards can offer a nudge, a shape, a form, a series of numerics that can be interpreted somehow.

And those numbers, 0, 1, 2, 3, 4, 5, 6, 7, 8, 9 and 0, presented as their whole or strung together to form a larger value, they can't lie, even if they wanted to. The rules are simple. I don't care for complicated rules, because complication brings anxiety, and it's cruel to make anyone worry any further.

We give meaning to things. We discern the pattern. There is no pattern unless we announce it exists. Maybe there is no pattern. Maybe this is all chaos.

It's only a game.
A card game.
Something simple.
Without stress.
Without worry.
I shuffle.

I stop.

I pull one card from the top of the deck, turn it over and face it up.
Past.
I do this for the next card, placing it to the right of the first card.
Present.
Finally, I take the last card, and set it down to the right of the present
cart.
Future.
Past. Present. Future.

A story told before us in numbers and pictures

Past: The Arrows / Las Jaras / Card number 31
Present: The Rose / La Rosa / Card number 41
Future: The Flowerpot / La Maceta / Card number 52

The reading follows the order of the images, and I recite the words
to each card's corresponding song.

Past: "The arrows strike where they hit."
Present: "Rosita, come, I want you here now."
Future: "They who are born to be a flowerpot do not go beyond the
hallway."

There's silence across the counter. A knowing, and lingering look
between the two parents.

"We called her Rosita," Gael says. He shifts his weight and takes a small step further away from Julia.

"And what of the numbers?" I ask, because the numbers always mean something.

"We started the adoption process when she was three years old. We brought her home when she was four years old. She went missing when she was nine years old."

I look at the last two cards, 41 and 52. The first number in each is four and five. Four and five. The sum is nine. The numbers always tell us a story.

"There's a pattern here," I say, scanning the cards. "There's something to do with a strike and a flowerpot. That's really all I can see here right now."

"I don't believe in any of this," Julia turns to Gael.

He takes a deep breath, his gaze remaining on the cards. "None of this tells us where she is."

I sigh. "I can only tell you what the cards show me."

"You're an awful psychic," Julia says.

"I'm not a psychic."

"Well, you're an awful tarot reader."

"Do these look like tarot cards? I don't touch tarot."

I feel a sharp pain at the top of my head. It radiates down my face. My hands reach up to my forehead, and I pull them away and stare at my palms, unsure why I'm even staring. I feel like I've been pulled away from the current reality, for just a moment. It's like déjà vu or something else. A calling. A reminder. A memory even. And just as quickly as that cloudy moment appears it's gone. The pain in my head. The confusion. It's all gone.

I return to Julia and Gael. "I just tell you what it is I see in the cards and you're seeing the same thing as I; a strike, the rose, the flowerpot.

I feel angry, and I don't know why. Perhaps because I was being questioned, and I did not lie. The cards did not lie. I had known enough deceit in my existence and would not deceive anyone. They look to one another again, searching for a reason or for a meaning for why they are even here.

"How much?" Gael asked.

I am insulted. "I don't charge for this. I only read for who my Aunt Angie sends me. That's it. I do this because it brings people comfort."

For a long time, I didn't want to believe in the cards, and at times I still struggle to believe in them. I thought it was sad for people to turn to superstition, legend, and folklore to provide them the answers they seek. I wanted to believe that the supernatural is not real, that ghosts weren't real. Nor vampires or werewolves or lumbering creatures lurking in the dark, stalking us. I wanted to believe that urban legends are just that, legends, children's stories, silly little fables, and delectable tales to explain away all of the awful things that happen in the world.

I believed that we should only accept fact, reason, and logic, not feelings or hunches, or beliefs that have been whispered from person to person across ages. But it was my Aunt Angie who taught me that I could believe in both numbers and superstition, that each carried power. It was also my Aunt Angie who encouraged that I share this gift with others. People would come to the coffee shop moments before closing, and they'd linger by the counter, waiting for me to make eye contact and when they'd ask: "Are you Rosa? Who reads the Lotería?" At first I'd roll my eyes and say no, but then they'd beg. A human desperate for an answer is the most miserable presence. And so, I'd shuffle, and I'd spread the cards and I'd recite the words to their songs, and allow them to interpret the order of the images and the corresponding calls at their will. It was not my job to make sense of the problems that hung over their life.

Perhaps I should have said no the first time and every time since, but I didn't, so it's equally my fault. I too have allowed myself to fall into a pattern, all because at some level I wanted to help. When I'm not here working at this coffee shop, I'm at home working on my dissertation. My life in mathematics in higher education has taken me from lattice reduction algorithms, to measures and integration, Fuchsian groups, symmetric presentations, Tribonacci convolution triangles, modern cryptography, construction of finite groups, simple and semi-simple Artinian rings, making models with Bayes, and more.

So much more.

Numbers exist in all of nature, in all of the universe. Everything is an equation begging to be solved, just like our life's problems.

The fact that I couldn't turn Julia and Gael away only confirmed my own flaws, that I am too afraid to hurt people, even though I had been hurt severely in my past. And perhaps because I had been hurt, I knew what it was like to live, or not live, with lingering pain. I knew what it was like to exist with this twisting yearn of never having answered all of the problems I had set out to map and solve. And so, they'd come, and I'd listen, and I'd shuffle, and we'd watch in silence as one by one a strange, yet familiar picture was presented. I would state the riddle and they would wander off into the night, satisfied or depressed by whatever they had experienced.

"Are you...sure?" Julia pressed.

"Yes," I snapped because I knew the moment she walked in the door that I did not like her. She had no redeeming qualities, just like my mother.

Julia exited first, leaving Gael there, stunned and staring at the cards.

"I miss her," he said, and I knew I couldn't offer any comfort in that moment other than with my silence and so I listened.

"Julia was never really kind to Rosita, and I knew that, but I ignored it. Maybe it's as much my fault as it is Julia's. I should have never left Julia alone with Rosita so long. I just knew..." He took a deep breath and rolled his head back, staring at the ceiling before meeting my eyes. "I just knew that something bad would happen, and it did. I came home one day from work and my daughter was gone, the little girl I promised to protect, she was gone, and while Julia cried and helped with the searches and posting the missing person's posters throughout the city, and speaking at interviews, and whatever program we could get on for attention, for Rosita, I always knew something was off about Julia's demeanor." Gael took a deep breath, exhaled and said: "Julia seemed almost relieved that Rosita was gone."

Gael pointed a finger at the Lotería card of the flowerpot. "She loved that beautiful flowerpot I had just purchased. She would hide behind it. Her and I planned on planting a tree there together. I never got the chance to do that with her. Julia went ahead and planted a tree there days after Rosita went missing.

AT HOME, I KICK my shoes off besides the door and hang up my bag. My apartment is bare. A studio. A bed. A nightstand. Plain clothes in the closet. Simple foods in the refrigerator. All of the things without complication. None of that mattered to me, when a great unknown galaxy danced above us with millions of questions and millions of answers pressing to be presented.

I sit at my computer preparing once again to search for the impossible solution I was cautioned to stay away from. In undergrad, and now graduate school, I was told that this is a siren song, ready to pull me away and drag me deep down into watery depths from which I will never appear. I was warned that by falling into this I would never do meaningful work again, but this was meaningful work. Sometimes the work that would define our lives was also the same work that would come to define our madness.

It's funny how our present sometimes holds glimmers of our past. I feel safe here, sitting and staring at the computer screen. I feel the same sort of comfort here in this quiet as I did when I was a little girl, alone and in silence in my room, working out math problems, because math problems didn't call you names or scream at you.

Yet, here and now I was placing my very existence at risk. I needed answers. Everything could be lost, my doctoral dissertation, my life, all because of my obsession that blossomed and bloomed in a spiral of numbers.

If there's anything I'm good at, it's not listening to warnings. And so, I allowed myself to fall, and here I now am. This is where I spend all of my time when I'm not at the coffee shop, searching and scanning infinity for a magic number I believe can unlock a mystery.

Everyone says it does not exist, but I know it must. There's possibility everywhere. Just like there's possibility in the Lotería cards, in the images and the numbers that are selected when we ask a simple question.

Every number, every possible scenario exists in the universe.

The problem isn't famous. It's infamous. It's whispered in faculty meetings, and when the name of that design, of that pattern is brought up in discussion there's laughter, because many people believe that the Collatz conjecture is an impossible problem, offering only painful consequences to any individual who chooses to work on it.

If you admit that this is something that you are working on, the mathematical world will believe there is something out of place and unsettled within you. Yes, numbers don't lie, just like the numbers of the Lotería cards. But some numbers and some sequences have their solutions tucked within threads that spin into infinity.

Yet, I'll admit, there is something wrong with me. There's a feeling as if being out of place, as if flickering in and out, and I feel it even now sitting here. I can think back to the coffee shop, and I see Gael there and Julia, both of them so vivid, and I see Gael's eyes, pink and watery and Julia's eyes narrowed and hard on the card of the flowerpot. The answers are always out there in the universe waiting to be plucked.

The mathematical problem of Collatz' conjecture sounds like a party trick.

Choose a number.

If the number is even, let's say two or four or six or eight, then divide that number by two.

If the number is odd, say three, or five, or seven, or nine, then multiply that number by three and then add 1.

Then, apply those very same rules to the next number in your calculation.

Let's start with the number 2. Well, based on the formula outlined above we'd get to number 1 fairly quickly.

2 / 2= 1

Let's now start with the number 11. With starting at the number 11 it would take us a few steps, a few operations, but still, we would land at the number 1.

11 X 3 + 1 = 34
34 / 2 = 17
17X3+1 = 52
52/2 = 26
26/2 = 13
13X3+1 = 40
40/2 = 20
20/2 = 10
10/2 = 5
5X3+1 = 16
16/2 = 8
8/2= 4
4/2 = 2
2/2 = 1

No matter the number, even or odd, you will end up at the number one.

Now, what happens if you apply the same rules to the number 1 is that you get trapped in a loop, from 1, 2, 4 and back.

An endless loop of just 1, 2, and 4.

But, it's still a conjecture, and so, we don't know if this opinion is true. Collatz only *believed* that if you start with a positive number and you apply these rules to that number that you will end up in an endless loop. And the reason it's still not proven true or false, is because one would have to test every single number to infinity to prove or disprove it.

There could be a number somewhere that starts a sequence of numbers that grows to infinity. For some reason, that number wouldn't obey the same rules as the other numbers.

Another possibility is that there exists a sequence of numbers that forms a closed loop beyond 1, 2, 4, 4, 2, 1. Mathematicians have tried and tested numbers up to 2^{68}, which is:

$$295,147,905,179,352,825,856$$

Every single number within this number comes back down to one and wraps into that infinite loop. We still haven't found the number that shoots up to infinity or that breaks the loop.

But I had time to go beyond that and more.

So is it true, or is it false? I want to prove that Collatz' conjecture is false, that there's some magical number that shoots up into infinity or an enchanted numeric that breaks free from this loop, this trap, this curse in which these numbers repeat themselves.

I stare at my computer and as it has been for months, it is cycling through another series of numbers, running down past hundreds of thousands of operations. And once again I watch in great disappointment as it reaches the end point of the calculation, back down to the number one. And there at that simple digit it falls victim, trapped in a prison of an infinite loop as the formula was applied back to it.

I watch as the numbers flicker on the screen, and the number 1 goes back to 2 and then 4, returning back on itself.

Its purgatory.

Cursed to repeat.

The computer waits to be fed another number. The last number I had entered before I went into work was the largest verified number in the world, $2^{1000000}$. This number had been verified previously, but of course, I wanted to verify it again. I had to. I scrolled back, checking the data report and found that after almost half a million computations, this number returned back to the number one and again, trapped in a cycle from which it could not break free.

I know the answer is out there. There is an answer for everything. Every question has a solution. There is no impossibility. There is only we have not looked hard enough, long enough, nor verified all sources. There is no great mystery in the world. All answers are reachable. We only need the motivation.

I think back to the Lotería cards from this evening: The Arrows / Las Jaras is 31, La Rosa / Rose is 41, La Maceta / The Flowerpot is 52.

Three. Four. Five.

A sequence. A pattern. I pull out the Lotería cards and place them next to my keyboard. It's silly what I'm about to do, but I'm tired, and to my graduate advisor and department I've already gone mad, so why not embrace it?

I enter in the number 52 and watch as a much shorter sequence than before plays out. It takes the program just a few seconds to cycle through this scenario, applying the same formula and theories, and then I have my string of numbers set out before me. All of the numbers are unique, and they all fall within the frame of the deck of cards in my hand.

I begin searching through the cards, one by one, until I have each selected and placed in order on the desk.

52 – The Flowerpot

26 – The Black Man

13 – The Little Hat

40 – The Scorpion

20 – The Bird

10 – The Tree

5 – The Umbrella

16 – The Flag

8 – The Bottle

4 – The Man

2 – The Little Devil

1 – The Rooster

I laugh to myself, because there is a story here, a narrative played out in pictures. I don't want to say my aunt was right, that superstition had designed any of this, but these images could be interpreted.

I run through each of the numbers, one by one, from number 54 to the number one once again, just to be sure that the number of cards within the deck of the Lotería don't magically point to the solution. I type each number into the computer, hoping that one of them will prove Collatz' conjecture false and break the cycle of the loop. Of course, none of them do, and once again we get to the number 1.

In the cards, the number 1 is represented by The Rooster.

Traditionally the song for The Rooster was: "The one that sang for St. Peter will never sing for him again." I didn't care for the religious identity of the line and so had simplified it for my readings stating simply "The one who sang will never sing again." It was just another way to signal the end of something. Then again, with the Collectz' conjecture, at least the way it stood now, it really didn't end, it just kept folding in on itself, in much the way we did. Because, we wake up each morning and go about our day not really knowing why. We just do these things we are expected to do. In many ways we are all trapped in a loop, and maybe some of us need to be freed from that cycle. I know I needed to be released from the ring I felt confined to. Each day felt like a repetition, and I wanted it to stop.

That night, I slept and dreamed.

I dreamt of a darling little girl seated on a blanket in a wonderous garden bursting with color, reds and greens, yellows and violets. Flowers vibrating with color. Leaves large and luminous against a brilliant sky. It was so bright outside her face was a shock of bright white from the intensity of the sun. In her chubby little hands she had gathered dandelions and had reached them out to me. Her lips moved but I could hear nothing. The world was silent. I took the dandelions in my hand and she smiled, very pleased. Beside her was a plate of watermelon and another with several prickly ears of cactus. She reached for a piece of cactus, larger than her hand, the needles pressing and puncturing deep into her skin. She moved the plant to her lips, opened her mouth and bit down and chewed. Her smile was a mash of green material, needles and blood.

IN THE MORNING, I ride my bike to the coffee shop and as soon as I open the door there is a line of people still asleep and stunted by the problems they fell asleep with and carried over into the morning. Many people seem angry when they order their coffee, the disaffected looks betraying nothing of the misery they have for their life and their upcoming day. They will down the caffeine, be jolted for a few minutes by the chemicals coursing through their blood and they will continue on, exhausted and upset that life did not turn out the way they had hoped, but here's what's curious; for those people who are upset for how their life turned out, did they ever even have a plan mapped out for what they wanted? For who they wanted to be? Did they ever speak into existence all of the things they hoped to accomplish, hold and have?

That's the true tragedy.

People are so angry because they say they don't have what they want. Yet they've yet to determine what it is they do want. It's that simple operation, a simple calculation that we must determine, but many of us don't, and so we are caught in this endless loop of misery.

The morning rushes by with a series of;

- Cappuccinos
- Espressos
- Flat whites
- Lattes
- Cold brews
- Black coffees
- Teas
- Anything with an extra shot of espresso
- Anything overly sweet with very little semblance to an actual cup of coffee

I could tell almost before someone opened their mouth what it was they were going to order by the way they looked at me or didn't, the way they fumbled around for their form of payment, where in their line of sight was their cell phone.

The morning dwindled from those eager to arrive to their offices before anyone else, to those that don't care what time they start work, to the parents with children in tug on their way to school, to those parents who preferred to get their coffee after school drop off, to those people who worked freelance and arrived late in the morning. I found myself with some quiet during that moment between late morning to early afternoon when people arrive for a second cup, or parents arrive before school pick up.

It is in those moments where I can work on calculations or slowly add to my dissertation:

Lothar Collatz posed the conjecture in the 1930s. Someone's intuition may say that the number you start off with will affect the number you end up with, but that is not the case. Collatz conjectured that if you start with a positive whole number and run the operation long enough, anywhere you start will lead to 1, and then once you hit number 1 and apply those same rules again, you will be confined to an infinite loop of 1, 4, 2, 1, 4, 2, 1.

I pause writing and turn to the Lotería cards once more.

Darkness drapes the windows, and I realize it is night outside. I'm holding the Lotería cards in my other hand and I do not recall what my intention was in handling them, and so, I pull three cards:

One. Four. Two.

One is El Gallo / The Rooster
Four is El Hombre / The Man
Two is El Diablito / The Little Devil

The pattern. It's there. I just need to read it.

One. Four. Two. One. Four. Two. One.

The rooster. The man. The devil. The man. The devil. The rooster.

As I go to lock the doors to the coffee shop, I find Gael standing outside.

"I'm sorry," I say. "I was just about to lock up. Did you need something?"

"Just one card," he says, his eyes are again pink and watery, a perpetual state of mourning. "I just have one question to ask."

Inside I stand behind the counter and gather the cards. I ask him for his question, and he says:

"Was it Julia?"

I shuffle. I think. I pull the card and place it down on the counter.

La Dama. The Woman.

I open my mouth to recite the accompanying song, but Gael shakes his head.

"There's no need. I have my answer," he says.

It's late. I'm tired. I'm confused and unsure of what exactly is happening here and so I ask: "What do you mean, 'Was it Julia?'"

He wipes away at his eyes and then shoves his hands in his pockets. "I asked if my wife murdered our daughter."

Gael pauses at the door, turns to me and says: "There's something about you that reminds me very much of my Rosita. I wonder sometimes if the universe bends in on itself, showing us what we want to see, what we should have seen. Some days feel like they're repeating themselves. Sometimes I feel as if I'm stuck in this awful loop, damned to repeat each painful day."

Gael takes a deep breath and sighs. "But it's only a game, right, Rosita? Lotería. All of this. Life. It's all a game."

At home that night, I wake to the computer beeping, alerting once again that it had whittled down another sequence and that once again, I failed. We were right back at the number one and again caught in that loop, that trap, that place of damnation, repeating itself.

I wondered then, is that what life was for some of us? A curse meant to be repeated? Ourselves trapped in an endless cycle reliving our pain, our suffering.

It was then that the numbers appeared to me. They had always been there, tucked within my memories. I don't know why it took me so long to recall them. A simple sequence of digits that I had not yet input into the computer. I place my fingers on the keyboard. I type the numbers in slowly, number by number and then hit enter.

I watch as the computer begins its operation, wrapping through the series of calculations. I sit patiently there in the night, because there is nothing left to do, but wait. I gaze at the numbers spread before me like the stars above punched into the night sky.

When the final number appears, the number 1, I watch and wait to see if it will repeat again, that loop of 1, 4, 2, 4, 2, 1, but it does not. I gasp as the numbers begin to shoot up, stretching and reaching as I hoped, as I suspected into infinity, numeric by numeric and it is beautiful and it is glorious, and then there is a loud beep from my computer. I scream as the numbers pause and then tumble, sinking down back to my prison, and then it is like a great door opening, and my memories rocket me back to my childhood, back to my garden, back to my beginning...

There is my mother, Julia, and there is the flowerpot, and I am shouting for my father, the very man I had just seen in the coffee shop hours ago, Gael, but I am not a woman. I am a child, his and Julia's child. I look up and find Julia holding a knife above my head. I scream as the blade comes crashing down on me with the weight of eternity.

I stumble back.

I reach up into my curls and I feel something wet.

I pull my hands away and look at them, and all I see is blurred and red.

In that moment, I am scared. I am alone, and as I open my mouth to scream, to cry, to call for my father I hear the words of my Aunt Angie begging me, pleading with me:

"Remember to find your way back. Stay on the path and go around and around."

I think of the numbers spiraling on my computer screen, and that is what I would do. I stay on the path. I go around and around, trapped in a loop myself, like Collatz' conjecture. There is a way to solve his great question, but it peers into the pain of reality, of our human cruelty. For this is all a game. Life. A wicked game of chance.

I hear my Aunt Angie so clearly now:

"Say it," I hear my Aunt Angie say.

"It's only a game," I say.

"Say it again," she says.

I repeat her words.

I hear her, in that faraway, never where place. It's an echo. A memory. A whisper.

"Remember to find your way back. Stay on the path and go around and around."

I look down and see the Lotería cards in my hand.

ACKNOWLEDGEMENTS

Thank you to Jason Pinter at Polis Books for bringing *Lotería* back to print.

Thank you also to Gerardo Pelayo and my children, Lane Heymont, Chantelle Aimée Osman, Michael J. Seidlinger, Hailey Piper, Karmen Wells, Kealan Patrick Burke, and everyone else who helped support this re-release. Thank you to everyone who read the original *Lotería*, who have read the new version, and thank you to those of you who have read any of my writing.

THE
SHOEMAKER'S
MAGICIAN

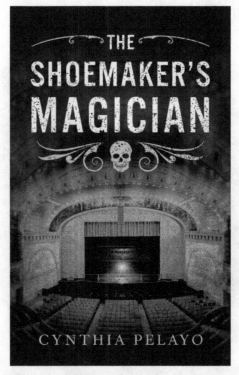

CHAPTER 1

THURSDAY EVENING: SEBASTIAN

Another murder.

A homicide. And what is a homicide but the intended and calculated killing of another person? There are so many ways to describe the methods and madness in which a human being can kill another. Homicide. Murder. Manslaughter. And we can break down the category of manslaughter even further with voluntary, involuntary, and vehicular. How prescriptive. As if any of those terms lessens the fact that someone's life was ultimately ended by someone else.

In all cases, we still have a body, like the one splayed before me. Arms and legs stretched out like Leonardo da Vinci's Vitruvian Man, or maybe like a snow angel. Or, perhaps, given the venue we are standing in, like a star.

I'm standing on the stage looking out at tiered rows of red-cushioned seats that stretch from the base of the stage to the exit doors in the back. Above, are more empty seats.

"What's that level called?" I point my chin in the direction of the multilevel balcony.

Detective Gutierrez is looking down at his dark wool jacket, dusting off snowflakes. He reaches down and then brushes away any snow remaining on his slacks. Like me, he's still wearing his outside gloves. It's his first week on homicide and he already looks the part, nice dark pressed suit, dark jacket, dark dress shoes. We look like a couple of morticians standing next to each other.

"You're going to get snow all over our crime scene," I say.

He shoots me a narrow look. "It's Chicago in January, Ramos. There's no escaping this stuff."

This is true.

Gutierrez takes a step downstage and points with one hand while loosening his black scarf with the other. "The level right above the main floor is the mezzanine, or box level. That's the middle. Then right above that you've got the dress circle or first balcony."

When Gutierrez got promoted to homicide, I knew I'd like working with him. He seems to know a little bit about everything, no matter how obscure, and if he doesn't know it, he'll figure it out.

I glance down at the mess around us, making sure to not step in anything that's going to get bagged or tagged later. I start removing my gloves to trade them in for latex. I'm trying to process what he said. Mezzanine. Dress circle. Balcony. I can feel the muscles in my neck stiffening. "What?"

He clears his throat. "The third floor is called the mezzanine level. The fourth floor is called the dress circle or first balcony. The level right above that is called the upper balcony."

Sometimes Gutierrez overcomplicates things. "Three balconies. Got it."

The auditorium is wider than it is tall, and there's so much red everywhere. Not just the seats, but the heavy, crimson curtains draped around exit doors and archways. The ceiling is a burst of gold, with hand-painted murals, and all along the cream-colored walls are decorative ornamental designs, floral medallions, cornice moldings, arches, and columns. That much

I knew because I know Chicago architecture. It's a passion. This town is a passion, and the historic Chicago Theater is a work of art.

Massive bronze crystal chandeliers hang along the space, highlighting the murals looking down on us. They remind me of blue, red, green, and gold stained glass that wraps around some churches. Pictures meant to tell a story.

I turn my back to the empty seats to face the reason we're all here tonight.

I've seen a lot of death, people frozen dead in alleys, kids stuffed in trashcans, torsos in abandoned buildings, gunshot victims still clutching their wounds where they took their last breath on a sidewalk, and more. Always so much more to look back on; a collection of people obliterated. I especially hate it when we have to pull someone out of the Chicago River. Bloated limbs. Skin slippage. Oozing.

It's a horror show.

Now, this. I cannot even begin to piece together the type of person that could and would want to do this. Perhaps the word "piece" here is insensitive. I can already feel Gutierrez's eyes on me, but I don't know what to say. This is an awful end, lying in one's own piss, shit, and blood, where just outside a bright marquee highlighted State Street. Right now, an audience should be speaking in hushed tones, above the crackle of snack bags, as the curtain is pulled back and performers hit the stage, and not me standing here staring down another body.

"Are those Reese's Pieces?" Gutierrez is shoving his winter gloves in his coat pocket now.

I nod. All of that candy makes this seem even more surreal.

We hear the doors leading to the lobby open. My gaze remains fixed on the yellow, orange, and brown discs of candy sprinkled atop and around the butchered corpse still wearing the bottom half of their theater manager uniform.

Boxes of M&Ms, Skittles, Snickers, Sour Patch Kids, and Twizzlers were emptied on the stage, their contents soaking in the thick red liquid on the floor.

"Dammit," I say through clenched teeth.

"What?" Gutierrez asks.

"Twizzlers are my favorite, and this asshole has gone and ruined them for me."

Puddles of liquid had spilled out from soda cans that were opened and tossed across the stage, and then there's popcorn. It's everywhere like confetti.

When we arrived at the entrance of the theater, Officer Jones and his partner Officer Delgado insisted we dig out plastic coverings from our car and slip them on our shoes. I figured, okay, maybe there's a little blood. Maybe there's shell casings. What I didn't expect was that there'd be corn kernels everywhere. Every step we take there's another crunch beneath our feet as we walk carefully across the hardwood floor.

"What's that smell?" Gutierrez asks.

"Buttered popcorn and urine," I say a little too quickly, but then catch a hint of something else. Wood polish. "Smells like the floor was just polished recently."

"Detective Ramos..." one of the uniforms below the stage says. I can already tell by the dazed look on Officer Jones's face, the sheen above his upper lip, and between the heat from the lights above and the smells of chocolate and popcorn mixed with fecal matter that he's not going to be able to hold it in much longer. I can always tell a rookie by how quickly their color shifts when they see a body for the first time.

"Jones!" his partner calls behind him as she sees him sway. She grabs his shoulder, spins him around, and lets go just as Jones vomits down the front of his jacket, covering his badge.

I tilt my head to the ceiling and let out a heavy sign. This is going to be a long night. I focus on Officer Delgado. "Get your partner back to the station."

Gutierrez has got a stupid grin on his face. "The show's obviously canceled tonight, right?"

"The show never ends for us," I say. "We gotta get those people out of here," I say, referring to the crowd standing outside in the negative wind chill on State Street.

I look around, searching for my new friend. "Officer Delgado!"

"Yeah, detective?" She's by the exit doors now, holding one door open as Officer Jones exits.

I shout. "None of those people outside entered the building, right?"

"Right, detective. They were all lined up waiting for the doors to open."

From behind me, Gutierrez says, "Are you really going to have them put up yellow tape all along the outside of the theater?"

I turn around and eye him. "You got a better idea?"

He lowers his eyes back to the mess we need to deal with, and I know what he's thinking. Downtown. Tourists. Media attention. And especially after last year, the mayor is not going to be happy.

"Delgado!" I call once more. "Are you sure everything inside has been secured as well?"

She hesitates. "It's a huge space. We'll double check we got everything."

"Your team better triple check, because this is gonna be a…" I pause, looking around. Then groan. "This is gonna be a thing." We all know what that means. McCarthy, the mayor, and the media, our three favorite M's, are going to be all over this within the next few minutes.

Officers Delgado and Jones exit the theater as more uniforms enter.

I hear Gutierrez's phone start vibrating, one text after the other. I'm sure it's Commander McCarthy on his way, probably texting while speeding through red lights, trying to hurry up and get here to try to control this situation, but it's already out of control.

Gutierrez reaches for his phone and confirms my suspicion. "McCarthy's on his way," he says, and shoves his phone back in his jacket.

With each text alert's buzz, I can sense McCarthy's blood pressure increasing. Then the noise stops.

"Either he's parking, or he finally had that heart attack he said we've all been trying to give him," I say, patting my coat pockets, wondering why he hadn't messaged me, but my empty pockets give me my answer. "I think I left my phone in the car."

"And your gloves too." Gutierrez hands me a pair of latex gloves.

He's already turning out to be the best work husband I could ask for. My last partner lasted less than a year, but maybe Gutierrez will hang around a little longer, considering all the good work he did in Humboldt Park last year.

"Guess I should message Hector?" Gutierrez says.

I slip on the gloves and say, "I think you need to text Hector and tell him we're not going to be home for a while."

"Already on it," he says, tapping away at his screen.

"Can you let Polly know for me?"

"Letting her know too."

This is the feature program for our evening, and probably for the next few nights. I know by looking at the scene that this isn't the work of a disgruntled employee or an upset theatergoer. This goes far beyond what I've ever seen in my decade on the job. This is dramatic. This is deviant. This is disturbed.

I look up to the last point that the theater manager saw before she died, a collection of bright stage lights that are managed by the control booth above the balcony. This woman bled out front stage center to an empty house. Who wants to die at work, especially like this?

"You said when we parked you got engaged here," Gutierrez says.

"*Phantom of the Opera* during intermission. It was December of 1999. Days before all of that Y2K insanity."

Like a good detective he already had his small notebook out ready to record details. "Sounds like it was special."

"It was. We were kids. Eighteen and nineteen."

"And now this…" Gutierrez kneels, careful to not get in the mess. "I can't even begin to guess what did this."

The white name tag which had likely originally been pinned to the front of her black jacket read Robin Betancourt. It was now pressed into her open right palm.

Gutierrez stood. "A scalpel. There's definitely at least some surgical training."

"Maybe, or lots of YouTube videos," I say, taking in the shape and skill of the Y incision, a deep line beginning at the top of each shoulder and running down the chest to just above Robin's pubic bone. An autopsy cut. The flaps of skin were pulled back to expose the entire chest cavity, for easy display of the lungs, liver, intestines, and more. The killer pulled back the flesh from her chest and then pinned it into her armpits so that all would remain exposed.

"YouTube videos about how to do an autopsy?"

"There's something for everybody on the internet," I say.

"What do you make of that?" Gutierrez motions to what I assume are her jacket and shirt, folded neatly next to the steps leading up to the stage.

"He probably had a gun and orders her to the stage. At first maybe she thinks it's a robbery or a sexual assault, but this is neither. He demands she remove her jacket, then shirt, and then bra. The killer wants all of her exposed."

Gutierrez takes a step back, kicking an M&M that rolls off the stage. "Our killer's creative."

The medical examiner is not going to be happy with this one, especially since part of their job has been started for them. No one expects to receive a body with a post-mortem examination in progress.

"Do you think she was dead first?" Gutierrez asks, and I know he doesn't want the answer. I don't even want to begin to think of the terror Robin lived through in her final moments, experiencing her chest cavity being hacked away and pinned back onto herself.

The sprays of blood, like red glitter, stretching far across the floor suggest her heart was still beating furiously as she was being ripped open. The victim was conscious as her flesh was opened like a curtain. The pain must have been excruciating, and I can only hope that shock, that biological wave of confusion, punctuated by a rapid heartbeat, cold sweat, and dizziness carried her away before she died from the deep gash that nearly decapitated her.

"What do you think did that?" I say of the wound in her neck. I scan the stage and then add, "Never mind. Looks like they used the popcorn scoop." The device is covered in blood and hair, and is resting inside an empty tub of popcorn near her foot.

"How?" Gutierrez's mouth falls wide open.

The stainless-steel scoop is sharp enough, especially if directing the right amount of pressure against someone's flesh. Anything with a dull blade can decapitate you, if someone is determined enough to try.

"Anything is possible if you're committed."

"What do you think about that?" Gutierrez motions to the smears around the victim. A circle within a circle, symbols or letters all painted with what looks like the victim's blood. It looks like the killer used their fingers to draw the design.

"I think we're not going to be sleeping for a while."

From somewhere behind us in the seats I hear a cough. I wasn't expecting a reunion.

"Officer Jones, we've got enough vomit over here," I say, not even turning around. I'm too focused on trying to make out the characters around our victim. "I told you to get back to the station."

It's Officer Delgado. She's holding a cellphone. "Your phone, Detective Ramos. You dropped it in the lobby."

"Just leave it there," I say, pointing to one of the front seats. "I'll grab it when I'm done here."

She pauses for a moment before setting it down.

"What now?" I throw my hands up. I can feel a migraine blooming above my left eye.

She presses her lips together tightly and then says. "Do you think...? I mean..."

"Get it out, officer!"

Officer Delgado stands rigid. "Do you think *she* may know anything about this?"

"Oh hell." I feel my eyes rolling to the back of my head. I did not want to talk about her today or any day. "She is not here, and if you mention her again you can join her."

"Sorry, detective," Officer Delgado says, and rushes to the exit.

Gutierrez is standing beside me now. He raises his arm and points to what each of us are avoiding. The laminated black and white poster pinned to the dead woman's groin. "What do you think that means?"

"I don't know," I say, already dreading asking the only person I know who's an expert in this area.

"It looks like a horror movie poster."

"The Chicago Theater is only a performing arts theater. They don't show movies here, right?"

Gutierrez wrinkles his brow. "It used to show movies, a long time ago."

Not a single spot of blood appears on the poster's surface. The killer took great care here, highlighting what needed to be known and shown. They want us to know that this poster is special, that this poster is a clue.

This movie poster is the star of the show, and the body on display and everything to come is just a side character.

Printed in the USA
CPSIA information can be obtained
at www.ICGtesting.com
JSHW022045171023
50259JS00001B/1

9 781957 957067